The NEBADOR series:

Book One: The Test

Book Two: Journey

Book Three: Selection

Book Four: Flight Training

Book Five: Back to the Stars

Book Six: Star Station

Book Seven: The Local Universe
2013

Book Eight: Witness
2014

Also by J. Z. Colby:

Standing on Your Own Two Feet:
Young Adults Surviving 2012 and Beyond

NEBADOR

Book Six
STAR STATION

an epic young-adult science fiction adventure

by

J. Z. Colby

and the short story

Neti's Temptation

by Karen Buchanan

Nebador Archives

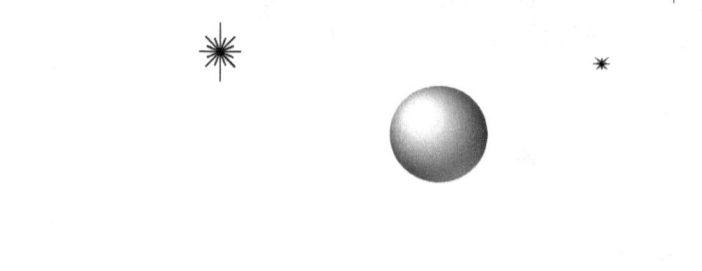

Cover art by Rachael Hedges and Sidney Oster
Illustrations by Sidney Oster and Casey Park

For other print editions, ebooks, dramatic audiobooks, previews, samples, biographies, comments, questions, artwork, writing contests, Ask Kibi advice, deep learning notes, Nebador citizens, and more, please see:

www.nebador.com

Nebador Archives
Kelso, Washington, USA

Library of Congress Control Number: 2012912322
Manufactured in the USA

ISBN: 978-1-936253-53-1
NEBADOR6PBG: paperback, 6" x 9", 183 pages, global edition
   (10-point Georgia type)

Greetings, young people of planet Earth,

We are all formed in the crucible of childhood.

"Slavery," in the sense of being "captive" by something that takes more than it gives, is often a part of our lives.

The "tests" begin early, even if just those boring days in school with countless multiple-choice questions to answer.

Some young people are called by a "journey" of growth, sometimes to get out of "slavery," sometimes in a very different direction.

The "selection" processes of our world can be very deceptive. Everyone wants to be a winner — but what are we winning, and is it worth it? The world will not tell us, for that would reveal its many games and scams. We must find out for ourselves.

"Training" is not so hard, *IF* we've had our eyes and ears open, with brain engaged, every minute since kindergarten. If not, we might have some catching up to do. A planet with tight resources and expensive energy will naturally have few people with comfortable lives, and many who are struggling to make ends meet. Training, at everything we can think of, is essential.

But occasionally, everyone needs to come home.

Does that mean we can just goof off? Since our parents are there, will they clean up our messes? Can we treat others however we want without getting slapped or bitten?

By stepping onto a star station, our beloved characters have left childhood far behind. They have, in some ways, even left adulthood behind. On a backward little planet like Sonmatia Three, being a grown-up just means staying alive until you die, and it doesn't matter who you step on.

On a star station of Nebador, it's not that simple.

Here on Earth, *we* must decide.

J. Z. Colby
2012

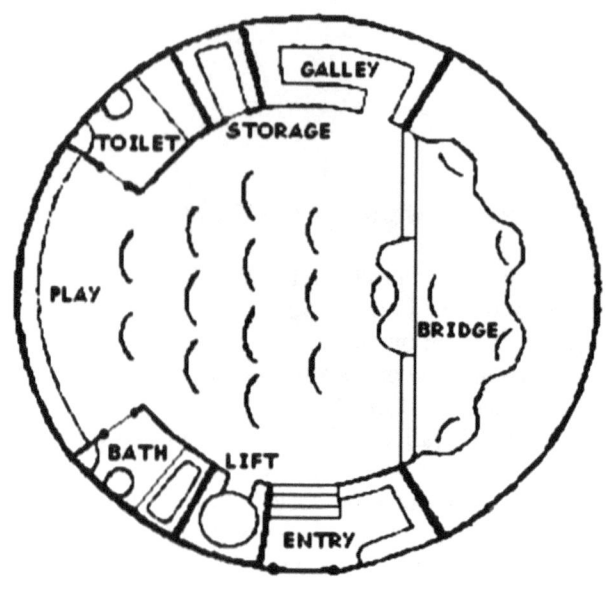

Acknowledgements

Wonderful people throughout the author's life provided unique and irreplaceable lessons and inspirations:

Juniper Russell
Vicky Ball
Linda Dezzutti
Jennifer Carolyn Gates
Rachael Bleich
Paula Wells
Sarah Satterthwaite
Ashley Riddle
Antonya Pickard

Esther Smith
Dottie Frisbie
Martha Higgins
Susanne Koller
Charleen Cox
Meredith Herzog
Patricia Sharp
Peter James

Valuable readers gave the author feedback after digging through early drafts of the book:

Ardith Libby   Cecelia Harper
Karen Oster

Excellent critiquers commented on thousands of passages, then provided reactions during in-depth interviews:

Sidney Oster, 11   Catherine "Cat" Harper, 13
Sarah Bray, 13   Dylan Oster, 13
Alex Chalcraft   Rachael Hedges

Careful publishing assistants, proofreaders, and technical helpers brought the final manuscript as close to perfection as possible:

Katelynn Persons   Cecelia Harper

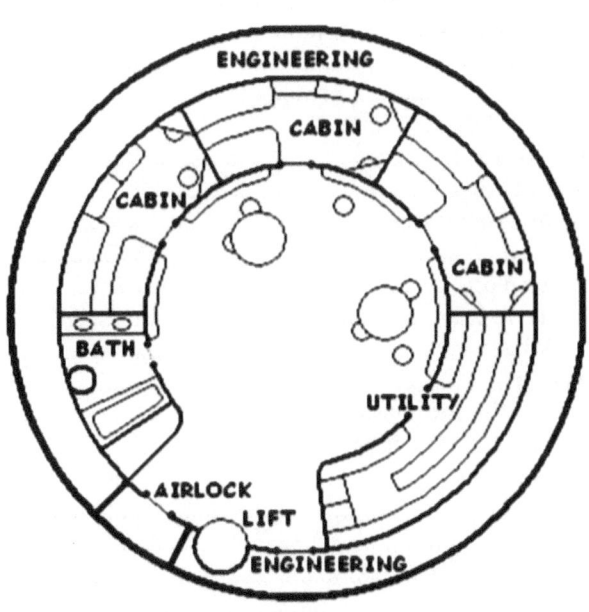

Contents

"It is not the purpose of the universe to get things done as quickly and efficiently as possible. That's a mortal preoccupation, especially strong in monkey mammals, but we all feel it to one degree or another . . ."

— Silmula Sorafax, in charge of the Great Transformation

Chapter 1: Star Station Approach

Their minds floated joyfully in the darkness.

The timeless, spaceless nothingness of star transit did not allow the crew of the Manessa Kwi to think, or even to feel. But somehow, a seed of awareness remained.

Then something changed, and thoughts began to form. Silence. Darkness. Life. Breath. A faint glow seen through closed eyelids.

"Take your time coming back," a soft voice suggested. "You'll be disoriented, maybe dizzy."

That's my lover, Kibi thought, and a smile curled her lips, but she felt so strange that she decided to keep her eyes closed a bit longer.

"We are in the Satamia star system," Ilika's voice continued, "on course for atmospheric braking around Satamia Five."

Sata opened her eyes and blinked like an owl. "Ma ... Mane ... Manessa?"

"Yes, Sata?" the deep-space response ship replied in her pleasant voice.

"Nav ... navigation status?"

"Four light-minutes to course adjustment at Satamia Five approach marker B. Relative velocity is point one seven light-speed."

Boro's eyes snapped open where he sat beside the navigator, still holding her hand. "I didn't know we could go that fast!"

"Normally we cannot," the ship explained. "The difference in universe motion between the two solar systems created the high velocity."

"Oh, okay. Engine status?"

"Repulsion field yellow. All other engines inactive. Anti-mass inoperative by request of Melorania, not yet overridden."

"Oh yeah, that."

Rini chuckled, squeezed the hand of the girl seated next to him, and stretched his arms toward the ceiling. "Manessa, sensor status?"

"Inter-planetary sensors active. All energy levels typical for this system. No objects on the flight path until approach marker B."

Beside Rini, Mati groped for her crutch. "Navigation markers! It'll be nice to pilot with some solid reference points."

"Okay," the captain said, standing up slowly and stretching, "let's take care of ourselves and be at stations in twenty minutes."

"There's a little dried peppermint," Kibi announced, "so I'll make tea!"

*

Mati got comfortable in the pilot's chair, touched a symbol, and her display glowed with the views and graphs she liked to have handy. Largest were the forward visual from Rini and the primary navigation chart from Sata. The red and purple gas giant Satamia Five, dead ahead, dominated both displays. Slightly to one side, a tiny white light pulsed with a regular pattern.

Also on her display, somewhat smaller but no less important, the engine list from Boro, and the internal ship summary from Kibi, gave Mati everything else she needed to know. "Since there's an approach marker for atmospheric braking, someone's had to do this before, right Ilika?"

"Yes. In a populated and well-traveled system like Satamia, there are navigation beacons for every type of ship and every kind of emergency. Back in your solar system, Sonmatia, we were in the wilderness. Here, things are more organized. Sata, would you teach the others about visual beacon identification?"

The navigator worked at her console for a moment and found the list she wanted. "Um . . . look at channel five."

The others tapped at their display selectors.

"All nav beacons transmit, just like the markers at Zolko and Memna on our fourth planet, so normally Manessa knows all about them. But if we just had visual, we could count the flashes."

"Three short and one long," Boro observed.

"Right. And there's only one beacon that flashes like that in the whole system."

"Satamia Five approach marker B!" Rini announced with a grin, reading his display.

"Okay," Mati interrupted, "we're almost there, so we need to do that course adjustment."

Everyone sat up straight and got serious. Rini touched several symbols. "Here's my fix, Sata."

The navigator made a selection. "Wow. We're almost one degree off!"

"That's pretty typical after star transit," the captain explained.

Mati peered at the numbers that flashed onto her screen. "All maneuvering thrusters, Boro. Inertia canceling."

"At least those still work. Green."

The pilot laughed nervously. "This will take about two minutes. How close can I come to the beacon, Ilika?"

"You can go right through it. It's not physically present."

Mati frowned for a moment, then shrugged.

The bridge was quiet as they watched the ship's heading slowly line up with the desired course. The correction was completed just moments before the little ship passed through the phantom navigation beacon, and continued its plunge into the gravity well of the swirling gas giant.

✳

Unlike the atmospheric braking around their own fourth planet, with its occasional dust storm, this one was done by instruments alone. By order of the pilot, a handicapped ex-slave from a medieval world, all visual displays were cancelled, lest her crew lose their peppermint tea, the last thing in their cupboards.

The deceleration from nearly one quarter light-speed took seven orbits through the thick and poisonous mists of the gas giant. Though smaller than the huge sixth planet of their home system, or the seventh where they had been trapped for two weeks preparing to die, Satamia Five hosted a completely different stew of elements, in addition to hydrogen, giving eerie shades of red, magenta, and purple.

The first three or four orbits went quickly. But as the pilot slowly increased the altitude, following graphs supplied by the medieval innkeeper's daughter in the navigator's chair, the process seemed to drag on and on.

The captain, a young man from a far-distant world he had not visited since childhood, noticed that some of his crew members were getting antsy. He was very proud of them for trying to stay within the engine restrictions set by Melorania, the head of the Transport Service. But with Satamia Star Station now so close they could almost see it, he knew their patience was being sorely tested.

"Boro," the captain declared, standing up, "you have command for the star station approach."

Kibi, the second-in-command, smiled from the steward's station, and had a hunch Boro would need a few pointers.

✳

Boro, a fifteen-year-old lad from a medieval cattle ranch, appeared both proud and nervous as he filled the command chair with his large, muscular frame. He had little to do but listen as the pilot and navigator worked together to complete the last few climbing orbits of Satamia Five.

Finally Sata turned and grinned at the boy in the command chair, the same boy she had just recently started kissing. "We're down to a thousand kilometers a second, but really can't go any slower, or it will take forever to get to the star station."

"Forever doesn't work with our food supply," Boro mumbled as he looked at the new chart that flashed onto the main screen directly in front of him.

Kibi chuckled from behind. "I *think* I can make one more pot of tea."

"The star station's only twelve light-seconds behind the gas giant," Sata continued, "in the same orbit. But that'll take us ..." She worked at her console for a moment. "... about three hours."

Boro sighed. "I hope there's a pot of stew on the stove when we get there."

Ilika smiled from the engineer's station. "Even the smallest star stations have everything you could want . . . except red meat, of course."

"I could go for an apple," Boro declared. "Status reports?"

✳

After getting routine matters out of the way, the commander turned to his captain. "Ilika, how are we going to slow down at the star station?   A thousand kilometers a second isn't a very friendly way to arrive."

"Good question, Boro. Maybe it's time to start talking to the star station."

Boro took a breath and wrinkled his brow. "Am I gonna be talking to a bird?"

Sata turned around and gave him a dirty look.

Ilika smiled. "You might be. Whoever's at docking control, I guarantee they'll know everything there is to know about getting safely in and out of the station."

"Um . . . okay. You do that, right, Sata?"

"Uh huh, as long as you're nice to whoever we talk to, even if it's a bird."

"It could also be an insect," Rini pointed out from the watch station with a gleam in his eyes.

Boro moaned, and didn't see the smiles on the other crew members' faces.

"Satamia docking control," Sata began, "this is the Manessa Kwi, eight light-seconds ahead of you in orbit. The commander has a question or two about our approach."

Boro moaned again.

A mammal with a snout and black nose, completely covered with brown fur, flashed onto the screen. "Greetings, beautiful monkey mammals of the Manessa Kwi! I see you are coming in very, very slowly. How can I help?"

"You're not a bird!" Boro observed with surprise.

"Not last time I checked my anatomy," the docking controller said, showing long, sharp teeth in the process.

"Sorry," Boro mumbled. "The only other person we've seen from Nebador was a bird."

The controller looked down at his console for a moment. "Oh, I see that you're a crew-in-training. What's this? Melorania made a note that you would probably be coming in slowly. Aren't her training challenges fun? Once it took me a week to get from one planet to another with nothing but maneuvering thrusters. Took *three* freeloading passes!"

Boro breathed easier and smiled. "Um . . . yeah, we're not supposed to use anti-mass. Actually, I'm the engineer. We did atmospheric braking around Satamia Five, but now we're wondering how to slow down the rest of the way."

"Well, we can handle that! I'll just send you the deceleration tractor . . . wait, what's this? I can't believe it! Only an hour ago, Melorania sent it to Satamia Two to help with something. She must really like you guys. Most new crews don't get *this* much tender loving care from the grand old lady of the Transport Service."

Boro chuckled, even as he absorbed the bad news. "It's probably because we're . . . monkey mammals."

"Could be. Your proper name is 'humans,' in case you don't know. We ursines can be a bit stubborn too. Anyway, back to our little problem. I'm not sure what else I can do on this end. Got any thruster fuel?"

"A little. We'll see if it's enough. Thanks."

"I'll stay on duty until you're safely in. For now, Satamia closing."

Boro sighed.

Sata smiled. "Manessa Kwi closing."

*

Ilika let most of the crew go off-duty. Boro sat down at his station, and with Ilika's help, transferred every drop of the old thruster fuel to a small holding tank, filtering and measuring it in the process. It came to twenty-three seconds at full-thrust.

Sata, the only one actually on duty, made some calculations at her console. "That'll get us down to about three hundred kilometers per second. Still way too fast for the maneuvering thrusters alone to stop us."

Everyone fell silent, Ilika wandered up to the big table to use a knowledge pad, and Boro began pacing.

"Found some dried parsley!" Kibi announced from the galley.

Her discovery brought smiles to all those within earshot, but no one grabbed a spoon.

"Stew on the stove," Boro mumbled to himself as he paced, "and we're gonna fly right on by unless we can slow down."

"When do we override Melorania," Sata asked from the front of the ship, "if we can't figure anything out?"

Ilika looked up. "Station approach marker A, which is one light-second out."

Sata looked at her chart and nodded.

"Wait a minute!" Boro suddenly boomed.

Everyone looked at him, including Mati and Rini who were just coming up the lift, arms around each other.

"Manessa," Boro began, "exactly what did Melorania say?"

"That we should not use the anti-mass drive until we arrived at Satamia Star Station."

Boro paced for a few more seconds, running his hands through his hair. Then he stopped dead in his tracks. "Manessa, exactly what does the word 'arrived' mean?"

"To achieve a destin . . ."

"No," Boro interrupted, "I mean *precisely* what does it mean, to a deep-space response ship, when coming to a star station? At exactly what point can you say you have arrived?"

"In that technical sense, a ship is considered to have arrived when it passes the inner navigation markers."

"Sata, how far . . ."

"I'm on it!" she declared, quickly switching charts. "The inner markers are exactly one kilometer from the station."

Boro began pacing again while rubbing his neck with both hands. "So . . . if we activated the anti-mass drive the instant we passed the inner markers, we wouldn't need to override Melorania's order. Right, Manessa?" he asked pointedly.

"Correct," the ship replied.

"But what about warming up the drives?" Kibi asked from the galley. "At three hundred kilometers a second . . . one three-hundredth of a second isn't enough time to do . . . anything!"

Boro lowered himself into the command chair, looked at the ceiling, and wrinkled his brow.

About half a minute later, his mouth snapped open. "Melorania said we shouldn't *use* anti-mass until we arrived, so it wouldn't matter if we *warmed it up* early. Right, Manessa?"

"Correct."

"And maybe *we* can't do that split-second timing," Sata said, "but Manessa can!"

Ilika was listening with interest.

"How precise?" Boro asked, still looking at Sata.

"Mati?" Sata passed the question up to the pilot at the table.

"Thousandth of a second."

"And in a thousandth of a second," Boro began with sparkling eyes, "we'd go less than half a kilometer, right?"

Sata grinned and nodded.

✳

Boro was clearly proud of himself, going from person to person to arrange every detail of the plan. Mati would do the deceleration thruster burn several minutes before arrival. Ilika, at the engineer's station, would warm up the anti-mass drive with time to spare in case anything went wrong and they had to override Melorania's order.

Judging by the expressions on Ilika's face, Kibi knew something was missing from the plan, and wondered if it had anything to do with Sata's wrinkled brow.

✳

As the last hour began, Kibi made more tea. She knew it wasn't providing much nutrition, but at least they wouldn't have to work on empty stomachs.

As she sipped her tea, the navigator looked at Boro with disappointment in her eyes. Kibi saw it, and was pretty sure everyone else did too . . . except Boro.

"I believe you have a job to do, Sata," the captain said over his cup of fragrant tea.

"I do?"

"Yes. You have something to report, and if you don't find your courage, the plan won't work."

Boro looked at Sata with surprise.

She took a deep breath and glared at Boro with smoldering eyes. "Are you *really* just going to go barreling in like a wild stallion without even *telling* the star station what we're doing?"

"Um . . . gosh . . . I thought it would be kinda fun to surprise them . . ."

The navigator rolled her eyes and slumped back in her chair.

"Sata," Ilika began, "why don't you explain to Boro the arrival procedures for a star station. You've studied them — he hasn't."

Sata breathed for a moment. "Sorry. I forgot you don't know this stuff. There are all kinds of ships going in and out all the time. You have to talk to the docking controller at the outer marker, there's a speed limit at the middle marker, and some ships have to let the controller guide them in past the inner marker. Big ships are sometimes parked outside the station. Inside the inner marker, people could be out in space suits!" When she finally finished speaking, she slumped into her chair, red-faced and breathing in gasps.

"Thank you, Sata," Ilika said calmly. "It's important for you to remember that you have an ability none of the other four have."

"I . . . I do?"

"Yes. You have the ability to trust, because you were raised in a working family where you could count on your mother, father, and brother to do their jobs and make good decisions about the inn."

Ilika looked around at the four ex-slaves. "The rest of you are used to assuming everyone in authority is against you, and cannot be trusted. I come from that background too, so I understand. You're learning to trust me, and slowly you will learn to trust everyone in the Nebador Services. The ursine controller you talked to is your brother now. You can trust him with your lives."

Boro took several breaths in the silence that lingered. "I . . . guess I should talk to the bear . . . I mean, the ursine controller."

Sata managed to force out a smile.

✳

"Wow, that sounds exciting!" the image of the furry docking controller said from the main bridge display. "I bet the whole station will come out to watch. Let's see what the boss-lady thinks, she's over in the Rontilia system . . ." He hummed as he tapped at his console. "Okay, she approves, and apologizes for not being able to greet you, but she's helping with a stranded ship."

"I've plotted a course," Sata explained, "that will take us *past* the station, instead of into it, if something goes wrong."

"Excellent! I'll clear the way of ships when you pass the outer marker. Satamia closing."

"Thank you. Manessa Kwi . . . closing," Boro managed to say.

Once the screen went dark, Sata looked at him with returning fondness.

"Thanks for . . . making me . . . do it right," he muttered.

She smiled.

✳

At Kibi's urging, Boro went over the plan in detail, twice, before they got to the first approach marker.

Mati asked the most questions, primarily of Manessa, as the pilot didn't want to approve a maneuver unless she was sure it was going to work. The braking thruster burn would be easy. Just thinking about the thousandth-of-a-second reaction time, needed to stop the ship just past the inner marker, made her stomach hurt.

Ilika smiled from the other end of the table and gave her a nod of confidence.

※

Finally Sata announced that outer approach marker A was at hand.

Boro called for stations, and ordered inertia straps, just in case.

The pilot peered at the deceleration graph, then made a decision. "Space thrusters, level five. It'll take a little longer than full power, but we've got the time."

"Good thinking," Ilika commented as he worked at the engineer's console. "Thrusters are green."

"Sata," the commander began, "Please tell the . . . controller that we're starting our approach."

Sata touched several symbols. "Satamia docking control, we are passing outer marker A, preparing to decelerate. The commander requests a pot of stew, preferably with fish."

Everyone on the ship chuckled, and the ursine controller roared with laughter as he tapped at his console.

Mati turned and looked at Boro.

The acting commander got quick status reports from Kibi and Rini, and glanced at Ilika to see if he was forgetting anything.

The captain nodded.

Boro took one more deep breath. "Slow us down, Mati. Use every drop."

※

The ship's inertia canceling kept the crew from feeling the deceleration that otherwise would have made them scream with pain. Sata listened for anything her dear friend and pilot needed, and called out the ship's speed.

"Seven hundred."

Rini watched for any ships or other obstacles.

"Six hundred."

Mati kept an eagle eye on their course with her three-D chart projection.

"Five hundred."

Ilika watched the thruster fuel get closer and closer to zero.

"Four hundred."

Kibi double-checked other parts of the ship from her console, and smiled at the thought of finally being able to fill her empty cupboards.

"Three hundred."

The thrusters began sputtering, and some of the jerks and lurches penetrated the inertia canceling. Boro felt his straps hold him tightly.

The space thrusters died.

"Two hundred fifty-three kilometers per second," the navigator reported. "Inner marker in . . . forty seconds."

Ilika's hands quickly went into action. "Anti-mass warming."

"Satamia Star Station ahead," Sata announced.

Everyone looked at their displays and beheld the glowing jewel in space, with countless facets gleaming from the yellow light of the Satamia primary sun, or the reds and purples of the nearby gas giant. It rapidly grew larger, and they seemed to be heading almost directly toward it.

"Anti-mass drive ready at level seven," the captain reported from the engineer's station. "All diagnostics good."

"The rest is up to Manessa," Boro declared with a trembling voice.

"Full stop, under ship's control, approved," Mati confirmed, still watching their course for any problems.

"Eight seconds," Sata announced.

The star station seemed to pick up speed and swoop toward them, making several of them gasp with fright. Suddenly it froze on the right edge of their forward view screens.

"Wow," Sata began, trying to catch her breath. "Relative speed . . . zero."

A heartbeat later, everyone on the little ship began clapping and cheering.

As soon as he could be heard, the captain spoke. "View to the right, please, Rini."

When the view angle changed, they could all see the gleaming crystal surfaces of the star station, seemingly just a stone's throw away. About half the facets of the giant jewel were clear, and hundreds of people, of all shapes and sizes, could be seen jumping up and down, swinging from the ceiling, leaping out of pools of water, or, if they had arms, waving them in greetings to the little deep-space response ship that had just passed another challenging test.

✳   ✳   ✳

Chapter 2: Docking Tunnel

"Kibi, would you take us in, please?" the captain asked.

"Whew!" Boro exclaimed and quickly hopped out of the command chair.

However, the captain didn't immediately let him retreat to the safety of the engineering station. He faced Boro and looked him squarely in the eyes. "Very good command, Boro. Thank you."

The fifteen-year-old blinked with embarrassment for a moment, then steadied his gaze and looked back at his captain. "Thanks. I guess . . . it was good for me."

Ilika smiled and let the younger man get to the comfort of his station.

Kibi was already on the bridge, chatting with Rini and Sata. The docking controller appeared on the main display. "That's one to make a story out of! I've already heard folks talking about Boro, the monkey-mammal engineer who out-smarted Melorania."

Boro cringed at his station, and busied himself checking fuel levels.

"So, who's in the hot seat for docking?" the ursine asked.

"Hi, I'm Kibi, steward and second-in-command."

"First, Kibi, I have to ask you for your honest and sound judgment, as commander of the ship. Do you need direct station control for docking? It's a maze in there."

Kibi looked at Mati, who returned the sternest frown ever seen on the handicapped girl's face. Then Kibi turned and looked at Ilika. He slowly shook his head.

"No, thank you," Kibi said firmly to the controller.

"Okay . . . you know the speed limits. Come to inner marker E and hold. I have a couple of ships waiting to get in."

"I need those speed limits," Mati urgently whispered as she located the marker on her chart.

Sata made a console selection and whispered back, "I'm adding them to the station chart."

Mati saw the area of space closest to the station take on a red tint. "Boro, anti-mass one, maneuvering thrusters."

✳

A minute later, Mati brought the ship to a stop beside the pulsing blue beacon floating in space. They arrived just in time to see a long, silver ship glide past and enter the dark, circular entrance to the star station. Half a minute later, a small round ship followed, with something gangly and irregular at the front.

"That looks like another deep-space response ship!" Sata announced with excitement, "but what's it carrying?"

Ilika looked up from the steward's console. "Planets who are just beginning to explore space often send little robot ships into the interstellar void. After they go dark and silent, we collect them and put them in a museum."

Rini peered at his display. "It's so ... flimsy ... compared to Nebador ships."

"Looks like a pile of sticks to me," Boro added.

"Manessa Kwi," the docking controller began, "follow the yellow path to sterilization and quarantine."

"What yellow path?" Mati whispered.

Sata made a selection. "This one!"

Lines in every color of the rainbow appeared on the pilot's three-D display, all going into the star station's docking tunnel. Mati took a moment to scan all her visual displays for other ships, then nudged Manessa forward.

Little breathing went on as the new crew approached the yawning dock entrance. Instead of a smooth circle, it appeared to be made of thick, woven strands, reminding the crew of vines or tree roots.

Sata touched a symbol, and Mati's chart was replaced by a plan of the docking tunnels. The colored lines continued into the depths of the star station, with one soon following a smaller tunnel to the left, and another entering a large docking area to the right.

"Wow, it *is* a maze," the pilot mumbled as she continued to follow the yellow line on her chart, deeper and deeper into the darkness.

✳

Just like the outside of the star station, most flat surfaces inside the docking tunnel seemed to be of crystal or glass, like the facets of a jewel. Between each surface, more roots or branches created an irregular matrix of rooms and spaces, some cozy for just a few small creatures, others roomy enough for hundreds.

"It's a ... it's a big plant, right, Ilika?" Rini asked, looking at his captain.

Ilika smiled and nodded, but put his finger to his lips.

Many of the surfaces glowed with subtle colors. Others were crystal clear, and creatures of all sorts could be seen inside, going about their business or watching the passing ships.

Boro smiled when he noticed water behind some of the clear surfaces, and occasionally a sleek creature swimming by. The small scar on his leg ached for a moment.

Sata glimpsed three pink-faced monkeys hanging by their tails from branches, and realized the resemblance to humans was strong, even though she and her shipmates didn't have tails.

Mati concentrated on piloting and didn't speak a word. After several minutes and five turns, only three colored lines remained.

The small ship with the spidery wreckage was still in front of them when suddenly part of the wreckage broke loose and began to drift and tumble silently. "Look out!" Boro boomed, grabbing the sides of his chair.

Mati blinked once. "Docking control, you want me to get that?"

"Hmm. I'm not supposed to ask student pilots to handle unexpected things . . ."

"You didn't ask, I offered," Mati said firmly, and started to move the Manessa Kwi toward the drifting junk.

"Hey, I like you! Mati is your name?"

She nodded, but was concentrating again. "Manessa, you ready to grab that stuff?"

"Yes."

Kibi glanced back at Ilika, and the sparkle in his eyes told her he was completely happy.

Mati slowed the ship as they neared the debris, placing the Manessa Kwi right in its path. Rini and Boro cringed at the scraping sound that came through the hull as the metal from a distant world made contact.

"Grapple complete," the ship said.

"*Now* I see why Melorania likes you guys so much!" the ursine controller declared. "You're not afraid to jump in with both feet! I'm holding the traffic behind you until we get this junk squared away."

"Thank you," Sata said. "Where do you want it?"

"Follow the other ship onto the green path."

✳

A few minutes later, they waited while the first ship placed its armload of wreckage in a storage bay, then Mati did the same with the rest. A shy reptilian navigator appeared and thanked them with few words.

"It's important to remember," Ilika began as they retraced their flight back to the yellow line, "that just because some species aren't as social as mammals and birds, they are no less sapient. I've worked alongside reptiles, and they're some of the most reliable people in the Nebador Services."

Boro looked at the captain. "I'd like to meet them. And that bear, the controller."

At the junction, they had to wait for three ships to pass. First came a round golden ship about three times the size of their own. "That's a life-monitor, which you already know about," Ilika explained. "This is heavy cargo," he said as another long, silver vessel glided by. "Only a small part is habitable." Finally, a somewhat smaller ship with a shiny blue hull moved slowly past. "About a hundred passengers, plus the crew. Nice big galley, plenty of recreation space, and a little medical bay."

"Have you worked on all three kinds?" Kibi asked from the command chair.

"Yes, and that exact passenger ship, the Palantia Lisa. Two engineers, and I was the junior, at about thirteen, working under an ursine who knew engines better than I ever will."

Boro grinned.

Finally they could continue their journey along the yellow line. It soon took them a different way than the other ships.

"We're all alone in here," Sata said in a sad voice as they moved along slowly, deeper into the star station, with no other ships ahead or behind.

The ursine controller appeared. "You folks ready for sterilization?"

Ilika grinned. "I haven't told them about it yet. But they handled star transit . . ."

"Pfff. Then it'll be easy! Trust Manessa!"

As soon as the controller vanished from the screen, they rounded a corner and beheld a blue sheet of light, pulsing and crackling with energy, that completely filled the tunnel. Mati instinctively brought the ship to a dead stop.

Kibi swallowed. "Is that . . . sterilization?"

Sata looked at the station plan. "Y . . . yes."

"Am I supposed to go *through* that thing?" Mati asked with a troubled voice.

"Manessa?" Ilika prompted.

"I will take us through by feel," the ship explained, "as all sensors must be deactivated. When we emerge, my hull will be clean."

Mati and Sata looked at each other, then looked at Kibi.

Kibi took a deep breath. "Shut down all sensors, Rini."

Mati turned back to her console. "I'm approving ship control for sterilization."

"Inertia straps," Ilika said. "It can be a little bumpy, as Manessa will be going through blind."

✳

The crew grinned and giggled as their hair stood on end, their skin tingled, and the air smelled like thunder storms. A few small bumps and a minute later, the ship announced that hull cleaning was complete.

Rini was quick to restore sensors, and Mati gladly took her flight control back in hand.

The ursine appeared again. "That wasn't so bad, was it? I've assigned you to quarantine dock B-Three, up ahead on your right."

They moved slowly past two other response ships, both held in place by large, blue and purple docking fingers.

"This is it," Sata said as they approached the third docking berth, its fingers currently open and empty, like the petals of a flower.

"Your captain will explain docking and quarantine. Congratulations to you all! I have no complaints about your piloting, Mati. I understand there's a medical surgeon waiting to meet you."

Mati grinned as she eased the little ship into the docking berth with the alignment display she had already used at the Monuments of Zolko. As soon as they were in position, the blue and purple fingers closed around the ship.

"Manessa says the docking clamps are secure," Sata reported.

"I'm going off-duty now," the controller continued, "as my mate has a big, juicy fish she's been keeping warm, and I'm as hungry as a . . . a monkey mammal!"

Everyone chuckled and thanked the ursine docking controller.

Mati brought the power levels, on both anti-mass and maneuvering thrusters, to zero, waited a moment to make sure the ship stayed in place, and took a long, deep breath.

Suddenly it dawned on her that she had just piloted a starship from her home planet, where she was a crippled slave, through many tests and challenges, to a star station in another solar system. Her hands started shaking and tears threatened to come, but she kept breathing while she reached for her crutch and looked around at her beautiful ship and loyal friends, and especially at one very cute boy at the watch station, who was looking back at her with smiling eyes.

Then, as she stood up, she remembered one last thing she needed to do. "Boro, finished with engines."

✳   ✳   ✳

Chapter 3: Quarantine

"Can we eat now?" the engineer asked after shutting down his station and spinning around.

The captain didn't answer the question directly. "Boro, all empty fuel canisters go by the airlock. Kibi, I'll work with you on swapping out waste containers. Sata, collect all trash from the galley, and Rini from the toilet rooms. Mati just had a very intense hour, and is off-duty."

"I'm still shaking," she admitted.

They all heard a dull thud against the hull.

Ilika looked at Kibi. "You did it! You explored the entire Sonmatia solar system, then endured star transit, atmospheric braking, and star station docking, without ever panicking and opening the main hatch!"

She looked back with mischief in her eyes. "There were moments I was tempted to open it with my fingernails!"

Mati and Sata howled with laughter.

"I believe," Ilika continued, "if you check your console, you'll find a boarding tunnel in place and breathable atmosphere outside the hatch."

"Whoopee!" Kibi cheered as she stepped to her station. "Yep. Permission to air out the ship, captain?"

"Granted!"

*

They could see a walkway through the hatch, going straight as an arrow through a clear, circular boarding tunnel, but they had a quarter hour of work before they could begin the journey. After gathering trash bags and canisters near the hatches, Ilika had them pack a change of cloths and other personal things. Interior de-contamination took an entire day, he explained, about as long as they'd be in medical quarantine.

"Manessa," the captain said as he shouldered his bag, "you are in command. Make sure the cleaning crew does a good job."

"They always do, but I will monitor the process, even though I cannot technically be in command, as you know."

Ilika smiled. "Thank you for . . . all the countless ways you kept us alive since the last time I remembered to thank you. We will see you tomorrow."

"You are welcome, and I look forward to serving with all of you in the future."

✳

The captain, four ex-slaves, and one innkeeper's daughter stood facing the hatch. They all bore rucksacks, save Mati. Rini's bag was heavier than the others.

"The cleaning, sterilizing, and quarantine is necessary because we just came from a primitive planet with all sorts of bugs and germs that might be harmless to us, but could infect others in the Nebador Services. Our time in quarantine will depend on what the healers find. Mati will probably begin chatting with the surgeon."

"Can we . . ." Boro began shyly, ". . . you know . . . buy some food somewhere?"

"There is no money here, Boro. Money is a way of rationing goods and services in a general society where some people would be lazy, or take more than they needed, if they could. People who do either of those are NOT members of the Nebador Services. This is a working civilization. We don't have time to be lazy."

"What . . . um . . . happens to someone who takes more than they need," Sata asked, "like maybe too much food?"

"If they can't grow out of it, they get a one-way trip home. I don't think any of you need to worry. Shall we go see what's cooking?"

Everyone nodded vigorously.

"Pilot and navigator, as you do in flight, would you lead the way?"

Sata held Mati's hand as they made their way down the steps, through the hatch, and slowly along the boarding tunnel. They could see in all directions, with crystal windows of the star station not far away, and thick roots and vines weaving it all together.

Boro and Rini came next. Boro's eyes were wide with wonder, but Rini wore a contented smile and looked like he was coming home.

Ilika and Kibi brought up the rear.

Soon the navigator and pilot stood at the end of the boarding tunnel and peered into a circular room, a bit larger than the main deck of the Manessa Kwi. About a dozen soft chairs and couches were scattered about. Around the edge, doorways with curtains, some open, led to little sleeping rooms. A double door on the opposite side was closed, and a large glass window, behind a strange machine, was currently dark.

The round table in the middle of the room, set with plates, cups, and serving dishes, drew their attention. From it came the aroma of hearty vegetable stew and baked fish.

Sata was about to dig in when she realized everyone else was slowly sipping pinkfruit juice. She remembered their warnings about eating too quickly after being hungry, turned to the engineer beside her, and looked into his warm eyes.

He smiled back and tapped his cup against hers when she held it up.

Kibi looked around the table with sparkling eyes. "What should we know about this place, Ilika?"

He set his cup down. "You have seen other sapient people in videos and on view screens. Now you must learn to walk among them, and get used to their speech. Most people here are far more intelligent than we are. Barely-sapient creatures, like Tera, do not roam about freely on a star station. There are four-legged people here, but they can think circles around you, I promise. We are just monkey mammals from backward little worlds. Remember that."

Everyone was quiet and thoughtful for a minute as they started eating their stew and fish.

"I know what Mati's doing here . . ." Sata began after taking the edge off her hunger.

The pilot smiled as she examined a strange vegetable on her fork.

"What will the rest of us be doing?"

"Ship maintenance, stocking supplies, getting to know the star station . . ."

Boro took another piece of fish. "Is this the center of Nebador?"

"Far from it. This is an outpost on the edge of the wilderness, like the little village of Nug in the mountains of your kingdom."

Rini chuckled. "But without the bones and flies!"

Ilika nodded. "While we're here, we'll get more comfortable with the notion that our lives are intertwined with beings much greater than us, like this star station."

"I know Manessa isn't sapient," Mati began, "but I think of her as smarter than me in most ways."

Ilika nodded. "There are also sapient beings here that make us look like children, but most of them are invisible unless they want to be seen."

"Like . . . Melorania?" Kibi posed.

Ilika nodded while chewing and swallowing. "We'll also get familiar with the Mission Assignment Room, where beings like Melorania are most often glimpsed. Mati will miss a few things, but she'll be doing something very important."

Mati nodded since her mouth wasn't currently free for speaking.

Suddenly Sata frowned, watching Boro take a third piece of fish. "Shouldn't we . . . stop eating soon, so they don't think we're taking too much?"

Ilika smiled. "No, Sata, I wasn't talking about having a hearty meal. Some people, when they have unlimited food, eat until their bodies blow up into blubbery masses of flesh they can barely move around with their own feet."

Everyone frowned at the thought. Boro breathed again, and dug into his delicious baked fish.

✳   ✳   ✳

Chapter 4: Healers

While the crew of the Manessa Kwi ate, the boarding tunnel closed and vanished. Manessa greeted old friends who arrived in space suits with cleaning and sterilization equipment. While they worked, they shared stories with the well-traveled deep-space response ship. The cleaning crew chuckled when they heard the adventures of the brand-new crew of monkey mammals, and promised the ship they wouldn't breathe a word after leaving.

*

Ilika explained that the only other door out of the medical quarantine room was actually an airlock. The inner door opened to his pull, and a cart for their dirty dishes stood within, but the door beyond was sealed and locked.

Suddenly lights came on behind the large glass window, and the entire crew gathered to peer at the examining tables and medical equipment within. A man with gray hair, reading a knowledge pad, strolled into view.

Sata's eyes lit up. "He's like us!"

The man looked up. "Is my timing okay? Did you have a relaxing meal?"

When Ilika didn't immediately answer, Kibi smiled. "Yes, thank you. I'm Kibi, steward of the Manessa Kwi."

"Greetings, Kibi. I am Dakalio, general healer. You've been on two primitive planets with atmosphere, I see."

"Um . . . yeah," Sata confirmed. "Sonmatia Three and Four. I'm Sata, the navigator."

"Welcome to Satamia, all of you!"

The others introduced themselves.

"As you may know, I'm looking for parasites and microbes that are best kept on their home worlds. Step onto the scanner, one at a time."

Ilika went first to demonstrate. Parts of the machine moved around him and shined dancing beams of light at him in all directions. He stepped down, and the others quickly found the courage to step onto the medical scanner.

"Hmm . . . hmm . . ." the healer muttered as he looked at a display screen they couldn't see. "Not bad . . . that little thing will be easy . . . hmm . . . Boro, there are two of you."

The engineer's face took on a sour expression.

Sata grinned at her friend and cocked her head. "Pregnant?"

Boro turned red.

"Nothing so dramatic," the healer said, "just an intestinal parasite. It won't take long to get rid of, but I want to wait until you've absorbed your meal, as we'll have to empty you out."

Boro became, if anything, even redder.

"Kibi," the healer continued, "you have a virus I don't like, so I'll be giving you some pills."

"Okay."

"Um . . ." Mati began, struggling to find the right words. "Can you . . . um . . . fix my knee? I'll do anything . . . scrub all the floors on the star station, or anything else you want me to do . . ."

The healer sensed the depth of her feelings. "Mati, dear Mati, you are a starship pilot. You have already earned anything and everything we can do for you. But I'm sorry, Mati, I do not have that skill."

Mati's face fell and tears started running down her cheeks.

"But the healer with that ability is in the next room right now. She is very gentle and wise, and is one of the most skillful surgeons in all of Nebador. Would you like to meet her?"

Mati quickly wiped the tears onto her sleeves and collected herself. "A lady healer? That would be nice. We knew a lady healer in the city we came from."

"I'll see if she's free," Dakalio said, and left the room.

Mati breathed deeply as she waited. Rini held her hand, and Sata put an arm around her shoulders.

A minute later, a large, green, gangly insect almost three meters tall entered the room and stepped up to the window, towering over the crew of the Manessa Kwi. Feelers quivered in the air, and claw-like mandibles played around the creature's mouth. "Hello, Mati. I will be your surgeon."

Mati's face turned white, and the world around her went dark.

Rini and Sata caught her.

When Mati awoke, she saw the faces of her beloved Rini, her dear friend Sata, and her captain, all smiling at her. A moment later, Kibi joined them.

"Is the monster gone?"

Sata nodded. "Only problem is, my friend, that monster is the only surgeon around who can fix your knee."

Mati sighed, sat up, and accepted a cup of water from Rini. "I thought I was okay with people being all shapes and sizes. But . . . it was so *big!*"

"After we put you in bed," Rini said, "we chatted with the surgeon. She's really nice, and says you can have a friend with you the whole time. Her name's K'stimla. Did I say that right, Ilika?"

He nodded. "But *you* have to make the final decision, Mati, and tell surgeon K'stimla yourself, perhaps with a little apology thrown in."

Mati flopped back down and sighed. "Can I think about it?"

The captain nodded.

Mati looked at her friends. "Where's Boro?"

Sata chuckled. "He's in a toilet room, and will be in there for a couple of hours."

Mati sighed again. "I wish a couple of hours in a toilet room would solve my problem."

Her friends laughed.

✳

When Boro finally emerged, the rest of the crew was at the table eating.

The engineer held his hands almost a meter apart and said, "It was . . . oh, never mind."

The others howled with laughter, except Mati, who cracked a smile but otherwise continued brooding.

Sata suppressed her laughter enough to speak. "There's a fruit salad here for you, Boro."

"I have *never* felt so empty, even as a slave," he said, taking a seat and grabbing a spoon.

"But we never got fruit salads!" Kibi reminded him.

Boro nodded, but was already chewing something tasty.

"Healer Dakalio says we should be out of quarantine by tomorrow," Ilika announced.

"Another healer looked at the scans," Sata reported, "and found a little something in me, so I'm taking pills now too."

Boro looked at Mati as he ate, but could tell she hadn't yet made a decision.

✳　✳　✳

Chapter 5: Different Paths

The following day, Dakalio scanned them all again. Three different healers peered at the results, then released the crew of the Manessa Kwi from quarantine.

Beyond the sealed door, each person, one at a time, unshouldered their rucksacks, shed their clothes, and entered a steamy shower room while their belongings went a different way to be sterilized. Mati's crutch was no exception, so Sata went with her friend through the shower.

On the far side, fresh clothes greeted them, and their packs soon emerged from a small door.

After dressing, each crew member stepped into the last waiting room and found places to sit on chairs or couches, some obviously designed for smaller or larger creatures.

Only one more door, of clear glass, separated the new arrivals from the interior of the star station, and they could see beings of all sorts walking, leaping, swinging, or flying along. Huge brown tree trunks soared upward, limbs and vines followed the edges of every crystal surface, and leaves spread out to catch the sunlight.

When all six had taken up their rucksacks or crutch, Ilika looked at his new crew, about to make the final step into a new civilization. Four faces showed excitement and eagerness to dash through the last door and into their new lives.

One face dripped with tears. "I can't do it Ilika. I can't go out there with you. I have to either find the courage to let the surgeon fix my knee . . . or go home."

Rini quickly declared his intention to stay with Mati, whichever road she took. The young couple got comfortable on a couch in the medical waiting room, snuggled close, and began whispering together.

Ilika swallowed several times, took a breath for courage, and led the

others through the glass door. So it was that he stepped into the main hall of
Satamia Star Station with only his steward at his side, and his navigator and
engineer, holding hands, close behind.

A wide open area spread out before them, with balconies and landings
rising four or five levels, all intertwined with rough-barked trunks and
quivering leaves. A bright pool of water, off to one side, churned with
creatures surfacing and climbing out, others jumping in, and some just
floating while they chatted.

The foursome, three of whom gazed about with wide eyes, hadn't gone
many steps when a large, sleek bird and a husky bear blocked their path.
Both wore scant clothing, not much more than a vest with pockets for a few
personal items.

"Bok. I was wondering if I could give my fellow navigator a tour of the
station, and show her that eating place I mentioned."

Sata grinned and stepped forward. "Drim-na!"

"Drrrim-na," the avian corrected with a slight bow.

"Dr-r-r-im-na," Sata attempted.

The feathered navigator cackled.

Sata looked at her captain and saw that he was smiling. "No problem
here, Sata. It looks like Boro is also getting an invitation."

The ursine docking controller bowed. "I have a mind to do some fishing,
and wondered if Boro would like to join me. He'll get a tour also, of course."

"Real fish, out of a stream?" the engineer questioned with wide eyes.

"Real, live fish. Stream or deep-water. I don't yet know if you swim . . ."

"I do, and love it!"

Ilika tapped at his mission bracelet. "Manessa is out of quarantine and has been moved to dock C-Thirteen. That's our meeting place."

Sata and Boro both strolled away with their new friends, leaving Ilika and Kibi among hundreds of different creatures, some walking, some running on urgent business, and a few just hanging from tree branches by their tails.

✳   ✳   ✳

Chapter 6: Sata's Tour

Drrrim-na ambled slowly through halls, along walkways, and up ramps or stairs as her new friend and fellow navigator peered this way and that. Sometimes a wide path circled around a great tree trunk. At other times the way seemed made of stone, molded into steps and decorative shapes.

Creatures they passed made pleasant eye contact, but didn't bother the pair except when Drrrim-na stopped to chat with another avian, and a bit later a small, furry mammal approached them to ask directions.

When they were alone again, in a passageway under a canopy of huge leaves, Sata tried to put her question into words. "Um . . . it seems strange that no one is . . . you know . . . trying to sell us something, or steal from us, or tell us what to do . . ."

Drrrim-na clucked with humor. "That's all monkey mammal stuff! Remember, I know — I work on a life-monitor ship."

Sata thought about it as they walked on. "What . . . monkey mammal things . . . should I be careful not to do?"

The bird opened her eyes wider. "All of them, bok! I mean, the ones about messing with others, getting in their faces, that kind of stuff. Bok. It's not just you. I'd *love* to peck holes in these leaves, eat ursine babies for lunch, and let my bowels go whenever I'm flying. Not here, bok!"

Sata rolled with laughter when she imagined the huge mess, and the angry bears right on her friend's tail.

"Here's that eating place I told you about. Bok. Great view!"

Sata's mouth dropped as they stepped into the room and beheld the red and purple gas giant Satamia Five through several large, clear windows. Even twelve light-seconds away, it still loomed impressively large, and seemed to glow with its own light.

When Sata finally looked around, she realized that most everyone in the room was avian. She spotted Drrrim-na at a small table with two chairs, and self-consciously shuffled over.

"I think I'm the only per . . . monkey mammal . . . in this place."

"Bok. You might be the only monkey mammal on the station, except for your shipmates."

"There's a healer."

"That's good. It's always a little hard having a different kind of healer."

Sata described Mati's situation.

"Do you think she can do it, bok? The mantidae are the best surgeons. They've saved my life more than once."

"I think so. Rini's sticking with her." Suddenly Sata looked uncomfortable. "What is there to eat? I'm not sure you and I eat the same things . . ."

Drrrim-na cackled. "You didn't think I was going to feed you *worms*, did you, bok?"

Sata shrugged and cringed with guilt.

"This place is known for its seed cakes," the avian continued. "Sort of like a dense, nutty bread, bok, but much easier to chew. They come with fruit and tender, peckable leaves and flowers."

"I'll . . . try it."

"Bok."

✳

The meal nestled in baskets with a handle, easy for the birds to carry to their tables. Remembering her years hauling food and drink from the kitchen to the common room, Sata was glad they served themselves at a counter, and would later clean their own table. She was amazed at how much she enjoyed the seed cakes, rivaling anything from Tori's bakery, except maybe fruit tarts.

She and her host chatted about the star station, then Sata shared her many adventures since they had first spoken. The avian listened intently to Sata's experience in the ice of Sonmatia Seven.

"Bok," the bird said slowly. "That is huge. I have never been tested like that, not sure I ever want to be, bok."

Sata smiled. "I'm certainly not looking forward to doing it again!"

Drrrim-na nodded agreement. "Bok!"

Just as they finished their meal, a noise of clucking and cackling came from the corridor outside, and about twenty avians crowded through the door.

"Bok!" the server at the counter yelled. "Need help!"

"Come on!" Drrrim-na said to Sata. "You have to learn how we do things around here."

Sata followed her friend. They quickly tossed their baskets into the washing room, and Drrrim-na pointed to a sink. Sata recognized the same dispensers they had on the ship, and washed her hands.

"Bok!" the server said with glee. "A monkey mammal can make baskets quickly!"

"I'll coach and carry, you assemble," Drrrim-na explained as she nudged Sata to a work table behind the counter. "Each basket gets a liner, seed cakes are in the warmer to your left, fruits and vegetables in the cooler on your right."

Sata opened doors until she found all the ingredients, spread them out on the table, and grabbed the first basket her friend placed before her.

"Two cakes, small bunch of jiba fruit . . . you remember what we had," the bird coached when she didn't have a basket in her beak.

"I think so. Just one flower, right?"

*

Sata worked quickly, both hands moving at once, to assemble the twenty baskets of bird food. When she glanced up, she saw the group of avians patiently waiting for their lunch, and obviously enjoying the sight of a monkey mammal working in the kitchen. Sata grinned. "I've been doing this kind of work all my life!"

Just as she was finishing the last basket, Drrrim-na staggered over with a huge basket she could barely carry.

"Huh?" Sata questioned.

"Fanators!" her friend whispered after dropping the basket on the table.

Sata looked up. Behind the last few birds about Drrrim-na's size, two giant feathered creatures waited in line, almost scraping their heads on the ceiling.

Another huge basket landed on the assembly table. "*Eight* seed cakes, *big* bunches of fruit, lots of leaves and flowers, and *two* cartons of maka worms, bottom shelf in the cooler. Fanators always want their maka worms."

"I thought you didn't eat worms," Sata said jokingly as she worked.

"Maka worms are for dessert! I said I wouldn't feed them to *you* . . . unless, of course, you have an open mind . . ."

Sata twisted her face. "I'll think about it."

*

When Sata completed the two large baskets, she looked up. The smaller birds were all seated, and only the two fanators remained at the counter.

"Greetings, skillful monkey mammal," one said.

"Hello. I hope you like your baskets."

"Thank you. You're new to Nebador, are you not?"

"Yes. I just arrived yesterday."

"Have you flown?"

"Well, yes," Sata said with a grin, "since I'm a deep-space response ship navigator."

"Excellent position. You'll get to see many of the mysteries of the universe. But I meant with us. I've been on a ship all day and need to stretch my wings after lunch. Would you like to come along?"

Sata swallowed. "Um . . . okay."

✳

The bird behind the counter thanked Drrrim-na and Sata for their help, then took over making baskets for the occasional guest or two who came in the door. The two navigators slipped out and peered over a railing. They could see several levels of the star station, and three or four thick branches of the great living tree that spread its leaves everywhere. Far below, small marine mammals played in a pool of deep water.

About a quarter hour later, the fanators joined them.

"I'm gonna find some still water to float in," the smaller female declared. "See you at the meeting!"

They clicked beaks together, then she hopped onto the railing, leapt into the air, and soon disappeared from sight.

Sata swallowed, and wondered what she had gotten herself into.

The male fanator stepped to a cabinet nearby. "There's supposed to be a harness . . . yes here it is." He slipped his head under a loop of shimmering fabric and the harness slid over his back easily. "I don't really like these, but it's better than getting feathers pulled out. If you like flying with us, there's a class you can take, and if you're really good, the harness is optional."

"You . . . um . . . carry people often?"

"Mostly on planets. It's a bit tight in here, but we'll make do. You coming along, little one?"

Drrrim-na nodded.

Sata smiled at her friend, looked back at the fanator, then blinked in surprise at the kinds of new friends she was making.

✳

The huge bird made sure Sata knew the two rules of flying with a fanator. Rule one, hold on or you'll fall and die. Rule two, no screaming or you might get *tossed* off.

Sata nodded that she understood, and placed her feet in the two lower loops of the harness. As soon as she had a good hold of the upper loops, the bird wasted no time hopping up to the railing, almost taking Sata's breath away in the process. Drrrim-na joined them on the railing.

A second later they were airborne, diving straight down.

Sata's mind screamed even though she managed to keep her mouth shut. A glimpse of her friend Drrrim-na, not far behind and looking very small compared to the fanator, gave her some comfort.

The giant bird soon spread it wings, flapped twice, and leveled out as it crossed the large open space in this part of the star station. Sata frowned when, seconds later, that open space came to an end.

The fanator clearly knew the station well, and banked sharply, entering a level passage that pierced a large block of rooms, taking them back toward the main hall. A few leisurely flaps kept them level and well clear of the furry and scaly creatures walking and hopping along the passageway.

They burst into the large main hall, causing Sata to gasp.

"Here's where we can really stretch!" the bird called.

Sata turned her head and glimpsed her smaller friend a hundred meters back, flapping with all her might.

Several powerful wing-beats brought them high up near the crystal roof of the hall, with nothing but stars beyond. Sata grinned, suddenly remembering that she was the navigator of a starship, and the universe was now her playground.

The fanator wheeled and swooped back across the open area, tucking his wings close when they passed a cluster of large leaves spread out in the sunshine. Sata giggled with delight.

Next the bird entered a narrow part of the hall, barely wider than his outstretched wings, and flapped several times to pick up speed. A solid wall of crystal, laced with branches and vines, blocked their way not far ahead. Sata closed her eyes.

The fanator suddenly tilted his wings back, beat the air twice, and they came to a dead stop in mid-air. Sata's eyes snapped open and her heart pounded in her chest.

The bird swiveled around in place, dove to pick up speed, then stretched his wings wide and they floated gracefully back across the main hall. The passenger couldn't help but shriek, "Weeeee!" A moment later, she added, "Oops, sorry."

"That was nothing," the bird replied, turning his head and glancing back with one sparkling eye.

Soon they entered another tunnel with no walkway below. Sata happened to look down. Several meters below stretched a clear, level sheet of glass, and she glimpsed a large rocky room with a number of lizard-like reptiles. The view was gone before she could make out anything else.

The fanator entered a smaller hall and banked several times, getting closer and closer to the floor each time. Finally he back-winged with powerful strokes above an empty place on the floor, and a heartbeat later landed on two feet without taking a single step.

Sata continued to hold the harness tightly.

"If you want more," the bird said, turning to look at his passenger, "you'll have to catch me later, as I have a meeting to attend in a few minutes."

Sata found her breath, and slowly loosened her grip. Half a minute later, she managed to step down to the floor, knees wobbling. "That was . . . wonderful!"

At that moment a furry monkey, smaller than Sata, ran up to the fanator, stretched out its arms, and the huge bird accepted its help slipping out of the harness. "Thank you, little one. Would you like to fly with me later today?"

"Yes, please!" it chittered, then dashed away with the harness.

Sata faced the huge bird, her heart still pounding. "If there is anything I can ever do for you . . ."

"You made my lunch," he said, eyes dancing playfully, "but I will keep your offer in mind for the future."

Sata grinned, and was suddenly moved to wrap her arms around the feathered creature.

He responded with a cooing sound.

She slowly let go and blushed with embarrassment.

Just then Drrrim-na landed nearby, quite out of breath.

✳   ✳   ✳

Chapter 7: Going Fishing

Boro glowed with pride as he walked beside the ursine docking controller. It dawned on him that the bear's swaggering gait was not too different from his own. "Um . . . that job you do . . . seems important . . ."

The larger animal chuckled. "Only if you want to get in and out of the station in one piece!"

Boro laughed as he continued to follow his host deeper into the maze of passageways and halls, passing thick tree trunks, doorways of all shapes and sizes, and ramps that went both up and down. "Um . . . I don't know your name . . ."

"Sorry. Ursines tend to be somewhat private about names and such. The part you can say, and that most people call me, is Glorm."

Boro tried the word with the same deep-throated intonation.

"Close enough."

"What do you . . . have to know to be a docking controller?" Boro asked as they descended a ramp.

"You have to be a pilot, and a navigator. Engineering and sensors don't hurt. Some command experience. And you absolutely *must* be able to juggle and dance."

Boro looked at the bear with a funny expression.

"I am deadly serious. A ship coming in with one of Melorania's little restrictions, like you had, is nothing compared to having two or three emergencies pile up in your face, and *you* have to figure out which one to deal with first, and what to do with the others who are screaming at you."

Boro was silent and thoughtful as they stepped onto another downward ramp. He was surprised to feel water on his feet.

Glorm laughed. "You're not used to the symbols, are you? Blue triangle back there. This is part of a whole maze of wet ramps, and you can go anywhere underwater, too."

"What if you . . . um . . . need to breathe?"

"Air pockets every eight meters. You'll see."

✳

A minute later they sat down beside a rushing stream. Water emerged from a dark tunnel on their left, and plunged into another tunnel just downstream. Roots stretched into the water on both banks, and large leaves blocked half the light that poured through a crystal window high above.

Boro frowned. "It isn't . . . natural — too smooth, no jagged rocks waiting to rip you open."

"Of course not. This isn't a planet. You'll get plenty of danger on your missions."

Boro laughed. "Had plenty on *my* planet!"

At that moment, a furry mammal about half the size of the bear, with webbed feet and a wide tail, emerged from the upstream tunnel. It grabbed a root and pulled itself onto the bank. "Glorm! Who's in the tower today?"

"M'sorpa, I think. This is Boro, response ship engineer, and fellow fisher."

The smaller mammal bowed. "Fish look good today, but I'm eating with my crew in an hour, so I resisted the temptation. Bye!"

"Don't shake until you're out of range!" the bear warned with a slight growl.

"I'll think about it!" the other said as he waddled up the ramp.

A moment later, they felt a few drops fly from above.

Glorm laughed. "He's fun. Works on a little ship that maintains navigation beacons. He and his mate are raising a cub right now, but he used to work on transport ships."

Boro was thoughtful for a minute. "It's hard to get used to all the animals talking, doing jobs, and being nice to each other. Where I come from, we would have just eaten your little friend for lunch."

The bear looked at Boro with intense eyes. "Just remember, there are planets where *monkey mammals* are eaten for lunch."

✳

After more chatter about the variety of planets that dotted space in the vast reaches of Nebador, Boro learned, to his delight, that none of the sapient species were fish, and amphibians were rare.

"I learned the difference between sharks and dolphins the hard way," he admitted, and went on to share his experience on the tropical island.

"You're lucky she only nipped you! Dolphins have serious teeth. You ready to go fishing?"

"Yeah, getting hungry. Do we use hooks, or nets?"

The ursine grinned. "No technology is allowed when fishing in the star station. We use our bare hands, and can only take what we eat."

Boro looked at the bear's claws, then at his own soft, pink hands and short nails. "I think . . . you'll have better luck."

"We'll see. If I get one first, I'll help a little if you want, but I'm sure you'd feel better if you got your own."

Boro's eyes glowed with a hunter's passion. "Yeah!"

✳

After hanging his vest on a peg by the ramp, the bear wadded into the water, then plopped down and let the current carry him. "Meet you at the first air pocket!" A moment later he disappeared into the far tunnel.

Boro breathed deeply for courage as he hung up his clothes. He stepped into the cool water, stood for a moment fighting the current, then sat down and let the water pull his feet out from under him. As soon as he entered the tunnel, most of the light faded and he was pulled down.

The current quickly slowed to a crawl as Boro blinked and looked around. Irregular but smooth rock walls seemed to glow with their own light. Behind him, air bubbles churned where the open stream plunged into deep water. Above him and ahead a few meters he could see the shiny surface of an air pocket, maybe two meters across, and a furry brown ursine treading water.

Boro felt with his feet, found the smooth bottom, and pushed off, aiming himself toward the life-giving air.

He broke the surface, saw a grab-bar within easy reach, and held on while catching his breath.

The ursine, also holding a bar, roared in welcome. "I had a hunch you'd be good in the water."

"This is easy!" Boro declared. "Clean and clear, not too cold, plenty of air ... what was that?" he asked with a start, looking down.

"Go down and see! Nothing dangerous in here."

Boro let go and dipped down, then kicked back up to the air pocket.

"Fluke or fin?" the ursine asked. "If fluke, it might be your next mission specialist. If fin, it's dumber than a cucumber, and fair game."

"Fluke," Boro said with a grin while chuckling.

"The best eating are the pink and silver fish, a meter long or more. They're slowed by age, but are still strong. Much under a meter and they're too young, and fast as lightning anyway."

Boro nodded.

"Don't worry about getting lost," the ursine continued. "I'll keep track of you, and lead the way back to our clothes after we've bagged lunch."

"Thanks. Anything . . . with a fin . . . I shouldn't touch?"

"The blue and green ones taste like bird feathers . . ."

Boro made a face.

"Yellow is okay, and sometimes easier to catch."

Boro looked around. "I've never seen a lighted air pocket before, with fresh air coming through a grill."

"You've never been in a star station before! Ready?"

The deep-space response ship engineer took a deep breath. "Yeah!"

✳

For the next half hour, Boro experienced the joy of using every muscle in his body, in water of a perfect temperature, with air and rest whenever he needed it. His friend was always nearby, but seldom did they talk. Marine mammals swam by, or paused to chatter in their own language that carried well underwater.

Boro noticed all the types of fish Glorm had mentioned, some darting by almost too fast to see, others lumbering fearlessly, especially the blue and green ones. Boro looked at them askance, and decided he wasn't *that* hungry.

The yellow fish were fairly slow, and several times Boro came close to grabbing one, even though he wasn't really trying. But at an air pocket, Glorm held up his pink and silver catch, more than a meter long. Boro decided it was time to get serious.

At first he focused on the delicious ones, but they were lightning-fast. After a quarter hour of trying, Boro decided a nice, tasty yellow fish would be okay, especially since this was his first star station fishing trip.

After missing a couple, he had one cornered in a tight place, the fish was obviously confused, and Boro was about to grab it when something silver flashed across the corner of his vision. Instinctively he jabbed that way with his opposite fist, caught the large fish against the wall, and for a moment it drifted, stunned.

Before Boro had time to think, the pink and silver creature started wiggling again, trying to regain its wits. Boro grabbed and smashed the fish's head against the wall, as hard as he could, until he was sure it would remain still.

As soon as the passion of the kill was over, Boro's lungs screamed at him to breathe, and the only question was whether it would be air or water. He clutched the lifeless fish tightly under his arm, looked up, and pushed off the bottom toward the nearest shiny, lighted air pocket.

As Boro gasped air in and out, fighting off a light-headed feeling, Glorm surfaced. "What's that under your arm?" the ursine said with grinning teeth.

Boro smiled even as he continued gasping, and didn't attempt words.

After Boro rested and regained his breath, Glorm led them slowly from one air pocket to the next. At one point along the way, a clear wall allowed Boro to glimpse a shallow pool where several lizard-like reptiles waded, two large ones wrestling playfully, a smaller one polishing a piece of jewelry.

"What was that?" Boro asked at the next air pocket.

"Last of their kind, poor fellows. We're looking for a planet for them, but they're very picky."

Boro shrugged and continued following his friend until a strong current pulled at them. The next thing he knew, they emerged into the air and light of the open stream, grabbed roots, and pulled themselves onto the bank.

"Where can we cook these beauties?" Boro asked as he dressed.

"They're better raw . . ." Glorm asserted with head cocked.

Boro squinted for a moment. "I guess . . . compared to what our pilot has to find the courage to do . . . I should try it."

The bear laughed. "If she can't find her courage, she wouldn't last long in the Nebador Services!"

✳

For the next half hour, ursine and monkey mammal sat near the stream, each hunched over his catch, passing Glorm's folding knife back and forth as they worked strips of meat off the bones of their fish. Glorm brought out a clear, flexible bag for the innards and bones. Neither spoke much, but occasionally they both looked up. Their sparkling mammalian eyes met, sealing their new bond of friendship.

At the end of the meal, Boro had to agree — it was better raw.

✳ ✳ ✳

Chapter 8: Mission Assignment Room

Kibi watched closely as Ilika paused to talk to former shipmates, old friends, and a stranger or two. Among the furry mammals, large birds, a quiet reptile taller than herself, and an eight-legged spider that made Mati's surgeon look cuddly, Kibi observed a common ritual of greeting that included eye contact and slight bows. She saw very little smiling, hand shaking, or hugging, and started keeping mental notes on what gestures might be unique to her own kind.

Ilika directed them into an eating place where they could choose from a dozen different meals, from a big bowl of leaves and flowers, to strips of raw fish. Ilika selected a little of everything, and Kibi grabbed cups of juice.

The eating tables in the courtyard bustled with activity and overflowed with all kinds of creatures sitting or standing. The pair of humans looked around, then exchanged grins when they spotted a quiet deck beside a pool of water.

Just as they got comfortable on the deck, a large dolphin breached the surface clutching a fish between rows of sharp teeth. Ilika quickly held the tray higher as a wave of water drenched the entire deck.

Kibi looked at Ilika and saw that he was smiling, so she did the same. The dolphin, still upright in the water, tossed the fish into the air, caught and swallowed it, and settled back to the surface. "Zalara Sim!" it said in a high-pitched voice, laying its head onto the deck.

"Krish-ka!" Ilika replied in recognition. "I haven't seen you in over a year!"

"Been in Nebula Seven-Two-Seven for months. Very glad to be back eating fresh fish!"

"Zalara Sim?" Kibi questioned, looking at Ilika.

"The name of my planet, in the native language, and *some* scientists have very good memories. I was the navigator on a stellar observing ship for a while."

The dolphin laughed in a very human way. "You have a girl now?"

"Krish-ka, this is Kibi, steward of the Manessa Kwi."

The dolphin rolled its head back and forth, looking at each of them in turn. "She is much more than your steward."

Ilika sighed and smiled. "Dolphins can read emotions very well," he said to Kibi. "Yes, Krish-ka, she's my dear lover."

The dolphin brought its wet snout close to Kibi. With only a moment of hesitation, Kibi offered her open hand. The snout nuzzled her fingers, but its teeth remained hidden. "Is he a good lover?" the dolphin asked softly.

Kibi grinned and looked at Ilika. "Most of the time. Enough to . . . you know . . . make me want to keep him."

Krish-ka laughed and started to slide back into the water. "Be good, Zalara Sim! I must go teach some young ones the difference between a star and an asteroid. Bye!"

When the dolphin was gone, Kibi laughed. "Even *I* know that much!"

✳

After eating a dozen foods Kibi had never seen before, she took on a thoughtful expression. "I feel . . . perfectly safe here. I've never felt that way before . . . anywhere."

"Just remember," Ilika began, "Nebador star stations are about the only places in the universe where that's true. And don't forget, we're on-call. Danger is just a mission assignment away!"

Kibi laughed. "I don't know about you, but I'm sopping wet! Does that count as danger?"

Ilika grinned at her while shaking his head. "That's just the price of working side by side with other sapient creatures. Ready to see the mission assignment room?"

She nodded and rose to her feet.

✳

In fresh, dry clothes, Kibi entered the huge hollow sphere with her mouth open. Thick tree trunks curved around the sides, and ramps connected platforms at many points in the large open space. Soft lights of different colors illuminated all the platforms and other places where creatures of all sorts sat or stood, some talking, others working at consoles.

Mammals and arachnids constantly moved up and down the ramps. Birds floated through the air from platform to platform. Marine mammals and reptiles worked in or near pools at the bottom of the spherical room.

Kibi tilted her head back. Stars and planets shined through every crystal wall. "But . . . how can . . . aren't we . . ."

Ilika smiled. "Yes, we're still deep inside the star station. The walls are all display screens, most of them of stars and planets far from here, anywhere some problem needs attention."

Kibi's skin tingled as she began to see more than mammals, birds, reptiles, and big spiders. Barely-seen fuzzy balls of light, of different colors and sizes, moved casually from one platform to another, or streaked away faster than the eye could follow, sometimes right through solid walls.

One large orange glow, almost a meter across, hovered near a furry black ursine at a console. As the bear worked, he often turned his head to the fuzzy light, listened for a moment, then nodded and went back to work.

At a platform close to a crystal wall, three small blue lights danced around each other. A large bird changed the view angle and magnification of the star field with sweeps of his wings in the air. After a moment, the blue lights vanished and the bird stepped to a console.

"Ilika . . . with all these glowing orbs . . . I feel like I'm back at Lumber Town with Melorania . . ."

"You can see them? I had a hunch you might. How many colors?"

"Um . . . three . . . no, four."

"There are eleven or twelve different types of non-material beings here," Ilika said, his head tilted up as he scanned the room, "and we experience them as different colors. You'll see them all in time."

"Wow. But . . . what . . ."

"Not all creatures in the universe are flesh and blood, my friend. You've met Melorania. We'll work with her often, since she's head of the Transport Service, but there are many others who will be involved in our missions from time to time. The one in charge of Satamia Star Station is here right now. Can you spot him?"

After a few deep breaths to master her fear, Kibi searched the room with her eyes. She was tempted to point to the orange glow, but changed her mind. The little blues were always coming and going, like messengers. Finally she knew, and pointed to a beautiful forest-green light, moving slowly from place to place, as if observing.

Ilika grinned.

"Makes sense," Kibi declared, "because the whole station's a big tree!"

*

They strolled along the ramps and observed the work at display screens or control consoles. Often, hurried conferences took place among flesh and blood creatures, fuzzy balls of light, or both.

Kibi was starting to think everyone was ignoring Ilika and herself, when suddenly she knew she was being watched. She slowly turned and discovered the forest-green light floating in mid-air not far away, and even though it had no eyes or ears, she knew with certainty it was looking at her, and listening to both her words and her thoughts.

"H . . . hello . . ." she managed to stutter out.

Ilika noticed and observed, but didn't interfere.

The glowing green fuzziness did nothing, said nothing, but a moment later Kibi's mission bracelet chimed. She flipped open the cover and peered at the little display. "Kibi," she read aloud, "please move the Manessa Kwi from dock C-Thirteen to C-Fourteen. Kerloran of Satamia."

Kibi looked up, and the forest-green orb slowly moved away. The feeling of being watched faded as he departed.

"Move Manessa? Me?"

Ilika smiled. "I *think* your name is Kibi . . ."

"You'll help me, right?"

Before Ilika could answer, his mission bracelet chimed. "Nope. I have to go talk to someone."

Kibi looked forlorn. "Do I get Mati?"

"No way! She's got enough to deal with, and Rini with her."

"At least . . . Sata?"

Ilika tapped at his bracelet. "Sorry. She's in flight somewhere, and it's not on the Manessa Kwi."

Kibi sighed. "And I'm sure that if I tried to find Boro, he'd be busy too, right?"

Ilika tried to suppress a grin. "Probably. I'd better go."

"But . . . I don't even know where dock C-Thirteen is!"

"Ask someone!" Ilika called back as he headed for one of the doorways that led out of the Mission Assignment Room.

✳   ✳   ✳

Chapter 9: Heat

A minute passed before Kibi worked up the courage to ask directions. She didn't want to bother anyone who looked busy, so she waited for the first creature who appeared to be off-duty. It turned out to be a sleek, furry mammal that walked on all fours and had feline teeth that could have made quick work of a donkey or horse.

"Um ... hello ... um ... do you have a moment?"

The animal's muscles rippled with strength as he sat on his haunches in front of Kibi, bringing his head level with hers. "Toran Takil, at your service, beautiful monkey mammal."

Kibi swallowed. "And ... you are very ... handsome. On my planet, mountain lions roam the land, and you remind me of them. But they are not sapient. At least ... I don't think so ..."

The powerful animal gazed into Kibi's eyes, and her rambling faded away. She felt nearly mesmerized, caught up in his penetrating glance. Her knees began to shake.

Seeing her mental state, he curled his lips slightly. "How can I help you?"

Kibi struggled to compose herself. "Um ... I need to find dock C-Thirteen, and move a deep-space response ship. Do you ... know where that is?"

The large animal yawned.   "Sounds like one of Kerloran's little confidence-building assignments. You are new here, or I'm a kitten."

Kibi smiled nervously. "*Very* new here. I can't even find my own ship!"

"I am free, and would be happy to guide you."

*

They followed three corridors and four or five ramps, but Kibi was so focused on her guide that she paid little attention to the turns they made or the signs they passed. As she walked along beside the sleek, powerful animal, she felt an unusual warmth fill her body. Soon they arrived at a comfortable little room with soft seats and a clear boarding tunnel that bridged the short distance to the golden ship. An intense desire to impress Toran Takil welled up inside Kibi.

"Um . . . I'd be very honored if you'd . . . come with me."

The huge cat curled his lips, then stretched forward and licked Kibi's neck, sending chills all throughout her body. Somehow she managed to get through the boarding tunnel without stumbling over her own feet, and he followed closely.

Driven by some deep need to look as good as possible to the animal watching her from the passenger area, words came to Kibi's mind that she had heard others say, but had never spoken herself.

"Manessa, short-range sensors, please, and the docking tunnel chart. Warm up anti-mass one and maneuvering thrusters."

Several consoles came to life with the requested functions. The chart flashed onto the main bridge screen and the pilot's three-D display.

"Close hatch, hull diagnostic, retract boarding tunnel. Select docking controller channel."

"Greetings, Manessa Kwi," a raspy insect voice said as an image of stick-thin legs and compound eyes appeared at the navigator's station.

"Hello, I'm Kibi, and Kerloran asked me to move the ship to C-Fourteen. No station control needed."

"This must be the shortest trip I've ever approved!"

Kibi grinned.

"The docking tunnel is clear, and your destination is about forty meters to your right."

"Thank you, Satamia control. Manessa Kwi closing."

Kibi sat down at the pilot's station for the first time. She glanced back at Toran Takil, saw his sparkling animal eyes watching her intently from the passenger area, and touched the symbol she knew would raise the flight control. "Manessa, release docking clamps."

As soon as the blue and purple fingers let go, she nudged up the anti-mass drive until she could feel the ship floating, then eased the flight control forward. Adrenaline filled her veins, and her heart throbbed in her chest. She felt more confident and alive than she could ever remember feeling.

Glancing at all her view angles, Kibi found the docking tunnel completely empty.   She cleared dock C-Thirteen, hoping her guest couldn't see her trembling.

Kibi grinned from ear to ear as they covered the forty meters to the next dock, and could feel the presence of the male cat every second of the journey. Finally she brought the ship to a stop, nudged it into the docking fingers, and breathed deeply when Manessa announced the ship secure.

"Manessa, shut down all systems and extend boarding tunnel."

Kibi was out of the pilot seat in a fraction of a second, and a heartbeat later stood before Toran Takil, breathing heavily but trying to look calm and confident.

"I am impressed," the cat said, and licked her on the neck again.

Kibi shivered and grinned with pleasure.

"Would you like to get some cold drinks with me, and I'll show you my favorite place in the station, a place few people know about, and fewer still ever go."

Kibi could think of no words to say, but nodded quickly and smiled.

✳

As they followed ramps and corridors again, Kibi dug deep into her courage and placed her hand on the large feline's back.   He didn't seem to mind, so she kept it there as they made their way through the station.   From that moment on, she had no awareness of where she was, other than beside a beautiful and powerful animal who excited her more than anyone ever had.

At a low table somewhere among the leaves of the station tree, Kibi knelt on the soft floor close beside her new companion.   She could feel his body heat, and sensing that he was comfortable with the closeness, she snuggled even closer.

The cold drink was probably delicious, but Kibi barely tasted it, and hardly noticed when they rose and wandered on.

Deep in seldom-used parts of the station, they followed narrow ramps and eventually arrived at a cozy patio among thick tree branches.   A little fountain bubbled, and a dark doorway stood at the far end of the patio, but otherwise the area was empty and quiet.

Toran Takil sat on his haunches and looked at Kibi.   She grinned and breathed rapidly.   He stretched close, licked and nibbled her neck, and let her feel his teeth without breaking skin.

Kibi sighed and giggled as shivers of pleasure shot through her body.

"I am Toran Takil, citizen of Nebador," he began.   "I stand and work beside the highest powers of the universe.   I go where the bravest people fear to tread.   I solve problems that planetary colleges and governments cannot even understand.   Kings and presidents sit before me and ask my advice."

Kibi suddenly felt an icy chill replace her previous warmth.

The large feline continued in a softer voice.   "If you want to play games with your heart, and other people's hearts, then you should return to your backward little planet as fast as you can.   If you have any intention of becoming a citizen of Nebador, then you need to do some serious growing up, right now."

Kibi swallowed hard and tried to blink away tears, but felt too ashamed to wipe them.

"The next time I look into your eyes, Kibi, I want to find an equal, a citizen of Nebador, strong and true. Right now I see a silly little girl. Beyond this fountain is a doorway. Within are powerful teachers who can guide you on the journey from . . . where you are . . . to where you could be, if you are willing to do the hard work."

With those words, Toran Takil licked Kibi's neck one last time, then turned and walked away.

✳

Kibi wrestled with her emotions for many minutes, knowing she was now the biggest fool in the entire universe. But somehow, she also guessed that Toran Takil would not tell a soul what she had done.

Eventually she managed to pull herself up straight. As she looked around the patio, she saw no sign of the big cat, and knew in her heart she would not see him again . . . at least, for a long time.

Kibi knelt down at the bubbling fountain and washed her face. When she looked up, she saw a little sign beside the door on the far side of the patio. Standing and going close, she read it.

Psychic Development.

She thought of Mati and her difficult decision. She wondered if Sata and her avian companion were becoming good friends. She tried to imagine Boro fishing with the bear. Finally, she thought of Ilika, and shame filled her mind and colored her face again.

After several deep breaths, she stepped through the doorway, not knowing what she would find within.

✳   ✳   ✳

Chapter 10: The Surgeon

An hour after Ilika and the others left the medical waiting room, Mati and Rini were still entwined on a couch, whispering thoughts and feelings to each other. The gray-haired human healer entered the room.

"Hello, Mati."

She tried to smile.

"Hi, Healer Dakalio," Rini said.

"If you'd like, while you're thinking about your options, I could do detailed scans. That way, we'll know more, and you'll know more, before you have to make any decisions."

Mati's mouth shifted back and forth in thought. "Um . . . okay. You'll tell me everything you find?"

"Everything. I promise."

* * * * *

For the next three hours, Mati allowed the mysterious machines to hover over every part of her knees, legs, and feet. What she didn't allow was Rini leaving her side, except once when he was beginning to cross his legs and do a clumsy dance.

To her surprise, the healer had his scanners probe both her knees, not just the bad one.

"We have to have something to compare to. Your left knee has had a hard life, but it's a lot closer to normal than . . . you know."

Mati smiled up at the healer for the first time.

He smiled back. "I think K'stimla would want to work on your hips and ankles a bit, too. After all, you have two or three hundred good years ahead of you."

"Wait a minute!" Rini challenged with a frown. "Even after I change that into base ten, it's still a lot longer than we live!"

The healer smiled slightly. "Maybe on *your* planet, but this is Nebador.

It's not easy finding good people, so we keep them as long as we can. I'm two hundred and fifteen."

Rini and Mati looked at each other with open mouths.

✳

For the next hour, Healer Dakalio explained many things he could see in the medical scans, and promised that K'stimla would see even more.

A shadow came over Mati's face. "How am I going to find the courage to let a big, green insect be my surgeon?"

The healer's eyes gleamed. "The first step has already been arranged. The four of us are having dinner together."

Mati sighed. "I don't suppose she'll eat me."

The older man laughed. "Not unless you're a frog! She *loves* frogs' legs."

Rini nodded and his eyes sparkled. "We do too!"

Mati sighed again. "All I have to do is eat frogs' legs with a big bug who's my only hope of walking again. Being a slave was *so* much simpler."

Both Rini and the healer laughed deeply.

✳

Mati desperately wanted to avoid sitting next to the huge green insect, so she quickly hobbled to the chair between the other two human chairs. Then she realized that would put her directly across the table from the big bug, face to face. She sighed and carefully sat down.

When the mantid surgeon arrived, a few minutes late, she perched on the floor in the remaining empty space and exchanged friendly greetings with her fellow healer on one side. Rini, on the other side, quickly joined in the pleasant conversation.

Mati was glad everyone was ignoring her.

Soon a cart arrived, pushed by a reptile wearing a funny purple hat, which caused smiles and laughter among almost all of those present. Bowls of fresh leaves came first, with a variety of sauces and sprinkles to choose from.

Mati tried not to look, but couldn't contain her curiosity. The surgeon ate with her two front-most legs, but the finger-like mandibles around her mouth did most of the work.

Both Dakalio and Rini steered the conversation toward topics that would give Mati some sense of what would happen, if she had the surgery, without ever referring to Mati or her knee. Hearing that surgery was done underwater piqued Mati's curiosity. A big pot of steamed frogs was placed in the center of the table, and bowls of dipping sauces completed the main course.

Mati noticed that K'stimla preferred the sweet-tart sauce. At first Mati avoided it, only using the savory garlic sauce. But when she started on her second frog, she took a deep breath, tried the sweet-tart sauce, and immediately understood why the surgeon preferred it.

Rini shared stories from their travels that made Mati smile. Dakalio, without ever looking at Mati, recalled times when patients would almost rather die than let a monkey mammal provide medical care. He clarified that those patients had not been Nebador citizens.

Mati felt about an inch tall. She also felt completely left out of the companionship and good cheer encircling the table. She suddenly realized that if she refused the surgery and went home, Rini might go with her, but their relationship would probably be reduced to ... something not much better than slavery.

"Um ..." she managed to squeak, her eyes still on her plate, "I don't think I could let *any* healer work on me unless Rini was at my side the whole time."

Mati looked at Rini with a questioning smile. Rini grinned at Dakalio. Dakalio turned to K'stimla.

"Actually," K'stimla began, "I wouldn't attempt this procedure *without* Rini there, because he's going to be my assistant for the surgery."

Rini's eyes grew wide. "But ... I don't know anything about ..."

K'stimla's hundred or more insect eyes looked at the lad. "You know how to draw breath, pump blood, and regulate body temperature. A machine could do all that, but it cannot love Mati as you do." The surgeon then looked directly at Mati. "Can you place your life in this boy's hands?"

Mati labored for a moment to swallow the huge lump in her throat. "Um ... um ... yes."

* * *

Chapter 11: Conference

Ilika entered the nearly-dark room with more than a little anxiety. He had been called upon to make many decisions during the previous year and a half of his life, ever since hiding the Manessa Kwi in the swamp near the capital city of a small medieval kingdom on Sonmatia Three.

He knelt and cleared his mind, knowing he had done what he had done, and could not now avoid the consequences of his actions ... or inactions. After a few minutes, he felt a presence. The presence slowly took on the form of a fuzzy glowing mist, then the color of a ripe peach. Ilika smiled.

For the next few minutes, as silence continued to fill the room, Ilika opened his mind and let the presence experience everything the young captain had seen, heard, and felt.

Judge yourself, Ilika Imni, the presence said softly without words.

Ilika breathed slowly to center his thoughts. "It was a good mission that taught me more things than I can remember. I made mistakes, as you know, and will again, but hopefully not the same ones."

Ilika felt a moment of humor radiate from the presence. *Judge the five you brought back.*

"Rini is as close to perfect as I could want. The other four have weaknesses, and will probably make serious mistakes, but I believe they will be citizens of Nebador someday. I will do everything in my power to help them on that journey."

Mati needs to spend more time with other sapient creatures, the presence asserted, *and her surgery and recovery will begin that process. She and Rini will work best together, especially after the surgery.*

Ilika nodded.

Boro will always be loyal, but will need help and encouragement developing his mind.

"I was thinking of cross-training him into navigation soon."

Sata has greater lessons to learn. Be watching for them, but do not interfere unless you must for the safety of others.

Ilika nodded.

Your biggest problem is your steward.

"I . . . sense that."

Never ask what happened today. You do not want to know. But be comforted — she has stepped onto a path that may bring her to citizenship. It may take her away from you, at times, but you cannot deny her that path without destroying her.

Ilika swallowed, took a deep breath, and tried to smile.

Overall, I am pleased, Ilika Imni, the presence continued. *You have earned the companionship of Manessa Kwi Habishu Glinta, and the task of guiding your chosen five toward citizenship. Your ship and crew are now active on the Nebador Transport Service rolls.*

"I am honored," Ilika said as a flood of warm emotions filled his body and tears of joy threatened to spring from his eyes.

The presence embraced him for a moment, then faded away.

Ilika, still on his knees, let the good feelings of success linger as he felt the cool, sweet air of the star station flow in and out of his lungs. Suddenly his mission bracelet emitted it's emergency chime. He quickly looked at the little display.

Manessa Kwi — prepare for immediate departure.

✳   ✳   ✳

Chapter 12: First Mission

Ilika's mind raced, and he quickly tapped at the tiny keys of his bracelet, marking Mati and Rini off-duty, and requesting location and status from the other three. Before getting any replies, he was on his feet, striding toward dock C-Fourteen.

"I'm about two minutes away," Sata's voice informed him. "Drrrim-na will guide me."

"Two or three minutes," Boro announced. "Glorm's asleep, but I found a big spider who knows the way."

"Less than a minute," Kibi said.

When Ilika jogged down the last ramp and could see the waiting room, Kibi was already there, stepping off a fanator.

"Thank you, sister," she said, embracing the huge bird. "Please tell Memsala I will redo that lesson as soon as I can."

"She knows," the bird said, turned and bowed toward Ilika, then walked up the ramp looking for a place to take off.

Kibi immediately grabbed Ilika and planted a passionate kiss on his lips.

"What did I do to deserve that?" he asked when she finally released him.

"Just . . . a tiny sample of what you're gonna get when we're alone in our cabin."

Ilika grinned just as Sata came striding down the ramp, with Boro close behind. They both turned and waved to the bird and spider who remained side by side at the top.

Ilika glowed with happiness for a moment, seeing his crew, except for those with a good excuse, all gathered and ready to work.

They stepped into the waiting room, but the boarding tunnel was blocked with a pallet of cargo that floated through slowly, followed by a small furry mammal with a wide tail.

"Ilika . . ." Boro began with concern, "we haven't restocked anything . . ."

"I know. I was planning to do that tomorrow. We'll have to . . . what would Drrrim-na say? Wing it?"

Sata chuckled as they slowly followed the cargo pallet into the ship. "I *doubt* Drim-na would say that!"

"Manessa," the beaver said as soon as he entered. "One pallet, and a seat for me, please."

The chairs in the passenger area rearranged themselves, leaving an open space in the middle. Kibi watched as the little mammal carefully positioned the pallet, then spoke to the ship again to anchor it to the floor. "All reasonable speed to Ubalora Four, Captain," he said after climbing onto the nearest seat.

"Pre-flight," Ilika ordered. "I'll cover sensors and helm. Kibi, I want you to get to know Rini's station whenever you can."

Kibi nodded as she stepped to the steward's console.

"No space thruster fuel," Boro reminded everyone with a worried tone. "Everything else will do for a short flight, I guess. Anti-mass and maneuvering thrusters ready."

"Docking tunnel, station departure, and Ubalora system charts on the board," Sata reported. "Controller on channel."

"Greetings again Manessa," the same insect said. "Nice to see you again, Kibi. Traffic is light, and you have first priority out."

Kibi grinned, and without a word from her captain, she closed the hatch, retracted the boarding tunnel, and released the docking clamps. She felt some desire to impress the little mammal behind her, but not nearly as much as she had felt earlier with the big, handsome . . . she stopped herself in mid-thought and remembered the huge trouble she had almost gotten into by letting herself fall for the first sexy male who looked into her eyes.

❋

The partial crew felt very comfortable with everything they had to do to leave Satamia Star Station. The discomfort began when the captain said, "Prepare for star transit."

Kibi, already studying the sensor options at the watch station, looked at her passenger. Without hesitation, he secured his inertia straps, relaxed, and closed his eyes. "Ship and passenger ready. No sensor warnings."

"Inner Ubalora entry chart is up," Sata said, then scrunched herself into a comfortable position.

"Star drive warming," Boro reported and closed his eyes.

If the passenger noticed the long delay before the star drive engaged, he didn't say a word.

❋

They popped back into space not far from the civilized planet Ubalora Three, and Ilika called for maximum ion drive to cover the five light-minutes to their destination, the fourth planet. During the half-hour flight, he gave his crew a sketch of the two sapient species, one mammalian and one avian, that shared the snowy little world.

The mammals were cave dwellers with thick fur, able to walk upright, but often preferring all fours to stay out of the wind. The birds ruled both the sky and the small seas when free of ice.

Sata looked thoughtful. "So . . . Ubalora Three has a civilization, and Four doesn't?"

"Right," Ilika began. "We only refer to sapient creatures as civilized when their society is willingly self-correcting. That means that any problem or imbalance that arises is fixed, and I mean really fixed — not ignored, not hidden, and not passed off to a future generation."

The beaver joined the conversation. "The avians have a complex society, but they love to lay eggs, so their population explodes, then crashes, based on the fish in the seas."

"What about the mammals?" Boro asked.

Ilika deferred to their passenger.

"More stable population, but they enjoy their tribal warfare. Thinkers and artists have very low status, along with women. Only warriors receive any honor."

Kibi frowned. "So what's Ubalora Three like?"

Ilika smiled. "Beautiful, every inch of it. They reserve large areas for different levels of social complexity. An entire continent is wilderness for those who want to live wild and free. And Ubalora Three welcomes the Nebador Services, and openly trades with us."

Sata smiled as she checked the ship's position on the chart. "Twelve minutes to destination. Our planet's a civilization, right Ilika?"

The long moment of silence that followed told Sata what she feared.

"No, not by our definition," he finally said. "My childhood planet isn't either."

After another moment of silence, the furry beaver looked at Ilika sternly. "Aren't you going to tell them?"

Ilika took a deep breath. "I guess I should."

Sata, Boro, and Kibi all looked at their captain.

"Every society *thinks* it's civilized. But by Nebador's definition, there are no human civilizations . . . um . . . anywhere in the universe."

Boro and Sata looked at each other, then both looked at Kibi.

"So . . ." Kibi began thoughtfully, "the *real* civilization on Ubalora Three . . . isn't human, isn't monkey mammal . . ."

"Right."

✳

The approach flight plan for Ubalora Four required them to stay high in the sky until right over a tiny, isolated valley deep in the most rugged mountains. After Ilika brought the ship to a stop eight thousand meters above the white peaks, Kibi poked at the watch console until she figured out how to get a down-angle view. Three domes, partly covered by snow, surrounded a small outdoor landing pad in a clearing among tall pine trees.

Ilika lowered the ship and selected a parking space.

"Welcome to Ubalora Four research station," the beaver said. "It is, believe it or not, the middle of summer."

Boro laughed nervously, gazing at his nearly-white display.

Their guest worked with his pallet of supplies. As soon as Kibi opened the hatch, the nearest door to the research station also opened. A mottled orange reptile emerged with another pallet, this one stacked with round canisters.

The beaver and lizard paused as they passed each other on the snow-covered landing pad.

"New monkey mammals," the furry one said. "Their first mission, I think."

"I know Ilika," the scaly one replied. "Stay warm!"

"Easier said than done in this place," the beaver grumbled in jest, then continued waddling into the heated research station.

✳

Unlike the quiet beaver, the reptile greeted everyone with bows, flowery words, and a flashing tongue that tasted the air between them.

"Ilika! You got yourself a ship and a crew, I see!"

The young man and the lizard embraced.

"I will never forget our deep-space missions together," Ilika said when they parted and looked at each other. "Everyone, this is Sss'rol'ti, one of our beloved Quanasia, and my second-favorite steward in the Transport Service."

Kibi grinned.

"Don't let the scales and horns fool you," Ilika went on. "Under his charms, the wildest beast will soon be sipping pinkfruit juice and watching videos."

The talkative lizard greeted Kibi and Sata, then came to Boro. After kind words and a taste of the air, his eyes swirled. "You've been eating my favorite fish! Did you save me some?"

"Sorry," Boro admitted with a guilty frown. Then he looked into the lizard's deep, multi-colored eyes and relaxed. "Glorm showed me the under-water part of the station."

"Glorm the docking controller? He's fun! But as always, I'm chattering too much. I guess we should get these samples back before they spoil."

Ilika smiled and gave commands to prepare for the return trip.

Once they were in the air, Boro received a message on his console from the navigator. *Take me fishing tomorrow?*

He turned and looked at Sata. Their eyes met, they grinned at each other, and he nodded.

"Prepare for star transit," Ilika said from the helm.

✳

The Manessa Kwi settled into Satamia Star Station dock D-Eleven. Sss'rol'ti chatted with the crew for another quarter hour, then floated his pallet of canisters down a ramp, humming a tune as he went.

Kibi looked at her console with surprise. "We've been awake almost a day and a half! It's almost breakfast time!"

Suddenly Boro yawned, and Sata couldn't stop herself from doing the same. "I don't need food," Boro announced through his yawn. "I need sleep!"

Ilika nodded. "Let's meet in eight hours and get this ship stocked."

"Yeah!" Boro agreed.

*

Ilika could feel Kibi's intense emotions as they made their way, with arms around each other, down the lift and across the lower deck. For the next several hours, he almost thought he had a wild animal in his cabin.

When they were finally exhausted, Ilika lay half-asleep beside his lover. He didn't know what change had come over her, and he wasn't going to ask, but he knew for sure he was going to enjoy every minute of it.

Suddenly the knowledge processor on Kibi's desk chimed. She groped her way to consciousness and staggered across the cabin.

"I have to go to a class, and finish an intro lesson I started yesterday. It's something . . . important."

"That place where we ate has nutrition drinks you can grab on the way."

Kibi nodded and was about to dash out the door. She stopped herself and looked at Ilika, recent memories causing her eyes to sparkle. "Thank you."

Ilika smiled shyly.

* * *

Chapter 13: Decision

Mati dreamed of slave owners telling her she was useless, guards yelling at her to hurry up, and a young goatherd informing her that none of her skills mattered. All of them were *her* kind, monkey mammals, humans. She squirmed and thrashed until Rini wrapped his arms around her and held her tightly. Even though she was already drenched in sweat, somehow the extra body heat made her relax.

The dream changed. A large bird glanced at her with friendly, sparkling eyes. A bear roared and offered her a fish. A giant green insect opened its arms to embrace her. In the dream, Rini stood by, watching and waiting.

Mati awoke, swallowed to wet her parched throat, and felt Rini's arms around her. "You awake?" she whispered.

"Yeah."

"Do you think ... maybe ... we could have breakfast with Surgeon K'stimla?"

Rini smiled. "I think so."

✳

Bowls of small fruits, nuts, and wiggling grubs were delivered by a spider almost as tall as Mati. She chuckled when he sampled them before bowing. "Have to make sure they're fresh!" he explained, a berry in one claw and a grub in another, leaving six legs to stand on.

K'stimla soon arrived, and clearly enjoyed the grubs most. Rini and Mati stuck to the fruits and nuts.

"Ilika has told us many times that we always have to keep growing," Mati began, pushing berries and nuts around on her plate. "A dream reminded me that ... it's been monkey mammals who have treated me badly all my life. Even the wild animals on my planet have never been ... you know ... evil."

"Evil requires sapience," K'stimla replied between grubs. "If a creature isn't self-aware, it might be dangerous, but can't be evil."

Rini nodded thoughtfully, but remained silent.

"I guess ... monkey mammals are the worst ..." Mati admitted with a guilty look.

"Not at all!" the surgeon interrupted. "Every sapient race is capable of selfish, terrible evil, using and abusing others, even their own kind. My people have a tendency to make beautiful planets into dark, ugly, polluted places where machines rule with iron claws."

"Oh ..."

"Being in the Nebador Services has *nothing* to do with the people we come from, and everything to do with who *we* are, as individuals. Very few humans, anywhere in the universe, could sit at table with me, and very few mantidae with you. But I can trust you to be my pilot, and you can, if you choose, trust me to be your surgeon."

The healer fell silent and dissected a piece of fruit with her mandibles.

Mati took a deep breath. "I ... would like you ... to be my surgeon ... if you can forgive me for being so ... thick-headed."

"I can."

Rini smiled and popped a grub into his mouth. It wasn't too bad, after it quit wiggling.

* * *

Chapter 14: Stocking the Manessa Kwi

Ilika didn't want to start ordering supplies for the ship without his steward, so he had a leisurely mid-day meal with Boro and Sata, and showed them some new parts of the star station. They were just stepping out of the museum, after looking at the last crystal cluster Sarto found twenty thousand years before, when Kibi skidded to a stop in front of them. "Sorry I'm late."

"We didn't set an exact time," Ilika reassured. "If I need you on-duty, your bracelet will scream at you."

Kibi grinned as they headed for dock D-Eleven hand in hand.

✳

On the last ramp down to the docking area, Sata noticed Kibi touching and working sore muscles. "Did you hurt yourself?"

"No, just wrestling."

"With what?" Boro asked. "A mountain lion?"

A shadow passed over Kibi's face and she was silent for a long moment. Eventually she cracked a little smile. "Just a very strong reptile."

Ilika sensed that this was the area of Kibi's life to avoid asking about.

As soon as they stepped onto the ship, Boro grabbed a knowledge pad. "I know what *I* want!"

"Let me guess . . ." Kibi began with a smile. "Pinkfruit juice."

Boro grinned. "Pinkfruit juice for Manessa. In other words, liquid number five, space thruster fuel!"

"You could fill that little tank on supply line fifteen," Ilika suggested.

Boro nodded. "Manessa's secret fuel stash! Would you like that, Manessa?"

"It's not very useful empty."

The four humans laughed.

"Want to help me, Sata?" Kibi asked. "We need *everything*."

"Sure. I just need a roll of paper for the chart printer, and it's already on my list."

The two girls took knowledge pads into the galley, and Ilika went down the lift with Boro. The captain wanted to make sure his excited engineer didn't start stashing fuel canisters under the beds.

✳

An hour later, with Ilika's help, Boro had a shopping list of fuel, a few other chemicals, and some power cells for the portable instruments.

When Ilika sat down with Kibi's shopping list, he immediately spotted a problem. "What are you going to feed avians, reptiles, and insects?"

Kibi grinned sheepishly. "Forgot about them."

Sata raised her hand. "I think I can make a list for the birds!"

"Go for it," the steward said, handing her a knowledge pad.

Ilika worked with Kibi, and they soon added preserved grubs and other things that Kibi had mistaken for cleaning supplies. The captain looked over the finished lists, marked them low-priority, and transmitted it all to the supply room. "It will be here in an hour or two. We can get stuff quicker in an emergency."

"That's all we have to do?" Sata asked with wide eyes. "All that stuff will just appear?"

"On a cargo pallet, in the waiting room. Then *we* have to put it away."

Just then Kibi's bracelet chimed. "Uh oh, class." She looked at Ilika with a guilty expression.

"Go. Sata and I can handle the food, and I'm sure Boro wants to personally stow each canister of fuel."

The engineer grinned and nodded.

Kibi slid her arms around Ilika's neck and kissed him tenderly. "I'll make it up to you."

"Yep," Ilika said. "You're in command of the next mission."

After a moment of thought, she licked him on the neck and dashed through the hatch.

✳

Ilika, Sata, and Boro got a light meal at a quiet little place that served fruits and vegetables, then returned to the waiting room of dock D-Eleven. For some reason, the supplies were late, not arriving until just after Kibi returned from her class.

"That's weird," Boro mumbled. "It's like someone's watching us."

Ilika smiled. "Things like that happen all the time in Nebador."

The two girls looked at the huge stack of supplies. Not even Sata had ever seen so much food in one place. She and Kibi danced around the pallet, grinning from ear to ear, as Boro clapped for them and tapped one foot.

Ilika stood watching and smiling. The small ursine who had delivered the pallet just shook his head.

✳   ✳   ✳

Chapter 15: Evening on Satamia Star Station

A couple of hours later, every fuel rack on the Manessa Kwi was loaded to capacity, and the galley, storage closet, and utility room were bulging with food and other supplies. Boro and Kibi both looked very proud.

Ilika's bracelet chimed.

"Want to have dinner with us?" Rini's voice inquired. "We have wonderful news!"

Ilika looked at the others, and they all nodded.

The four wandered through the vast main hall of the star station, with its many levels of balconies, thick tree trunks, ramps, stairs, and pools. But they noticed a dramatic change. The light in the huge room was dim — the Satamia sun had recently slipped below floor level as the station slowly turned. Shafts of colored light occasionally flashed from devices on balcony rails, as if being tested. Some of the lights changed color, while others moved or flashed.

Most normal activity in the main hall seemed to have stopped, and those people who remained were busy cleaning or putting up decorations. Pallets of supplies floated out of tunnels and made their ways into the many kitchens on the edges of the big space. Cooks within were busy preparing food and drink, but didn't yet have any customers. A many-legged insect on a balcony tested his musical instrument, filling the hall with a flurry of pure tones for a moment.

Kibi stopped in her tracks, looked around, and grinned.

"What's . . . going on?" Sata asked.

"Evening. Party time. Don't worry, it won't get started for an hour or so, plenty of time for us to eat with Mati and Rini."

"But . . ." Boro began with a frown, "we came through at about the same time yesterday, and nothing like this was going on . . ."

"That was yesterday based on Manessa's clock, set to your planet's rotation and occasionally modified by Kibi. A day on the star station is about five times as long."

Kibi seemed lost in wonder, but somehow found her words. "Can we . . . go to it?"

"Of course, as long as we remember that this is Nebador, and the Mission Assignment Room, or your teachers, Kibi, can call at any time."

Kibi nodded, but her mind was elsewhere, up in the balconies with the colored lights, glittery streamers, and musical instruments.

Sata grabbed her hand and pulled her along to catch up with Ilika and Boro.

Rini and Mati knew nothing of the preparations in the main hall, and listened eagerly. The dinner cart arrived, and Mati proudly explained which dipping sauce was best with the steamed frogs. Bowls of vegetables and fruits rounded out the meal, and Rini even had a small cup of grubs. After eating a few, he passed the cup around, but it returned to him with the same number of grubs. He laughed.

"This is my last meal before . . . you know what," Mati announced, pulling a frog apart on her plate. "I don't get any breakfast, and K'stimla says the surgery will take most of the day."

"But she'll get nutrition right into her blood," Rini explained as he took some vegetables, "and I'll be with her the whole time. We already met the glowing purple guy . . . person . . . being . . . who will link our minds, and he said . . ."

"I thought it was a she," Mati asserted.

"Yeah, could be. She said part of the link would remain for the rest of our lives."

Mati smiled with pride. "He also mentioned that the link would be strong for several days, and that would help with my recovery."

"Are you each doing this of your own free will?" Ilika inquired.

The couple looked at each other and nodded.

Rini turned back to Ilika. "A really serious-looking spider came by to make sure we knew all the risks, and recorded our answers with his knowledge pad."

Everyone enjoyed their food in silence for a minute.

"You know," Mati began without quite looking at Rini, "*you* could go out and enjoy the party. I'm the one getting ready for surgery . . ."

Rini scraped the meat off a frog's leg with his teeth. "Nope. I go through that door when you do . . . on two feet, both of us. Wanna watch a video?"

Mati rolled her eyes, but was smiling with happiness.

When the four active members of Manessa's crew returned to the main hall, preparations for the party were just about complete. A group of reptiles played bits of music to test their instruments, and trays of drinks and snacks lined many tables.

Kibi turned circles in wonder, remembering the simple pipes and drums that played under torchlight back in her kingdom.

"Ilika!" a deep human voice called from somewhere above them.

Ilika looked up. "Sorrano!"

The others could see a man with long brown hair, wearing a shimmering orange robe, leaning over the railing of the first balcony level.

"Can you help? Some wonderful avians are trying, but making monkey-mammal food really does need hands."

"We'll be right up!"

As the others followed Ilika to the nearest ramp, Sata explained that this was how things were done in Nebador. She strode into the kitchen, found it similar to the one she already knew, and pointed to the hand-washing sink.

The birds were relieved and gladly made way for the crew of monkey mammals. A tall yellow-haired lady, in a shimmering blue robe and apron, bowed and thanked them.

"I'm Rossilia," she said, greeting the crew with a friendly smile and gesturing for them to gather around the assembly table. "I was hoping to make these little treats, until I learned there were hardly any humans on the station. Ilika, you've made these before."

"Years ago."

"A sheet of dried seaweed, a layer of sticky rice, then strips of veggies and fish. Roll them up and slice into single bites. Easy . . . if you have hands."

The crew went to work while Rossilia attempted to fix the ones made by the birds. "Each roll can be a little different."

While they worked, Sorrano sliced fish and chatted with Ilika. The three had worked on a ship together when Ilika was quite young. "I had a hunch you'd become a captain someday," Sorrano said. "You always liked seeing the bigger picture. I never got over being space-sick half the time, so I decided to stick to star and planet stations."

"He likes flying," Rossilia revealed, "but only by shuttle or fanator so he can see the ground."

"I've flown on a fanator!" Sata boasted. "I only screamed a little . . ." she continued more humbly.

Ilika looked at Kibi, busy holding in a smile.

"It's required for my training," she revealed, "and anything else I'm uncomfortable with."

"Oh!" Sorrano began, "you must be in the Psychic Development program!"

Kibi nodded. "What do you know about it?"

"Not much. I flunked out after a week. It's not required for citizenship, only if you want to walk and talk with Kerloran and such during the toughest missions."

Kibi swallowed.

"I'm just a supply clerk, power cell technician, and occasional cook," Sorrano continued. "I helped make up your pallet today. Your cupboards must have been bare — I thought I was stocking a transport ship!"

Kibi grinned and nodded as she took the last piece of fish.

"And he's a very good singer!" Rossilia added. "He's on the schedule tonight."

Ilika smiled as he sliced his last fish and vegetable roll. "That'll be a treat! I've always envied your rich, deep voice."

Sorrano brushed off the compliment with a jerk of his head as he cleaned up the pile of fish bones. "The party's about to begin. Let's get these goodies out there!"

As Kibi helped carry trays of food and drink to the serving tables, she fell in beside Ilika. "Have you done the Psychic Development training?"

He nodded. "It's required to be a captain."

In that moment, while carrying a tray of party food, Kibi became absolutely sure that she was going to go all the way through the program, and someday be Toran Takil's equal on all the hardest missions . . . *and* Ilika's faithful lover.

The music had just begun when Ilika and his partial crew descended to the main floor. On a landing above the largest pool, a spider worked a keyboard with most of his legs, while a lizard held an instrument that produced tonal sweeps. On another landing, a monkey with a long tail perched before a console that controlled a hundred dancing, flashing, changing lights, all coordinated to the music.

Several birds were already on the dance floor, hopping from foot to foot, or spreading wings upward and turning circles.

Kibi looked at Ilika. "I can just . . . go out there and dance?"

"That's the idea. Just don't step on anyone!"

As eager as she was, Kibi started slowly, watching those around her to see what they were doing, and being very careful where she put her feet. Deep down inside, she knew she was born to dance, but her only opportunity so far had been on the Manessa Kwi when off-duty. She was just figuring out how to move to the piece played by the spider and reptile when her bracelet chimed.

Sit, until I release you. Memsala.

Kibi's face fell and she stood motionless on the dance floor, fighting with her feelings. Ilika noticed, stopped dancing, and stood near. After more than a minute, she sighed and dragged herself to a couch in a dimly-lit area off to one side.

To her surprise, Ilika plopped down beside her.

"*You* don't have to stop dancing," she said with a hurt tone, wearing a pout. "*Your* bracelet didn't chime."

Ilika smiled. "I bet the message didn't say anything about eating, drinking, snuggling, or kissing!"

Kibi struggled with herself for a long moment. "Thanks."

"What are lovers for?"

They shared a long kiss while a quartet of furry apes began a new song with smooth horns and deep-toned strings.

"You ... um ... deserve to know about something," Kibi began with obvious difficulty once their lips parted.

Ilika nodded slightly and took her hands in his.

"I ... almost made a huge mistake recently with ... another male ..."

"Oh, Toran Takil?"

Kibi's mouth opened in surprise, but she managed to nod slightly. "How did you know?"

"When you licked me on the neck, I guessed. That's sort of his trademark. And if you'd met him, but *hadn't* felt his magnetic qualities, you'd be about the only female, of any species, who could make that claim. Even some of the males ..."

Kibi burst out snickering, and Ilika joined her. With that load of guilt off her chest, she felt much better. Still, she really wanted to dance, and kept twisting this way and that to see what the other dancers were doing.

Eventually she swiveled around to see what was behind her. She hadn't realized it until then, but the couch was not far from the medical center. Silhouetted behind the glass doors, she could see two small human figures holding hands, one leaning on a crutch.

Somehow, that helped her to relax.

Sata felt for Kibi, but knew it was Ilika's place to comfort her. She continued to hold hands with Boro, and even though she had never danced in her life, she felt drawn to the dance floor. As she watched the other dancers, she realized that few of them had any dancing skill. They were just prancing, hopping, or swaying to the music, each type of creature in a different way.

Occasionally someone with real skill would take to the floor, and others would give them room and watch. Most often it was a large bird with vivid green and blue feathers, or one of the reptiles that walked on two legs. The monkeys with tails could prance up a storm, but not very gracefully.

Sata tried to nudge Boro toward the dance floor, but became aware that he was trying to nudge her toward the food and drink. They both stopped and looked at each other with embarrassed smiles.

"How about . . ."

"Yeah, maybe . . ."

"Uh huh."

"You first?"

"No, you."

"Um, okay."

Sata guided Boro onto the edge of the dance floor, in a little-used area, far from any of the fancy dancers. She started moving her feet to the music. The only other dancers nearby, a pair of clumsy birds, continued hopping from one foot to the other while nuzzling each other with their beaks, and paid no attention to the new arrivals.

Boro tried shuffling his feet, but quickly became embarrassed. "I'm terrible . . ."

"Me too," Sata assured him. "Remember, we always have to keep learning."

Suddenly Boro remembered something Glorm said. To be a docking controller, you had to juggle and dance. Boro started moving his feet again, and thought he might have almost found the rhythm of the song just before it ended.

Sata offered her hand, and together they headed for the snack tables.

Boro realized with surprise that he was looking forward to the next song, and hoped he could get his feet moving to its beat.

With the help of a neck massage from Ilika, Kibi began to relax on the couch and accept the situation. "I guess . . . I was sort of all full of myself when I started dancing, thinking I was going to go out there and impress everyone. Now . . . watching the brightly-colored birds, and those fast-footed lizards . . . how do they always know our weaknesses?"

"Who?"

"You know, the people in charge, and my new teachers."

Ilika chuckled. "They can see right through us, my friend. It used to bug me too. Where I grew up, just like on your planet, no one knew or cared what anyone else was thinking or feeling."

As the entire main hall had become quiet, both Ilika and Kibi fell silent and looked around. All the dancers were finding places to sit, perch, or hang. The previous musicians put away their instruments, and a group of six rather large reptiles were setting up big drums on part of the dance floor.

"Oh, I know!" Ilika let slip.

"What?"

"You'll see. If he's gonna sing what I think he is, you'll see more than a thousand Nebador citizens nearly moved to tears. There are few songs that deeply touch all the different sapient species. If my hunch is right, this is one of them."

"Who!" Kibi demanded.

"Sorrano."

At that moment, the first drummer, the smallest of the six reptiles, began to beat a simple rhythm. Half a minute later, he was joined by another drummer, creating a richer sound, and soon a third added emphasis every fourth beat.

Birds and reptiles all around the dance floor sighed with anticipation.

The next drummer began a complex rhythm on several smaller drums, and the fifth drummer added a similar, but slightly different, rhythm that seemed to balance the first.

"There he is," Ilika whispered as a spotlight lit up a small landing about halfway between the main floor and the clear crystal ceiling. Sorrano stepped into the light, breathing slowly and deeply.

The last drummer finally added the deepest and loudest sound of all on a drum more than a meter across. The leaves of the great star station tree began to quiver, and the floor seemed alive with vibrations.

Suddenly the deepest drum stopped, its player silencing it instantly with his claws. At the same moment, Sorrano sang out in a deep, clear voice, creating an image of fire and flames in every listener's mind.

Five of the drums continued their simple or complex rhythms, and the largest resumed when Sorrano ended a verse. Kibi felt her heart beating in time to the drums, and wondered if everyone experienced the same thing.

A few of the most nimble dancers took to the floor, flailing wings or arms in wild expression to match the fury of the music.

The deep drum again ceased and Sorrano began a new verse, bending the theme into the fire of passion and love. Howls rose up. Arms, tails, and wings reached for companions, and the dances became slower and more sensuous.

The deep drum took over again, letting Sorrano breathe and recover. The other drums held their steady rhythm. The six drums were as masters, and every creature's heart was enslaved.

With a slightly softer voice, Sorrano altered the theme once more, pulling it to the fire of the mind, the search for truth and meaning, and the love of justice and wisdom. The dancers and listeners responded, the lighting changed colors, and the entire mood of the star station shifted.

Kibi's eyes sparkled and she grinned, letting the music take her emotions along on the journey.

Again the largest drum returned, and the deepest passions of the dancers resumed.

Suddenly all the drums but one fell silent, the dancers froze, and Sorrano sang of the subtle fire of the spirit. The entire room of more than a thousand sapient creatures was so enthralled, and so quiet, that Sorrano's voice filled the room, perhaps the entire station, with ease.

When he completed the last verse, he bowed, all the drums resumed, and nearly everyone jumped onto the dance floor.

Ilika felt Kibi start to spring, then catch herself. Instead, she wrapped her arms around him, the only thing she could do to express the deep emotions created inside her by the beautiful music of another of her kind, a simple monkey mammal.

Boro had no trouble finding the rhythm of the six drums as soon as Sorrano's song ended and Sata pulled him onto the dance floor. Once his feet were loosened up and moving on their own, he had time to look around at the other dancers. A green reptile caught his eye, moving slowly to the drumbeats, its strong and supple back curving this way and that like a snake.

Boro began to experiment with his own back, and found it not nearly as flexible and expressive as the reptile's long spine. But a thought came to him, and he added his arms, sometimes over his head, sometimes out in front, and discovered they gave him the extra length he needed to fully move to the music.

The only thing he still might wish for was a tail. No, he decided, he could do without that.

Sata didn't find much inspiration in the lizards dancing nearby, but could glimpse a trio of shimmering blue avians whose motions would have been beautiful even if their feathers were not. Her arms also began to move over her head, out to one side or the other, or in front as she ducked her head to mimic the graceful motions of the birds. She was not extending her spine, as Boro, but creating wings that reached for the crystal ceiling, or spread out as if to take flight.

Suddenly both Boro and Sata became embarrassed at the same moment. About a dozen other creatures had gathered around to watch the two graceful monkey mammals dance.

The reptilian drummers bowed and carried away their drums. The changing lights revealed a quartet — an ursine playing small drums, a green mantis with a complex stringed instrument, and two avians with keyboards. They began a slow, sensuous song that had most of the dancers swaying in twos or threes.

Kibi sat on her couch, swaying while holding hands with Ilika, completely lost in the flowing music as if carried along by warm water.

The song ended and dancers entered or left the floor. A lively tune began, carried by the keyboards and supported by the quick paws of the bear at his drums.

Kibi was completely happy, still sitting on the couch but moving her body to the rhythm and melody. Her bracelet chimed.

Last song. Dance with all your heart! Memsala.

Kibi looked at Ilika.

He grinned at her, hopped up, and motioned toward the dance floor.

She was quickly on her feet, pranced in place for a moment to loosen her muscles, then followed Ilika to a clear space.

As Kibi found the rhythm with her feet, and began to express the feelings of the music with her arms and hands, she realized something. At the beginning of the dance, she didn't know what it meant to dance with other Nebador people on a star station. Now she was beginning to understand.

She wondered how Memsala knew.

Chapter 16: The Link

To Rini's eyes, Mati had been more relaxed as she prepared to die on Sonmatia Seven.

She clutched at her dear friend constantly as Healer Dakalio and two helpers, both ursine, carefully prepared her for surgery. They got her comfortable on a strange bed that sensed when its shape was not just right, and changed without a word from patient or healer. They connected her blood to something Rini guessed was half creature, half machine.

Breakfast arrived. Rini received a tray, and Mati could feel the sugars and proteins enter her bloodstream directly. She grinned up at the love of her life as he chewed fruits and nuts.

Mati's bed tilted up and the entire lower half of her body was immersed in a clear, warm liquid. Surgeon K'stimla arrived, and several more helpers. Bird, reptile, and spider all greeted Mati and explained what they would be doing.

After the surgeon and her helpers arranged all the tools they would need, there came a moment of silence. It reminded Rini of star transit. Into the silence came a fuzzy purple ball that seemed to float down from the ceiling, then slowly swirl around Mati.

She giggled. "It tickles!"

Rini smiled just as the purple being came to him. He had only experienced his mind and soul touched so deeply once before — by Melorania.

When the fuzzy ball finished with Rini, it placed itself directly between the two young humans, one hoping with all her heart to walk again, the other craving to prove his love.

The mantid surgeon touched Mati's hand with one of her claws. "In a moment, Mati, you will sense that your companion is with you, and he will remain with you while you sleep and we fix your knee. Don't be surprised if you have some strange dreams."

A moment later Mati began to sense Rini's presence, as if they were snuggled together by a campfire whispering secrets to each other. "That's okay," she mumbled in a slurred voice. "I've always had strange . . ."

✳

Mati's mind slept, but her body quivered on the edge of terror.

Rini's outer senses dulled as the purple being of light linked his mind with the sleeping girl. He felt her awareness slip away, and sensed the nervous tension throughout her body.

"Find her breath," K'stimla instructed. "Take charge of it and breathe as one."

Rini sensed the last shreds of Mati's willpower fade away just as they began to breathe in unison. As a test, he held his breath for a moment, and Mati also stopped breathing. Then she took a big breath when he did.

"Good. Find her heartbeat. It's faster than yours right now."

Even as he listened for Mati's pulse, Rini was surprised to discover he could control his own — a little slower or faster — just by thinking about it. He guessed he shouldn't go too far in either direction. Suddenly he heard Mati's heart in his mind, racing faster than his own. He tried to slow it by sheer force of will, but nothing happened.

A subtle smile appeared on his face.

Rini speeded his heartbeat until it matched the pulse of the girl beside him — dangerously fast, it seemed to him. Soon their hearts beat in unison. He willed both hearts to slow. Mati's heart followed his for a moment, then slipped away and sped up. Three times Rini had to let his heart return to a faster rhythm, then slowly and gently coax his beloved's heart slower.

"As you can see, Rini, that's more difficult. There, that's a good pulse. Now for the hardest part of all. Mati may be asleep, but she's still tense, and that's causing high blood pressure. Caress and massage every part of her body until she relaxes."

Rini had massaged Mati's arms and shoulders many times, and sometimes even her back, but never from the inside. Now he willed himself to explore every part of her sleeping form, to coax every muscle to melt under his soothing mental touch. He smiled when he came to parts that were different than his. He frowned when he sensed the broken bones and misshapen muscles around her knee.

"Good. Take your time. Blood pressure is coming down. Don't forget her feet."

Rini smiled as he mentally massaged Mati's feet, one at a time. He was surprised to find bone and muscle damage in the ankle of her good leg. He cringed, suddenly realizing that Mati was probably in pain whenever she walked anywhere. Without opening his eyes, he told K'stimla.

"Yes, we know about that, Rini, and will fix it, along with minor damage in several other joints."

Rini was happy that all of Mati's wounds would be healed. He continued to work his way through her body, coaxing each part to relax, some muscles requiring three or four passes.

"Good, Rini. Breathing is okay. Heartbeat a little slower, please — yes, that's good. The surgery will now begin."

＊

For the next hour, Rini felt dull sensations as the surgeon cut into Mati's knee and began moving pieces around. He kept watch over breath, heartbeat, and muscle tension, but the fuzzy purple being would no longer let him focus his attention on Mati's bad knee, and he guessed why.

"This is going well, Rini, and I'm putting Healer G'sonk in charge of the bone reconstruction while I start on the left ankle."

Rini kept his eyes closed, but sensed the spider begin work.

"A little stronger heart rhythm, please, Rini."

He smiled shyly, realizing he had let Mati's pulse get too slow. He matched his heartbeat to hers and slowly strengthened both.

＊

After another hour, K'stimla put the reptile to work on Mati's ankle and came back around to observe the spider's work. She spoke with Healer Dakalio about blood sugar levels, then suddenly noticed the frown of concentration on Rini's face.

"What's wrong, Rini?"

At first Rini thought he could take care of Mati's slow pulse himself, as he had done earlier. Now he was beginning to worry. "I . . . I've tried three times, and her heartbeat keeps slipping too low," he said without opening his eyes or ceasing his effort.

K'stimla looked at some displays. "Try again."

Rini concentrated once more, slowing his own heart to match, then using all his willpower to bring Mati's back to a strong, steady rhythm. "It starts to follow me, then slips away."

The surgeon spoke with Dakalio again, and he adjusted the nutrients going into Mati's blood while watching the displays. "Not responding . . . getting weaker," he reported.

She checked the progress of the spider and the reptile, saw no problems with either surgery site that should be causing Mati distress, and looked at her displays again while her mandibles twitched with worry.

"Rini, I think you'll have to go into Mati's mind. Something is causing her distress, and I can't find it anywhere else. This is more dangerous . . ."

"I'll do anything you need me to do."

K'stimla smiled as only a mantis can. The purple being seemed to glow a little brighter as it deepened the link between the two humans.

＊

As Rini willed himself to enter the mind of the sleeping girl, he was amazed by all the activity. Voices whispered, talked, laughed, or shouted. He glimpsed scenes from dozens of places around their kingdom, and a few from more recent months in the Manessa Kwi, as if someone was holding up pages from a picture book. Some scenes he recognized, but many he did not. Although nearly overwhelmed by the sights and sounds, Rini focused on looking for something, anything, that would cause Mati's heart to slow.

For what seemed like hours, he explored, searching for anything that could be the cause, but finding only noise and fragmented memories.

❋

K'stimla quickly assigned the bird to care for Rini, and without his knowledge, monitors were connected to his hands and nutrition added directly to his blood.

"He is strong, bok," the avian healer announced after studying the displays, "but has a difficult task ahead."

K'stimla nodded.

❋

What seemed like days, maybe weeks later, Rini found something that made him nearly cry out with relief. A single nerve pulsed with the same rhythm as Mati's heart, down to about half the speed of his own. Wasting no time, Rini followed the nerve deeper and deeper into Mati's mind.

The voices and other noises became louder, the flashes of visual memory more frequent, and both seemed to be from earlier in Mati's life. The mental spaces Rini traveled were tighter now, and he sensed he was slowing down, as if trying to push through dense bushes in a forest. He clenched his teeth and forced his way through, still following the pulse of Mati's heartbeat, desperately looking for the reason it was too slow.

❋

K'stimla worked quickly but calmly, talking with her helpers, watching their work, and beginning the minor surgery needed to repair Mati's right hip. Two ursines fetched anything the surgeons needed, while Dakalio monitored blood, breath, and nutrition. The spider announced the completion of Mati's new knee cap, and the reptile carefully re-attached leg muscles to ligaments and ligaments to ankle bone.

❋

Rini was drenched in sweat and trembling from the effort of exploring Mati's mind when he finally cried out, "A dark place! Cold and creepy. Very tangled. The slow heartbeat is coming from there."

Memory voices assaulted him constantly, all yelling or screaming to hurry up or work harder. Flashes of whips and sticks made him cringe, and he felt the pain as if he was receiving the blows himself. Mentally, he held up his hands and arms, protecting himself and Mati as best he could. "I can't get in there, it's too tangled! But I have to! Mati can't live with that pain!"

K'stimla looked at the purple being of light and they talked silently in her mind. After a minute, she nodded.

Rini, the purple spirit said to his mind, *if I deepen the link enough for you to enter that place in your beloved, your minds will be linked for the rest of your lives, and you will never be free of each other's thoughts and feelings. A link that deep drives some creatures insane. Humans are especially prone.*

Rini swallowed. *And if you don't?*

It appears that she will not survive the surgery.

I could not live, knowing I let that happen. Mati and I live together or we die together.

The glowing purple being quickly brightened, and Rini discovered he now had the power to dive into the deepest, darkest part of Mati's mind.

✳

He soon came upon a tangled bundle of nerves, glowing with a faint light from deep inside, but blackened, battered, and broken on the outside. Mean voices and heartless images hurled themselves at it constantly, and with every blow, another tiny part turned dark blue, cold, and icy.

"I found it," he whispered.

The avian at his side heard and repeated for the other healers.

No more! Rini mentally screamed.

The hurtful memories paused, laughed, and resumed their attack.

Suddenly Rini realized he couldn't fight this enemy with anger. He knew what he had to do. He took several slow, deep breaths, smiled, and moved forward, wrapping himself completely around the vulnerable part of Mati's mind.

Now there are two of us! he warned the voices and the painful memories.

✳

"Pulse is coming up," Dakalio announced.

K'stimla studied the display. "How's Rini?"

"Smiling. Heartbeat slow but getting stronger, bok."

The head surgeon breathed a deep sigh of relief and continued reconstructing the layers of muscle and ligament in Mati's right knee.

✳   ✳   ✳

Chapter 17: Sharing

Sata noticed the pride in Boro's posture and smile as he guided her down ramps toward the sound of rushing water.

"The blue triangle means we're entering one of the wet ramps. We can walk carefully, or just . . ."

Sata had the idea, so she plopped down in the shallow water and found the bottom smooth and slippery. Just then, a high-pitched voice called from higher up the ramp. "Look out!"

Sata turned her head and saw a gray dolphin barreling down the ramp toward her. She quickly pushed with her hands to get moving.

Boro jumped and landed with his legs wide apart.

Sata slid under and was picking up speed, but the marine mammal was a split second behind, wiggling to slow itself, but still going twice Sata's speed.

"Eeeeek!" it shrieked as it collided with the female monkey mammal who didn't know that wet ramps were for *sliding down*, not *sitting on*.

Boro turned and watched helplessly as Sata and the dolphin tumbled together the rest of the way down to the river, with legs, fluke, arms, and flippers all tangled up.

When they finally splashed into deeper water, Sata quickly grabbed a tree root and coughed out the water she had inhaled. The dolphin began churning the water with its tail to stay in one place while looking at Sata.

Boro arrived at the water's edge, but remained silent.

As soon as Sata recovered enough to realize what had happened, she poured out sincere apologies. "I'm so sorry. It's all my fault. I'm just a stupid . . ."

The dolphin opened its snout and started laughing.

Sata grew quiet.

"Are you hurt?" the marine mammal asked between rounds of laughter.

"Um . . . no."

"Me neither. Wanna do it again?"

Boro threw his head back and howled with laughter.

*

Trekila Spimalo was a fresh-water ecology specialist who traveled all over Nebador, helping star stations and planets to understand and correct imbalances in their water. She sensed the bond between Boro and Sata, who sat close together at the water's edge. With a gleam in her eyes, she told them about her own handsome lover, currently on a deep-space mission.

"Are there . . . deep-space response ships full of water?" Sata asked with wide eyes.

"Only half-full. We have to breathe, just like you!"

Sata chuckled.

"And sometimes we need to bring along an avian or a reptile, and once in a while . . ." she paused for dramatic effect, "a silly monkey mammal!"

Boro and Sata both laughed.

"Farewell, new friends! I must go taste the fish, then get some water samples!" Trekila Spimalo danced on her tail, then turned and dove into the tunnel that led to the underwater world of Satamia Star Station.

*

Sata snuggled close to Boro, and smiled when he put his arm around her. She looked up at him with sparkling eyes and a glowing smile. Boro felt his heart pounding as their heads moved together and they shared a tender kiss.

"Yeah . . . okay . . . so . . ." Sata began when they parted, as if grabbing something solid after feeling dizzy. "I think I just learned something."

"About kissing?"

"No!" she said with a friendly frown. "About what Nebador people do when accidents happen. They laugh. They forgive each other, have fun, and make new friends. Right?"

"Um . . . yeah. Way different from our planet."

"I know. But we have to learn how to do it. At least . . . all but Rini, who already knows how."

Boro chuckled. "I think Rini was born smiling."

"Mati's gonna need all the smiles he can give her, today and for many days to come."

Boro nodded thoughtfully.

"Okay. I'm getting hungry. How do we go fishing in this place since we don't have long rows of sharp teeth like Trekila?"

Boro grinned.

*

Sata only hesitated a moment before following Boro into the water tunnel. He watched from below to make sure she was comfortable with the deep water. For the next hour, they swam from air pocket to air pocket, exploring the underwater world below for as long as each breath would allow.

Sata was almost as strong in the water as Boro, and he enjoyed teaching her the rules about catching fish. With the ursine docking controller Glorm,

Boro had made a new friend, another male, quiet and strong like Boro himself. Swimming with Sata, Boro had a different experience, admiring her graceful strength and female curves whenever he was in a position to take a good look.

For that first hour, the fish eluded them, so they discussed tactics at each air pocket. Sata clearly intended to stay as long as it took to catch a fish. Boro was reminded of the many times they had worked together on a navigation problem on the Manessa Kwi, which sometimes took hours, and he smiled with happiness that they could also share other areas of life. Maybe someday, he pondered, they could share . . .

Suddenly a huge surge of water burst into their air pocket, and both of them held their breath while the wave passed. As soon as they could see, they recognized Kibi as she reached for a grab-bar, her dark hair plastered to her head. They had, however, never before seen a turtle with a head the size of a man's, and a shell more than a meter long. The giant sea turtle nodded a greeting while treading water.

To their surprise, Kibi just breathed deeply, but didn't try to say much. "Only get . . . eight seconds. Psychic . . . Development. Bye!"

At that moment, her bracelet chimed, she took one last breath, then slipped down into the water. The turtle followed.

Boro blinked. "Wow. Some kind of *serious* training."

"She found out Ilika's done it," Sata said, "but she started even before she knew that. Something happened that made her want to, or need to, commit herself to it, but she won't say what."

"I wonder if we should do it."

"First . . . maybe we should see if Kibi survives."

Boro chuckled. "Ready to try our new plan?"

"Yeah!"

✳

The fish easily avoided Sata, waving her arms, by darting around a large rock. One of them didn't see Boro hiding in the dim light behind the rock. He proudly carried the yellow fish, three-quarters of a meter long, up to an air pocket.

"Hurray!" Sata cheered when she surfaced.

Boro made sure the fish was dead before stashing it on a ledge near the fresh air outlet.

After breathing deeply for a minute, they went down again. This time Sata crouched behind the rock and Boro herded the next school of fish that came by.

Boro struggled with himself back at the air pocket when he saw the pink and silver beauty Sata held up, easily a full meter long.

✳

Back at the river bank, Boro was even quieter than usual, and Sata could sense that her dear friend was challenged by the situation. "Knife?" she requested.

Without a word, he pulled if from a pocket of his dry clothes and handed it to her.

She eyed the meaty fish before her, judged the halfway point between gills and tail, and hacked the fish into two pieces.

"What are you . . ." Boro started to ask.

Sata handed him half the pink and silver fish, and the knife. "We worked together, so we share."

Boro looked at her for another moment, found his smile, and set to work cutting the yellow fish into two equal parts.

✴   ✴   ✴

Chapter 18: Memsala

Kibi sat on the soft floor of the dimly-lit room, toweling her hair dry. "That was fun! Exhausting, but fun."

"I'm glad you liked it," Memsala said from nearby. "What did you learn?"

"Um . . . lots of things. That swimming in warm water is really . . . more than fun . . . deeply satisfying. Where I come from, all the water is bitter cold, except little hot springs."

Memsala nodded her head, a barely-seen silhouette.

"And . . . I was amazed how little I needed to breathe. For a while I thought I was going to die, then the buzzing in my head went away, and eight seconds at each air pocket was plenty."

"What did you sense around you?"

"Fish!" Kibi chuckled. "Mostly avoiding me, of course. Some of the underwater plants tickled. I saw four or five dolphin types, two beavers, and one ursine. Oh, yeah, two monkey mammals. They're on my crew."

"You missed the most important thing . . . or didn't recognize it."

Kibi let the towel drape over her slender shoulders and searched her mind. "I . . . can't think of anything else."

"Did you taste the water?"

Kibi laughed. "More than I wanted to!"

Memsala made a deep sound that might have been a chuckle. "Did it all taste the same?"

Kibi concentrated on the question. "I think . . . wait. There was one place . . . near that jumble of rocks that aren't really rocks . . . I have a vague memory that the water seemed a little . . . off."

"Off?"

Kibi scrunched her face to try to remember. "Almost like . . . the smell of fear. Can you taste fear underwater?"

Memsala's shadow nodded. "A small marine mammal, newly arrived on the station, was lost and afraid, hiding in the rocks."

Kibi frowned with guilt. "I'm sorry! Is it okay now?"

"Yes. I sent a message, and a member of its crew came. How is it that you sensed the fear, in a place where there is rarely any fear, and didn't respond?"

Kibi hugged her knees and buried her face for a long moment. "I . . . I guess I was thinking about Mati. She was in surgery all day."

"How much of the time were you thinking about Mati?"

"I don't know, maybe . . . half the time."

"So, dwelling upon someone who was surrounded by all the care she needed, caused you to miss someone alone and in distress."

Kibi started crying silently.

"I know this moment is painful, my dear Kibi. To learn humility, we must be humiliated, over and over again. There's no shortcut."

Kibi tried to speak, but her throat had trouble forming the words. ". . . better . . . next time."

"Breathe and center."

Kibi tried to collect herself by sitting up straight and steadying her breath.

"Let me ask you a question. While you're on duty as steward, do you spend half your time and attention checking the levels in your water tanks?"

Kibi tried to laugh, but only a cough came out. "Impossible! I have about a hundred things I have to keep my eyes on."

"By choosing Psychic Development, you have set foot on the path to becoming, in a sense, a steward of Nebador. Now you have a million things to keep your eyes on, not to mention your ears, nose, tongue, and intuition."

Kibi wiped the tears from her face with the towel. "I . . . don't suppose . . . I get a checklist . . ."

Memsala made her deep laughing sound again. "No. You have left that level of simplicity behind. However, your mind is quite capable of scanning the universe around you for those things that need your attention. Ilika Imni does it. Toran Takil leads some of the most challenging missions that flesh and blood creatures can handle."

Kibi breathed slowly, holding back a nearly-dizzy feeling as she pondered the huge responsibilities she had taken on by stepping onto Ilika's ship, and then into the Psychic Development program at Satamia Star Station.

Memsala pulled her head back into her shell and slipped into the shallow pool beside her.

* * *

Chapter 19: Dreams

Even though no one had made an official plan, the entire crew of the Manessa Kwi gathered at the medical center when the dinner hour, ship's time, approached. Rini was ready for them, and delighted when Sata handed him a container of raw fish slices.

Mati was still asleep in a recovery room, half her body in a healing tank, and would remain asleep until the following day. Rini already had a pot of vegetables steaming in the little kitchen attached to their sleeping room, and soon located a baking pan as he chatted with his crewmates.

"It was the most intense day of my life!" he declared as he sprinkled salt and spices over the fish. "I fell dead asleep as soon as the surgery was over, and dreamed about spiders with slave whips, and goatherds that turned into mantidae!"

Everyone laughed.

"Sounds like you got some images from Mati," Ilika speculated. "Maybe the link hadn't yet faded."

Rini suddenly looked guilty, and everyone noticed. "Well . . . um . . . Mati had some trouble, and I had to go way deeper than we planned. It's . . ."

"Permanent," Ilika finished with large eyes.

Rini cringed and nodded.

Ilika took a slow breath. "I hope you two are still happy with each other, because it would be very difficult to ever be close to anyone else."

Rini smiled and nodded as he poked at the vegetables with a fork. "These are done."

Sata hopped up and held plates as Rini served.

"So, did everything else go okay?" Ilika asked.

"Yeah, when I woke up, about an hour ago, K'stimla said everything went just as she expected. She'll be making adjustments, but she knew that. Mati's sleeping and dreaming."

"I bet she's dreaming about surgeons with green mandibles!" Boro speculated with a grin.

"Nope," Rini declared. "I know exactly what she's dreaming about. The purple guy said this is normal for a deep link. When only one of us is asleep, they'll dream what the other one is doing. Mati's dreaming she's cooking veggies and fish!"

Ilika smiled and the others snickered.

". . . except that things get exaggerated and distorted in dreams, so she might be dreaming about steamed pine trees or baked whales!"

Kibi laughed deeply and passed a plate to Ilika.

Boro and Sata talked about their fishing trip, and with a reassuring girl's arm around his back, Boro admitted he had to nurse a wounded ego after catching the smaller fish. That gave Kibi the courage to mention the lost marine mammal she had sensed, but failed to help.

Ilika's eyes sparkled with pride as he listened to his crew members. He was just about to share his day when five bracelets chimed at once.

They all looked and saw the same message.

"Rini, you are on-duty," Ilika declared, "but let me know if any more surgeries are scheduled."

The slender lad nodded and started grabbing empty plates as soon as each person inhaled the last few bites.

"Kibi is in command, and is cross-training with Rini during non-critical times. Also, Sata with Boro. I'm your pilot."

They all drained their cups and headed for the door.

✳

Rini, his hair brushed back and his face glowing with power and masculine charm, picked up an entire pallet of heavy boxes, and without effort, strode into the ship.

A chicken came next, clucking and tapping at a mission bracelet on her left wing as she guided the next pallet.

Boro flexed his huge arm muscles, showing them off to Sata, who swiveled her sexy hips in response. When he tried to lift a pallet, he grunted and strained, but it wouldn't move. He kept trying until Rini strode back out, grabbed it with one hand, grinned, and re-entered the ship.

Finally, taller than all the rest, Ilika came behind cracking a whip as beams of light flashed from his green eyes. "Work! Faster! Don't forget that the square root of the semi-major axis is equal to the velocity of the anti-mass drive at inner navigation marker C near the liquid-gaseous boundary on Sonmatia Seven!"

All four crew members saluted and scurried to their stations.

"You're in command, Kibi!" Ilika boomed. "I want to play games on my knowledge pad."

The chicken clucked loudly, hopped into the command chair, and laid an egg.

✳

Mati startled awake.

An avian healer wandered over from another part of the quiet, dimly-lit recovery room. "Bok. Hello, Mati."

"Did K'stimla . . . did I . . ."

"The surgery was completely successful, bok," the bird explained as she studied the blood chemistry display, "although there will probably be minor adjustments during the next few weeks. Our bodies sometimes do not heal the way we want them to, bok. How do you feel?"

"Weird dreams."

"Would you like a knowledge pad, bok, so you can record them?"

Mati thought for a moment. "No, not those dreams."

The avian chuckled as she tapped at the blood console. "A very deep link with your partner was necessary to overcome some stressful memories, bok. You and he will have some work getting used to that link. We will help, of course. Hungry, bok? Thirsty?"

"Um . . . no. Sleepy."

"Good. I'm increasing your sleep medication slightly."

"Okay. Good ni . . ."

✳

Several hours later, Rini soundlessly stepped into the recovery room. The avian met him and guided him into an office where they could talk.

"She woke up for a few minutes, bok, and reported strange dreams, probably because of the link."

"That's funny, it was a very uneventful mission — two pallets to a mining camp on an asteroid. The steward was in command, and we didn't have any problems at all."

"You know how dreams can be, bok."

✳ ✳ ✳

Chapter 20: The Scrub Brush

Sometime the following day, after half an hour of guided meditation, then a lecture by one of the avians on the Psychic Development staff, Kibi received her next assignment.

She stepped out the door into the quiet patio with its bubbling fountain, remembered Toran Takil, and wondered if he had also endured humiliating assignments. Somehow, it was difficult to imagine the big cat, or Ilika, the captain of a ship, doing what she was about to do.

She looked at the scrub brush in her right hand and the bucket of blue solvent in her left, and sighed.

With heavy feet, she dragged herself along the paths, ramps, and stairs that eventually brought her to a balcony overlooking the main hall of the star station. The Satamia sun flooded the room with light, and the large leaves of the great station tree reached out to catch the rays. With a look on her face close to a pout, Kibi realized it would be many, many hours, nearly three days by her reckoning, before the next evening dance party.

Kibi leaned over the balcony and looked at the huge floor below. She judged it to be about the size of the entire marketplace in the capital city of her kingdom. Again she sighed.

Creatures of all sorts came and went, or lounged on couches, perches, or in pools. She noticed a group of four reptiles whose bracelets all chimed at once, and they hurried away. Kibi could only guess what their mission might be. She glanced at her own bracelet and wondered if it would save her from the task at hand. "Dream on, Kibi," she mumbled to herself. "You're probably off-duty until the floor's spotless."

Her mind wandered back to her parting words with Memsala.

The whole floor? But . . . where should I start?

Start . . . in the middle.

Kibi looked over the balcony railing again. The middle of the huge room was the busiest part, with people going every which way, pallets of stuff floating by every few moments, and avians taking off and landing.

Kibi sighed once more, then pointed her feet in the direction of a downward ramp.

✳

As she stood in the exact middle of the great room, bucket and brush in hand, many things came to mind that seemed better than getting down on her hands and knees and scrubbing the floor. Slavery. Death. Lots of things.

People passed by going in all directions. Some moved quickly while reading bracelet displays or knowledge pads. Others were more relaxed, surveying the available eating places.

She knew she didn't have to do it. Sorrano had quit. Probably many others. She could just march back up to the Psychic Development room and tell Memsala . . .

Two voices came out of her memory, and listening, she put off making a decision.

First, she heard Ilika. *Kibi, you have command of the Manessa Kwi.*

It was not the words themselves that touched her heart, but rather the feeling deep inside herself every time she heard them. As a slave, nothing she did mattered much. If she died in the middle of a job, the owner would just get another slave to do the same job.

But the Manessa Kwi was a deep-space response ship, the fastest ship in the universe, ready to go into the farthest reaches of the unknown. She had been on the star station long enough to know that most citizens of Nebador looked up to the Transport Service crews, and the majority of those citizens, for one reason or another, did jobs that were simpler and easier.

Then she heard another voice from the recent past.

The next time I look into your eyes, Kibi, I want to find an equal, a citizen of Nebador, strong and true.

Deep inside herself, Kibi looked forward to that day. She wanted to look into Toran Takil's eyes again, and know in her heart that she had earned her Nebador citizenship, the stewardship of the Manessa Kwi, and Ilika's loving touch.

She wasn't aware of it, but a look of determination was forming on her face. Without further thought, she knelt down and started scrubbing.

*

Rini was giddy with excitement when Mati finally awoke, and K'stimla had to give him a stern look. "She still needs lots of rest, and with your new link, she can't get that unless you relax too."

Rini smiled and took several deep breaths.

Once Mati was lifted out of the healing tank, the surgeon and two assistants examined all the surgery sites. "The skin is healing quickly, bok," one healer said.

K'stimla looked at the reptile.

"True," he said, "but the muscles will knit much more slowly. Nutrition is now extremely important."

The surgeon nodded. "You two are in charge of that. Be firm with Rini."

Both assistants nodded, and Rini blushed.

*

Kibi's moment of willful determination quickly wore off. She didn't dare look around, but knew everyone was staring at her. She kept scrubbing.

She could almost feel their glaring eyes, burning holes in her back. She could easily imagine their thoughts, gossiping about the stupid monkey mammal scrubbing the floor in the middle of the busiest room on the star station. Tears started coming, but she continued scrubbing.

She kept her eyes on the floor, but could almost feel feet and claws getting ready to kick her or rip her clothes, maybe even her skin. She started crying freely, and her tears mingled with the blue solvent, but she didn't dare look up. She scrubbed harder and faster, hoping beyond hope that she could finish before they killed her.

✳

Mati's special bed was floated into their little room and placed beside Rini's bed. A tray with a strange variety of fruits and vegetables arrived, and Rini began feeding his beloved friend, telling her about recent events while she chewed. Between bites she shared what little she remembered since they had last spoken, including images from her strange dreams.

They soon discovered that when one or both of them were eating, they didn't have to cease sharing thoughts and feelings, as their mouths and ears were no longer necessary.

✳

Kibi nearly jumped out of her skin when the claw-like feet of a large spider appeared next to her. She steeled herself to be laughed at, poked, and bitten.

The arachnid raised two of its legs, and Kibi flinched, but at the same moment she noticed something on its feet. The spider plunged both legs, and the small scrub brushes they held, into the solvent bucket, then began scrubbing the floor where Kibi's work left off.

She began laughing and crying at the same time.

✳

About an hour after they finished the tray, the young couple was still chatting, sometimes silently, sometimes aloud. The avian healer came in and announced it was time to let Mati get some sleep.

The young couple agreed, and Rini got comfortable with a knowledge pad, his place marked in a book about the evolution of stars.

Even though no more spoken words were heard, giggles or chuckles slipped out every few minutes, and Rini made little progress in his book.

✳

Kibi finally found the courage to look.

All around her, creatures of every kind were arriving with scrub brushes. More buckets of solvent appeared. Some of the helpers worked alone, but she also spotted entire crews of six or eight of the same kind. Soon the clean spots on the floor were merging with each other and connecting with Kibi's own small area.

Kibi stretched up from her knees and beheld several birds setting out purple marker cones, then moving them as the work progressed.

She dried her face on her sleeves and plunged her brush into the bucket.

✳

An hour later, Mati's thoughts became sluggish. *Okay, I really am getting sleepy, so you have to take a nap too, or go find something to do.*

He kissed her on the lips. *I'm gonna read a little, then maybe take a nap too. Good night!*

Mati mumbled something, then let sleep take her.

✳

From her knees, Kibi met the captain of a passenger transport ship, an avian whose entire crew of twenty was skillfully moving the marker cones so people and pallets could get by while the scrubbing work continued.

She thanked the captain with bird-like bows of her head as she dipped her brush again.

All around her, more and more teams of helpers appeared, set to work, and quickly had marker cones keeping people off their sections of wet floor. Kibi estimated it would all be done in another quarter hour.

The next time she glanced up, something strange caught her eye. Not far away, a lone scrub brush appeared to be moving all by itself. Kibi blinked several times, but still saw no one pushing it. Then, on a hunch, she let herself shift into a meditative state of mind.

Slowly, she began to perceive the forest-green glow that hovered over the scrub brush.

"Thank you, Kerloran," she said softly.

Kibi heard no words of response, but had the impression that someone hugged her gently, just for a moment.

✳

The steward of the deep-space response ship Manessa Kwi scrubbed until every part of the floor was clean. Then she wandered around the huge room, thanking all her helpers, exchanging bows and kind words, receiving names and offers of friendship. As she wandered, she picked up marker cones when sections of floor were dry, and stacked them in the storeroom the avian captain showed her.

When she finally arrived, alone with her scrub brush and empty bucket, back in the Psychic Development room, Memsala was with another student, so Kibi sat and meditated.

Perhaps an hour later, Kibi felt the presence of the old and wise giant sea turtle. She took some grounding breaths and opened her eyes.

"So, my dear Kibi, what did you learn?"

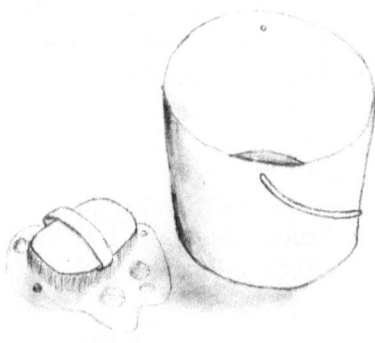

Chapter 21: Juggling Lessons

A new day, ship-time, brought the four who slept on the Manessa Kwi to the breakfast table in good spirits. Nothing was planned for that day, and Kibi had a day off from her classes. She and Sata giggled and schemed together at the table, and soon dashed off to explore parts of the star station they had not yet seen.

After doing dishes, Ilika had his nose in a knowledge pad and mumbled something about advanced training for captains.

Boro felt a little lost.

He busied himself for a few minutes by cleaning up his cabin, then started a load of laundry. When he could think of nothing else on the ship that needed his attention, he wandered out to the dock's waiting room, and from there up a ramp to the nearest main corridor.

A shaft of golden light streamed in from a crystal window at the far end, lighting up the balcony above where several birds stretched their necks into the warm rays. Above them, near the ceiling, large green leaves dangled from a gnarly limb of the great station tree to catch the light.

Boro took a slow breath and smiled, relaxing in the good feeling of being a part of this wonderful place, even though he still didn't completely understand it. He was the engineer of a little ship, and knew he still had much to learn, but had been doing it long enough to know it was within his ability. Someone needed the Manessa Kwi, and other ships, to do the things they did, and they provided food and all the other necessities of life to him, his shipmates, and the many others who worked on the star station.

The larger purpose of it all was still unknown to him, and he wasn't sure it mattered. The kingdom where he was born and raised didn't seem to have a larger purpose. People lived as best they could, accomplished a few things during their lives, or didn't, and it mattered little one way or the other. Yet the question hovered in the back of Boro's mind, not fully formed, but never completely fading away.

Always keep learning and growing. Many times, someone on the crew had asked what they needed to do to become citizens of Ilika's civilization, and had received that answer. Boro rolled the idea around in his head as he stretched his arms toward the ceiling, enjoying the warm light of the Satamia sun. Then he remembered questions he had put to his new friend Glorm, a bear who could think, work, and swim circles around him, and one of Glorm's answers stuck in his mind.

Boro spotted a knowledge processor on the wall across the corridor. At that moment a cargo pallet floated by, lightly loaded so that it's operator, a large cat-like creature, sat on the pallet instead of walking behind. Boro smiled, waited for it to pass, then strode across.

He opened his mouth to speak his request to the device, but became embarrassed. Although it took some concentration, he managed to enter his question into the key pad.

Juggling lessons?

A list of classes flashed onto the screen. Some were clearly for other species. Most required previous training. Then Boro spotted the one he wanted. *Beginning, any species, new students any time.*

With the touch of a key, the knowledge processor displayed a map to the class location. Boro studied it for a minute, thanked the device out loud, and wandered along the corridor, looking for a ramp to the upper levels.

He didn't see the small, fuzzy blue light that hovered near the knowledge processor.

The little patio Boro found at his destination contained a small, bubbling fountain. Beyond, a simple doorway was marked with a sign that said *Juggling Lessons.* Boro smiled.

Inside, an aged, gray-haired monkey greeted Boro while keeping three balls in constant motion with his hands and tail.

Boro's eyes grew large. "Um . . . I don't think I can do *that!*"

"Of course not," the monkey replied. "If you could, you wouldn't need lessons. Are you willing to learn?"

Boro remembered his captain's words. "Y . . . yes."

Boro's new teacher immediately tossed him a ball, which Boro caught.

"Hot potato!" the monkey said. "Pretend that if you hold it for more than a second, it will burn you!"

Boro quickly tossed it up. "When do I get to try three?"

"When you're good with two."

"When do I get two?"

"When you're . . ." The elderly monkey stopped and grinned.

"Let me guess," Boro began as he continued to toss one ball up and catch it, "when I'm good with one."

"You're learning already!"

Boro grinned as he continued to toss and catch.

"Your first lesson is to walk about the star station while tossing, with complete awareness of everything, and complete attention to all your responsibilities."

Boro continued tossing. "Doesn't sound too hard."

The monkey smiled, bowed, and disappeared into an inner room, leaving Boro alone with his one juggling ball.

"Complete awareness of everything, and complete attention to all my responsibilities," Boro mumbled to himself as he tossed the ball up, first in the patio with its bubbling fountain, then as he slowly walked along pathways, ramps, and balconies.

He thought he was doing very well, until he stumbled into a bench on the side of a path. His leg throbbed painfully, but seeing that he wasn't bleeding, he picked up the ball and resumed tossing. As he slowly limped along, he mumbled to himself, "Complete awareness of everything ... complete awareness ..."

The small blue light came silently behind.

To Boro's surprise, no one laughed at him, or even asked what he was doing. The next hour of wandering about the star station saw three more minor accidents. The stair step, planter, and tree root seemed to suffer no damage. Boro judged that his feet and legs, although painful, would heal.

The faint blue light that witnessed each accident did not express an opinion.

As lunchtime approached, Boro started wondering if it was possible to eat and toss at the same time. There were certainly plenty of eating places where he could grab a cup or a plate with one hand. Since it was his first day of juggling, he decided to play it safe, and got a nutrition drink in a closed cup with a straw.

Even so, the new activity split his attention into three parts — walking, tossing, and drinking, and soon another bench sent cup and ball flying. Boro caught the cup, and after hopping on one foot for a minute while remembering some strong words from his native language, he retrieved the ball from where it had rolled.

A quarter hour later, with a liquid lunch in his belly and the pain in his legs dulled by time, Boro was leaving his cup at one of the dishwashing windows when a reptilian voice from within caught his attention. "Hey monkey mammal, we could use some help in here if you're not busy."

Boro looked into the dishwashing room and saw the reptile, a lanky mammal he didn't recognize, and two birds, all working together to process huge stacks of dirty plates, bowls, and cups. "Um . . . I'm supposed to keep tossing this ball . . ."

The reptile made a slight growling sound. "Sorry. I thought you were a Nebador person."

The fuzzy light above and behind Boro said nothing.

Boro became red with shame, and suddenly remembered Sata talking about making bird-food baskets. He looked at the little ball he continued to toss into the air every few seconds, and also remembered his juggling teacher's words. *Complete attention to all your responsibilities.*

After another second of thought, he pocketed the ball and pointed his feet toward the door to the dishwashing room.

Within half an hour, Boro had learned the routine, shared names with his fellow workers, and had an invitation to go tree climbing with the strange lanky mammal, also an engineer. Many plates, bowls, and cups left the room clean, but almost as many dirty ones replaced them. Boro was completely enjoying the work and the companionship when his mission bracelet chimed, startling him.

"Hi Boro, it's Glorm! I'm at work in the docking control room, and there are no students here for the next hour. Want to come watch, listen, and learn?"

Boro's face lit up, and he half-turned to take a step toward the door. Then he saw the sad look on the bird's face on one side, trying to hand him scraped plates, and the disappointment in the lanky mammal's eyes, waiting for the plates Boro was supposed to spray. He shuffled his feet for a moment, moaned under his breath, and finally set his jaw. "I wish I could, Glorm, but I'm in the middle of something, and people are counting on me."

The blue light near the ceiling glowed a little brighter.

"No problem. We'll find a time soon. Gotta go, ship coming in!"

Boro returned to his work, and the next time he glanced at his co-workers, he was greeted with smiling eyes and respectful nods.

Nearly an hour later, the dishwashers were finally catching up with the dirty dishes. Boro's bracelet chimed again.

After reading the message, he touched the key for audio. "Ilika, could Sata cover my station? I'm doing some work I'd like to finish."

Ilika didn't get a chance to reply. The reptile in charge of the dishwashing room had been looking over Boro's shoulder. "No, Boro. Your primary work *always* has priority over helping out here and there. Go, go, go! And thank you!"

Boro verified to his captain that he was two minutes away, hung up his apron, and bowed to his new friends.

The engineer of the Manessa Kwi dashed along the balcony and down a ramp. Just as he emerged into a corridor, he was startled by an avian bursting through a cluster of leaves. It back-winged desperately, but was too close to the wall. Boro cringed as the beautiful bird smashed helplessly into the vertical surface, slid to the floor, and lay twitching and gasping.

Boro glanced at his bracelet for a fraction of a second, gathered the injured avian into his arms, and began striding toward the medical center.

On the way, Boro's bracelet chimed twice more, but he made no attempt to answer.

The elusive glowing light hurried along behind.

Two hours later, the unlucky bird was still in surgery, but was expected to be okay. Mati was asleep, and Rini was beside her, reading. The Manessa Kwi was long gone, and Boro used a knowledge processor to learn that his ship and partial crew would be back in about three hours.

He wandered slowly through the station, wondering what to do in the meantime. The dishwashing room contained a completely different crew that wasn't in need of help.

After strolling up a ramp, he happened to feel the juggling ball in his pocket. After tossing it up a few times, he realized he wasn't in the mood. But he felt like talking to someone, so he continued on up to the little patio with its bubbling fountain.

As he waited on a couch just inside the door, he tossed the ball some more, just to stay in practice. Soon the gray-haired monkey appeared. "How was your first day of juggling?"

"Well . . ." Boro admitted, "I didn't get much practice. Other things kept coming up."

The simian's lips curled into a smile, and he appeared to be holding in laughter. "From what I heard, your entire day was *filled* with juggling practice!"

Boro looked into the monkey's sparkling eyes, and after a long moment, chuckled aloud at himself.

The fuzzy ball near the ceiling faded from sight.

* * *

Chapter 22: On Her Own Two Feet

Mati began another day in the medical center of Satamia Star Station with her usual routine.

Rini noticed the Satamia sun getting low, and knew a day on the star station, about five of their own, was coming to an end.

Mati's breakfast of strange foods, some of which she had never seen before, made her long for a bowl of simple porridge. Rini looked at her with smiling eyes when she tried to hide a slice of bitter fruit under the rim of her plate. She laughed out loud, remembering that she could never again hide *anything* from this freckled boy.

After finally eating — or choking down — everything on her tray, Mati spent an hour in the healing tank as a reptilian coaxed her through all the exercises designed to strengthen her muscles and joints. Rini sat in a chair beside the tank, wearing his usual contented half-smile, silently sharing her frustrations of trying to make muscles work that had not practiced in a very long time.

When they were nearly finished, the mantid surgeon K'stimla arrived, with the human healer Dakalio and two avians close behind. As Mati was lifted from the tank, the healers peered at displays and talked. After Mati was comfortable on an examining table, all the healers gathered around and used sensitive instruments to look deeply into Mati's knees, ankles, and hips.

Rini noticed the smile K'stimla formed with the mandibles around her mouth.

"Mati," the surgeon began, "it's time for you to walk out the door."

✳

For the next quarter hour, Mati was nearly in a state of panic. K'stimla talked about the low-gravity pathways throughout the station that would allow her to start at one-eighth what she was used to, and slowly work up to normal. The young pilot hid her feelings well — from everyone but Rini.

He knew she was back on the slave auction block, feeling the emotions she had experienced there many times, fearing and dreading what was about to happen, holding onto her only possession, her precious crutch, for dear life.

Rini wrapped himself mentally around the fear and dread in Mati's mind, and said aloud, "We'll bring your crutch along, in case you want it."

After a moment, Mati wrinkled her face in thought and took several deep breaths. "Um . . . that would be pretty silly. You'll be at my side, right?"

He nodded.

*

Even though they would be living in the medical center for another week, Mati insisted they clean and tidy up the sleeping room before going out. She refused to do less than half the work, so it went very slowly. Lunchtime arrived before they got anywhere.

Rini had never seen Mati take so long eating a meal, but he smiled. She savored the fish, sipped the chalky nut milk, and carefully nibbled the bitter fruit.

After lunch, Mati insisted they send their dirty laundry to be done. Rini smiled. Mati was suddenly very particular about what was dirty and what wasn't. She held onto furniture with one hand as she moved slowly around the room, sniffing and examining things.

Soon it was mid-afternoon.

Rini looked at Mati, and for perhaps the first time in his life, he wasn't smiling. "Want to ask for an early dinner?"

She turned red. "I'm sorry. I want to laugh and cry. I want to curl up in a little ball and just let you hold me."

"You can do all those things. Anything else?"

Mati went to the door of the little apartment and looked out. The bright yellow walkway started right at their door, curved through the inner waiting room, and continued through the doorway that led to the outer reception room and the main hall of Satamia Star Station. As she looked, a feline healer walked through the room on his way to another sleeping room, and when he came to the yellow path, floated right over with one slow step.

Rini appeared beside Mati. "That's your path to freedom, and someday Nebador citizenship."

Mati swallowed and listened to her racing heart.

*

As they stood looking through the open door, an avian came by with dinner menus for those patients who had choices. As Mati's diet was completely pre-planned, she was puzzled when the bird stopped at their door.

"No dinner for you two tonight, since there's a *feast* waiting outside, bok!"

Mati frowned as the avian healer moved on.

Rini stood patiently at her side.

A minute later, she carefully stretched her right foot over the yellow walkway. It felt light as a feather. She let it touch the yellow surface, and felt no discomfort. To her surprise, neither did it feel like the healing tank, where the zero gravity did not allow her any control at all.

Rini held her right hand and waited.

She leaned forward, and without breathing, let the weight of her body move over her right leg, something she hadn't done since early childhood, and had no memory of doing.

Nothing happened. Her knee did not collapse under her, and no pain shot through her leg. She looked at Rini and grinned.

After that, a step onto her left leg was nothing.

The second step onto her right leg was taken very slowly and carefully, and the third with a little more courage.

Suddenly Mati looked at Rini with shock. He was holding her right hand, but had not taken any of her weight.

Since he knew exactly what she was thinking, he responded even before she spoke. "I'll be there if you need me, but so far, you don't need me."

Mati's mouth opened in surprise, and she looked back toward their room. They were three steps from the door. Suddenly she giggled. "I just walked!"

Rini smiled.

✳

As each step toward the door became a little less timid than the one before, Mati formed a thought. *It doesn't really count until I can do it at full gravity.*

Rini pondered the notion for a moment. *Does only the last leg of a flight plan count?*

Mati chuckled with embarrassment as the door in front of them opened, allowing them to see the main reception room of the medical center. A few other creatures were sitting or perching, talking softly among themselves or reading. The bright yellow path continued across the room and through clear glass doors into the star station's main hall.

"I haven't been through those doors yet, Rini. Why is it so scary? I can pilot a starship. Why can't I just walk out there?"

Rini shrugged.

Mati took several more slow steps, and was half-way across the reception room when she focused on the activity outside. Strong ursines were moving furniture and planters around, musicians carried or wheeled their instruments, and monkeys swung from branches as they hung glittery streamers and shimmering lights.

A bird looked up from a knowledge pad. "Party time! Just my luck to break a wing. A big, kind monkey mammal brought me in. I think his name was Boron."

Mati sparkled. "You mean Boro! He's our engineer. Rini's the watch, and I'm the pilot."

"Oh! You're the . . . never mind." The avian quickly went back to reading, or at least pretending to.

"I think . . ." Rini began. "Never mind."

A split second later, Mati read his thought. "You think? No! Look, it's a mess out there — they're still setting up."

"You're right. Couldn't be."

Mati knew he was lying.

＊

As soon as the last door opened to Rini's touch, a musician plunged furry fingers into his keyboard and brilliant chords sprang forth that stirred the heart of every creature in the room. It was also a pre-arranged signal.

What seemed like the leisurely process of setting up for the star station's evening party, suddenly changed. Within seconds, as Mati and Rini slowly made their way along the low-gravity walkway, many hands and claws quickly cleared the middle of the room.

The path ended in a yellow circle, and Mati smiled when she recognized K'stimla on one side of the circle. Then she spotted Ilika not far away.

People of all shapes and sizes lined the yellow path, and suddenly arms and claws stretched toward her with plates and trays of finger foods and small cups. Mati giggled with embarrassment.

Now I see why we don't get any dinner! Rini said silently. *If we eat one tiny piece of each thing, we'll be stuffed!*

Mati laughed aloud.

The music continued as the couple moved slowly along, sampling the foods and sipping the drinks. Everything was delicious, with none of the bitter fruits or chalky nuts Mati had bravely consumed since her surgery.

As they neared the yellow circle at the end of the path, Mati could see most of the healers who had cared for her, and near Ilika stood Kibi, Sata, and Boro. But for some reason, a large space at the very end remained empty, even though people were crowded several deep everywhere else.

Suddenly the air in that space began to shimmer, the shimmering began to whirl, and the whirling took shape. A beautiful lady in swirling blue gowns looked at Mati with ancient youthful eyes.

"Melorania!" Mati breathed with a grin.

The music stopped on a final pleasing chord and the room fell silent.

"Mati, dear Mati. You have followed a long and difficult path to finally arrive here in the main hall of Satamia Star Station, and you have arrived on your own two feet!"

Cheering and clapping filled the room. Mati glimpsed Sata wearing an understanding grin.

When the room fell silent again, the head of the Transport Service continued. "Citizens of Nebador, I present to you, Mati of Sonmatia Three, the pilot of the Manessa Kwi, who began her training by riding a barely-sapient, often-stubborn creature called a donkey, who could have bucked or kicked Mati to her death at any moment if they didn't share a strong bond of love and loyalty."

The cheering resumed, and the musicians added a flurry of notes and chords.

Reminded of Tera, Mati couldn't hold back tears. Rini held her hand tightly in case her knees got wobbly.

Melorania spoke again. "And after she and her ship-mates handled everything I threw at them . . ."

Many voices laughed or moaned with understanding.

". . . Mati went on to become the only pilot in the last twenty years to perform her first star station approach and docking *without* station control!"

Everyone cheered. Mati turned red and her knees started wobbling. Rini wrapped his arms around her.

Melorania became a swirling blur, enveloped Mati and Rini for a moment, then shot away into the upper balconies of the main hall.

Two ursines quickly carried a couch into the low-gravity circle, and Rini lowered his beloved onto the cushions. They sat close together and looked around with amazement. In every direction, and above on balconies and landings, creatures of all sorts continued their preparations for an evening of food, drink, music, and dancing, as the Satamia sun slipped out of sight for another day.

Mati craved to dance, but her muscles were far from ready. Even though she stayed in the one-eighth gravity yellow zone, moved her feet slowly and carefully, and Rini held her hands constantly, she was exhausted a few minutes into the party, and asleep on the couch before the first hour had passed. Everyone else was just getting warmed up.

Boro and Glorm carried the couch, sleeping pilot and all, back to the medical center. When she felt a soft blanket cover her, Mati awoke just long enough to make Rini promise he would return to the dance party so she could at least dream about it.

And dream she did. Sata grew feathers, and soon blended in with the blue and green birds, both in appearance and dance skill. Boro tossed a huge ball, easily a meter across, high into the air as he danced or nibbled snacks, sometimes bouncing it off the crystal ceiling of the main hall. Ilika and Kibi swung each other around until only a blur remained.

Every female in the star station approached Rini, who glowed with masculine charm. They begged him to dance with them, but he refused them all.

Chapter 23: Meeting

"Is anyone bored?" Ilika asked when his entire crew had settled at the large table on the upper deck of the Manessa Kwi.

Sata, still in a blue and green skin-tight dance suit that made her look like a nimble-footed avian, and feel completely naked, grinned and shook her head.

"You were impressive last evening," Ilika said with admiration, "and I saw some green birds watching and learning from your movements."

Sata shrugged and ducked in a very bird-like manner, then blushed as only a monkey mammal can.

Kibi looked at her knowledge pad and sighed. "I learn to trim the station tree later today, while dangling from the ceiling on a rope!"

"That was hard for me," Ilika admitted. "Makes orbit excursions seem easy."

Boro pulled a small ball from his pocket and tossed it up a few times. "From the fish and salad place in Orange Hall, third balcony, to the ship, without dropping it or running into anything!"

Ilika smiled. "Someday, you'll get to do it with raw . . . oh, never mind."

Boro's eyes grew large.

Rini turned his knowledge pad for Ilika to see — a diagram showed the layers of a red giant star, Nebador type two, stage three.

Ilika smiled. "I'm glad you're making good use of Mati's recovery time."

"I've been looking up at the stars all my life," the freckled lad said with a smile. "Now I get to really know them."

"I'm learning about stars too, whether I like it or not," Mati announced with a mixture of humor and irritation. Then she glanced at Rini, and the irritation melted. "It's okay, I just wish my muscles would heal faster. K'stimla says I can go to one-half gravity tomorrow, *if* she likes what she sees at my exam this afternoon."

Ilika smiled at his pilot.

"I have a question," Sata suddenly said with a wrinkled brow.

Ilika looked at her.

"There are so many things going on — dance lessons, getting to know the station, helping out, visiting Mati, mission bracelets chiming — sometimes I don't know what I'm supposed to do first!"

Boro cleared his throat. "I think I can help."

The captain looked at his engineer with a knowing smile.

"Emergencies come first," Boro declared from recent experience, "and if it's personal, where *you're* the one who has to do something, then that's the most important kind of all . . ."

＊

Mati and Rini took the long way back to the medical center. At four different knowledge processors, they looked at the possible low-gravity pathways, then took turns picking the most interesting route.

The last path they chose, promising to return them to the main hall and the medical center, passed a small theater-like area where a number of creatures sat or perched while peering into a large window.

Rini was curious, so he stepped to the nearest knowledge processor and asked for a brief explanation. The one-way window looked into a large cavern-like room that simulated the home planet of a unique species of sapient reptiles. The planet was no longer livable, and the three hundred reptiles within were the only remaining members of their kind. Efforts were underway to find them a new home, but a suitable planet had not yet been found.

While Rini read, Mati stood at the back of the theater and gazed into the rocky desert environment visible through the one-way window. The reptiles wore no clothes, but jewelry shimmered on their necks, arms, and tails. They spoke to each other in deep-throated rumbles and hisses, often shared affection, and sometimes got into fights. Mati's heart went out to them, and she craved to somehow help them.

Rini stood at her side until her legs began to tremble with exhaustion. He held her hand tightly as they made their way back to the medical center along the low-gravity pathway.

The small, fuzzy blue glow that had been following them went a different way.

"I can tell by your blood chemistry that you really pushed yourself today, Mati," K'stimla said during the exam.

"Yeah, we went exploring, but I stayed on the orange path. Rini almost had to carry me the last hundred meters, but I made it!"

K'stimla's mandibles twitched. "If you tear something, we'll have to start all over."

Mati turned white. "I'm sorry."

"I'll let you go to one-half gravity tomorrow, but I want you to rest tonight, get lots of sleep, and take shorter walks tomorrow. No more than a hundred meters, then rest and eat something."

"Okay."

"I'll make sure," Rini promised from a chair nearby.

Mati flashed him a momentary frown, then smiled.

✳ ✳ ✳

Chapter 24: Dance Troop

Sata couldn't stop smiling.

She had just been offered membership in a dance troop. True, it was all students, but two were blue and green birds with natural skill, and one, her assigned dance partner, was an agile green reptile, one of the super-friendly Quanasia. She was glad her dance partner was a reptile, and even more glad that he was married. She didn't want Boro to get jealous.

After practicing some steps, and arm or wings movements to go with them, their teacher, a blue bird who could dance circles around any of them, shooed them out the door. "Do not stop dancing until you arrive at Violet Hall, but always with complete awareness of your environment, and complete attention to your responsibilities!"

Once outside, the eight of them practiced their steps in a circle around the little bubbling fountain for a minute. Faint music came from the troop leader's mission collar, just loud enough to stir the blood.

Sata looked back at the simple doorway, marked *Dance Lessons*, and knew she had found another home.

A moment of sadness washed over her, and she lost the dance step as she remembered the sand dunes in the desert, the monastery in the mountains, the hot spring terraces, and most of all, her parents' inn. All of those places were home. She focused her attention and found the rhythm again.

As her troop wound its way along paths and ramps away from the patio, Sata smiled. The Manessa Kwi was more than her new home. Since it was a ship, it would always be near, and she could go there for safety and companionship any time she needed. Her gentle but firm captain would be there, and her dear friend Mati, who would soon be walking, maybe even dancing.

They pranced along a corridor, and passed a small theater of benches and perches that clustered around a large window. Sata was curious, but couldn't learn anymore while dancing.

Sata thought of quiet Rini, and was glad he was staying at Mati's side. When Kibi's smiling face appeared for a moment in her mind, she felt a deep respect for the steward and second-in-command, and looked forward to learning that job someday.

Warm, almost hot feelings welled up when she thought of Boro, who was now learning the basics of navigation. It wasn't easy and natural for him, but neither was she comfortable working with the many engines on the lower deck of their ship.

Suddenly a group of children, two small ursines and a young monkey, came dashing toward the troop. The bird in the lead formed a tunnel with his partner, and Sata and her reptile partner did the same. The children laughed and chittered as they ducked through.

Soon the green reptile's mission bracelet chimed. He waved and pranced away. A little later, one of the birds' mission collars sounded, and he found a clear space and took flight. Sata paired up with a colorful bird, and spent the rest of the time learning from her bold wing movements.

Finally arriving in Violet Hall, the leader danced them right through the door of a little eating place, then silenced the music from his collar. They stood together, listening to their strong hearts and looking into each other's happy eyes, then turned and looked over the food and beverage options.

Having seen them dance in, the large spider at the counter had six cold, fruity drinks ready before they even asked.

After sharing a meal and saying farewell to her dance troop, Sata felt drawn back to the little theater and its window. The people watching and taking notes before had left, but others had taken their places. Sata slipped into a free spot on a bench.

The window looked into a large open space with a sandy floor, rock walls, and at least a hundred reptiles scattered about. Some just talked in small groups. Others exchanged pieces of jewelry after shaking claws about some business deal.

Sata smiled when she saw a large green reptile strutting and speaking in melodic tones to a smaller blue one. For a while the smaller one acted uninterested, but eventually her eyes sparkled and she walked beside the larger one toward a cave.

A little later, a lone reptile climbed onto a rock and began grumbling in a loud voice. Others gathered to listen. Soon his audience was nodding and pushing in closer.

Sata focused all her attention on the reptile giving the speech. Even though she couldn't understand a word, she knew from his gestures he was talking about their living space, and his audience was rumbling with anger.

Just then Sata's mission bracelet chimed, and her attention returned to the halls and balconies of Satamia Star Station. Those around her continued to take notes while watching the drama within. Using the tiny keys on her bracelet, Sata confirmed her status, and rose from the bench with a thoughtful frown.

✳ ✳ ✳

Chapter 25: Observation Tunnel

Mati stepped out of the examining room at the medical center onto a normal, full-gravity floor, and stood on her own two feet, steady and confident. She was greeted by her five fellow crew members, six or seven healers, and a handful of other well-wishers, including Glorm the docking controller and Drrrim-na the navigator. They were all clapping or stomping, smiling or calling in gleeful voices.

Mati turned red. "It doesn't count," she muttered. "There's still a long list of things I can't do."

Sata noticed that her friend was holding in a grin. "Dance?" the navigator inquired.

Mati looked at the knowledge pad she carried. "In about . . . thirty days, real Satamia days."

Sata bounced up and down, clapping.

Mati sighed. "I can't do *that* for almost a year!"

*

The entire crew helped Mati and Rini move their things back to the ship, then partook of a relaxing meal on a balcony overlooking the star station's main hall. When their plates were empty, Ilika announced a training experience that would help them understand something they had all glimpsed in passing.

After opening a heavy door on one side of a little-used corridor, the captain led his crew along a winding, dimly-lit tunnel. The walls were sometimes smooth and solid, at other places like the insides of hollowed-out boulders, and transparent.

At one point, Boro stood still for a moment, watching a green female lizard feed grubs to her scaly infant. If the tender morsel wiggled, she dangled it within reach until the child's tongue shot out. If the grub was limp and lifeless, she tossed it aside.

Sata waited for Boro to catch up, but soon found herself watching four large, blue males playing some kind of game in a small cave. At times, it seemed like a game of chance as they tossed bones onto the sand. At other times, it became a game of strength when two, after roaring about a roll of the bones, grabbed each other and wrestled for a minute.

As Kibi watched a lanky male caress a plump female, she felt Ilika at her side. "Are they mates?" she asked in a soft voice, fearing to disturb the intimate scene so close at hand.

"Yes. She's carrying three girls and one boy, and the birth rate is so low right now, they'll be carefully protected, probably spoiled."

Kibi smiled for a moment, then frowned. "They know it's not a real planet. I can tell."

"Yes, they know. They're very intelligent and sensitive. That's one reason the birth rate is so low."

Rini looked at everything with curious eyes. "You're sure they can't see us, Ilika?"

"It just looks like rocks on the outside. Light and sound only passes one way."

Mati moved slowly, with Rini or Sata always near. She looked and listened at each observation point, and often wore a frown.

✳

The crew members of the Manessa Kwi observed public meetings in large caverns, tense with disagreement. Hushed business transactions in dark corners sometimes ended with bows and other gestures of respect, more often with a fight. Intimate encounters between males and females occasionally resulted in mating, but usually just snapping and hissing.

"Why are we seeing all this?" Mati suddenly barked. "It seems like . . . it's none of our business!"

Rini squeezed her hand.

"Training," Ilika replied after considering Mati's question. "This is one of the things we do. These noble creatures would be extinct right now, but for the efforts of the Nebador Services, guided by much greater knowledge and wisdom. To help them find a new home, we have to understand them."

Ilika watched until Mati nodded, then continued to lead them along the tunnel.

The captain and crew witnessed several more glimpses of the public and private lives of the homeless reptiles. Their temporary lodgings were nothing but a simulated desert environment on a star station orbiting a star called Satamia. The reptiles had no knowledge of that star, except as a point of light, like any other, in the night sky they once knew.

The frown soon returned to Mati's face.

A small blue glow followed at a distance.

After half an hour of walking along the tunnel, Ilika could see that his crew was tired and hungry. He didn't linger at the last few observation points, and walked right past a closed door.

Mati, at the end of the line, paused to read the words on the door. *Caution: simulated environment beyond.*

Sata waited for her friend at the next bend in the tunnel.

Mati stood at the door, frozen, her brow wrinkled with indecision.

"Mati!" Sata called. "The others are almost at the exit door! What are you doing?"

Mati hesitated one more second, then pushed on the door in front of her. She heard a soft beep, and felt the door move slightly at her push, but her new leg muscles began screaming at her. "Sata, help me!"

The navigator glanced along the tunnel, and saw Boro disappearing through the exit door into the star station corridor beyond. She looked back at her pilot, still trying to open the door with its words of warning. After one more breath, and a few quick strides, she was beside her friend. The door responded to Sata's greater strength and opened a little.

"That's enough," Mati declared, seeing sand and small rocks on the ground beyond the door. She quickly kicked at the ground until a pebble bounced onto the door sill. "I just want to give them a chance."

Sata's heart throbbed as she watched Mati ease the door most of the way closed, but could see by the yellow symbol that it had not latched.

When Sata and Mati finally arrived at the exit door, Boro was holding it for them. "What took you guys so long?"

"Just taking one last look," Mati replied with a smile.

Sata didn't dare open her mouth. As she stepped into the corridor, not far from the observation window with its benches and perches, she wondered how long her heart would continue to throb loudly in her chest.

Rini turned and looked at Mati. *I don't know if that will do them any good, but I'll always be at your side, no matter what.*

Mati smiled at him.

The fuzzy blue light remained in the tunnel near the door to the simulated environment.

✳   ✳   ✳

Chapter 26: The Guard

"Tar'gn'ja has discovered a Rip in the fabric of the universe."

"An anomaly? A dis-continuity? Can't be!"

"It is. And you knew it was coming, just as I did. The stars have been wrong for months."

"Yes. Water does not flow like it should."

"Directional instincts have been off."

"Few females are mating. They sense something's wrong."

"It's as if our world ended, and we didn't notice, when we moved out of the collapsed cavern and into this one."

"Tell us about the Rip, Shun'gsh'ta!"

"Tar'gn'ja says a huge boulder floats, and he can move it with one claw. He only peeked beyond for a moment, then became frightened. He mutters about small, glowing eyes in the dark that do not move, but sometimes change color."

"Spirits?"

"Demons?"

"Maybe both, I don't know!"

"We must activate the Guard."

"The Guard? It has not been used in our lifetime!"

"It must be used now. I am one, as are you."

"True, but in name only. We know nothing of the old skills. After we destroyed our enemies, one and all, there was no purpose to the old training."

"There is purpose now. We must find out where we are, and how we can return to the world we knew. This . . . tear in the fabric of the universe . . . may be our only chance."

"I am with you, although I wish my grandfather was here to lead, or at least advise us."

"So do I, my friend. So do I."

*

"There are seven of us," Shun'gsh'ta declared as he looked over his fellow reptiles.

Five males and one stout female looked back, all wearing the jewelry of the Guard, long an honorary order without training or duties.

"I cannot tell you what we will find when we go through the Rip."

"Is it another dimension?"

"A time portal that will take us to the past or future?"

"The demon-filled Underworld?"

"I don't know!" Shun'gsh'ta snapped. "It is the unknown. Are you willing to go, knowing that if even one of us returns alive, with information that will lead us back to the world we knew, it will be worth the sacrifice?"

Silence filled the cave for a long moment. The female was the first to raise a claw. After that, none of the males dared show cowardice, and six claws were quickly held aloft.

"I am proud of you. I, too, tremble at the thought of stepping through the Rip. My scales rattle and my claws shake. But we all know that something is wrong, deeply wrong, with our world. We must find out what before all the females refuse to mate and we are doomed."

The others nodded.

"Because we know nothing about what lies beyond, we are all scouts. Explore for an hour at the most, always marking the way. Return to tell your tale. I can say no more."

The seven members of the Guard, with their hearts in their throats, crept to the mysterious boulder that opened into ... they knew not what. The others gasped as Shun'gsh'ta easily swung it open to reveal a dark tunnel going in two directions. They stared at the strange symbols on the other side of the floating boulder, but only shrugged.

Finally, not knowing what else to do, four of them went to the left and three to the right, trembling as they paused at each nook that offered any cover or protection.

Small blue presences followed in both directions.

*　*　*

Chapter 27: Refugees

"That looks good," the spider declared, dangling from his own thread. "Let's go lower," he directed as he played out more silk.

Kibi glanced down at the floor of Blue Hall, twenty meters or more below, then closed her eyes to steady her stomach and nerves. Soon she heard and felt wing beats very close.

"You okay, Kibi?" the large bird asked, hovering nearby.

She forced her eyes open. "Yeah. As good as a monkey mammal can ever be, high in a tree."

"Your ancestors lived in trees, swinging from branch to branch."

"That was when we had tails! You want this basket of trimmings?"

"Yes, please, unless you want to eat it for lunch. They're very tasty."

"No thanks," she replied, pressing the release symbol as soon has the bird had his beak on the handle. "Already tried them, at Drrrim-na's suggestion, don't know why you like them."

The bird made a laughing sound in his throat as he backed away, then tucked his wings to dive toward the floor far below.

Kibi looked down, saw the spider waiting for her four meters lower, and wrapped her fingers around the rope controls. As she slid down to the next tangle of leaves and vines that needed trimming, she noticed unusual activity below.

An orange reptile dashed on all fours across the hall, looked around, and quickly disappeared behind a trunk of the station tree.

Three small bears ran into the hall and turned circles, clearly looking for something.

Kibi looked at the spider. "Should we help them? It looked like one of the homeless reptiles, and I saw where it went."

The spider looked back with hundreds of eyes. "Do you *know* the reptile is dangerous, and the ursines are doing the right thing?"

"Um . . . no . . . I just thought . . . I don't know . . ."

"Because it was *one* reptile and *three* ursines?" the spider asked pointedly. "Majority rules?"

Kibi looked embarrassed. "Is that . . . one of those monkey-mammal bad habits?"

The spider nodded. "However, you're probably right, in this case." He scanned the room again. Two young monkeys had joined the small bears, and four little birds landed soon after and began talking with the other five. "It looks like the children are taking care of it. If we're needed, we'll be called. Let's trim this tree."

A bird arrived with a basket, Kibi clipped it to her line, and pulled a pruning tool from her vest.

*

Rini was spraying dirty dishes when a reptilian claw suddenly reached into the dishwashing room and grabbed a piece of food someone had left on a plate. Rini blinked in surprise, but his jaw dropped when a half-dozen young birds swooped into the room and swarmed around the fleeing reptile, who dove under a bench.

Still in his apron, Rini dashed out of the dishwashing room, ran to the bench, and jumped on top. "Stop it! He's alone and afraid!"

The birds settled onto the floor and ducked their heads in shame.

At that moment, a deep-green glow began to form nearby, took on more substance as seconds passed, and quickly became a green reptile with leaves twined around his head and neck.

Rini had never seen this exact shape before, but somehow knew who it was, and had a good idea why he was taking the form of a reptile. "Kerloran . . ." he whispered.

Thank you, Rini, the master of Satamia Star Station said directly to Rini's mind. *They are young, lacking in wisdom, and hopefully will remember what you just taught them. I will take this poor fellow back to a place he understands.*

Even before he finished communicating with Rini, the majestic green reptile gathered the trembling run-away into his arms and floated toward the simulated desert environment.

*

Boro and three fanators, with lots of help from others with time to spare, were coming to the end of scrubbing the blue-green floor of Cyan Hall, when a gray reptile burst from a corridor with three young ursines right on its tail.

Boro stood up to take in the situation, just as the bears succeeded in cornering the frightened lizard. He immediately saw the danger. "No! Be careful!"

Before anyone could heed his warning, a spiked tail flashed out, the bear children went flying, and blood splattered everywhere. Boro wasted no more time, ran and dove, and a second later had his strong arms and legs wrapped around the cornered creature. He felt his own skin pierced in several places by scales and horns, but nothing he couldn't handle.

Boro could hear the fanators helping the injured ursines, but could see nothing, and didn't dare allow the reptile to gain any distance and use its claws or tail.

The reptile tried to wiggle free, but had no success. After a long minute of effort, it began to relax.

Several minutes later, as Boro continued to hold the lizard tightly, he heard a voice in his mind. *You're very lucky that's a female. The males are much stronger. Thank you, Boro, I'm ready to take her back now.*

A green mist formed around them, and the reptile went completely limp. Boro, with some hesitation, released his grip. The mist-enshrouded lizard floated away, and Boro found himself sitting on the floor in a small pool of something red. A moment later, a large spider arrived and opened a medical kit.

✳

Sata and Mati sat nervously in the waiting room of the medical center, wondering why they had both been called in. They soon discovered why no one had time to talk to them.

A stream of injured creatures, of all kinds, began arriving — ursines and felines, avians and reptiles, monkeys and spiders. Both girls quickly noticed that most of the injured were children, but had no idea why.

A little later, four more stretchers came in the door. The first two held small bears with minor injuries. Both looked sad, but occasionally exchanged words with their attendants.

The third stretcher brought Mati and Sata to their feet. It came slowly, without urgency, a cloth covering the victim. From the shape, and an uncovered paw, they knew an ursine child was beyond help.

The next stretcher kept them on their feet.

Boro looked out from under a blanket, and when he saw them, quickly said, "I'm okay, just some little cuts and scrapes."

When all four stretchers had passed into the medical center, Mati and Sata tried to relax, but had no hope that anyone would have time to see them, or even tell them why they were there.

✳

Even before the stream of injured creatures were all treated, Ilika and Kibi received a call to a special meeting.

Melorania glowed a bright blue. *I hope you are comfortable enough with Nebador now, Kibi, that I don't need to bother with a material form.*

Kibi swallowed, then nodded.

Many people were tested by the situation that arose today. Of the young ones that Kerloran asked to help, most of them learned some valuable lessons, and they all dealt with the death of one of their fellows.

Feelings twisted Kibi's face for a long moment, but she eventually took several deep breaths. Ilika held her hand.

Rini and Boro helped, and even though they both responded well, they have much to learn about dealing with frightened, confused mortal creatures.

Ilika nodded.

After a few days of healing, we must take your pilot and your navigator from you for a time. I have high hopes that both will survive the project, and return to you stronger and wiser.

"I . . . hope so too," Ilika whispered.

Melorania faded and disappeared.

Kibi squeezed Ilika's hand. "What kind of . . . project . . . was she talking about?"

Ilika took a slow breath. "I'm . . . not sure."

✳ ✳ ✳

Chapter 28: In Trouble

For the next day and a half, Satamia time, things seemed to return to normal. The many injured children, and a few adults, including Boro, were treated in the medical center and returned to their lives. The entire crew of the Manessa Kwi attended the memorial service for the young ursine who had not survived her encounter with a full-grown, cornered, frightened reptile.

*

At the end of that long Satamia day, the evening party featured many excellent musicians, including a reptilian singer who chanted a lament for the deceased ursine that brought tears to many eyes, and other signs of sorrow to those without tears. But before it ended, the song changed into a spirited celebration of life that had nearly everyone dancing with joy.

Mati, of course, had to mostly watch, and she found she had lots of company. A transport ship from a far-away star system was in the station, a variety of creatures she had never before imagined. Most of the music and dancing was strange to the new arrivals, so they stayed on the edges of the main hall, and talked with whoever was available.

Mati learned they were students, and had come to observe something called the Great Transformation. She admitted she knew nothing about it, that she was just a simple response ship pilot.

To her surprise, the students' eyes opened wide and they begged her to tell them of her adventures. Soon she had twenty or more creatures gathered around her couch, about half of them floating in the air nearby. They listened intently as she recounted the time she accidentally backed into a ruined building that collapsed onto the ship, and how she eventually got it out.

Rini came and went, bringing his beloved what she mentally requested from the snack tables. Sata, Boro, Kibi, and Ilika stopped by less often, and smiled when they heard Mati tell of planets they had explored, places on her home world they had seen, and even locations visited on donkey-back.

Some of the students sensed the deep mind-link that she and Rini shared, and when Mati ran out of stories, they begged Rini to tell them how it came about. He was not as comfortable talking to other people as Mati, but satisfied their curiosity.

* * *

During the five days, ship time, between that evening party and the next, life for the crew of the Manessa Kwi seemed to return to normal.

Ilika and Kibi had several meetings they had to attend, and said little about what went on at those meetings, but were almost always on the ship for the minor missions that came up. Twice Kibi was deep into tasks assigned by the Psychic Development program, so Ilika marked her off-duty, and covered her station. Once, for the first time, Kibi commanded a short supply run without Ilika on the ship. She was very glad she had her pilot back on duty.

Boro finally got to spend time observing Glorm as he directed station traffic, and was amazed at the responsibilities of the job, but could almost see himself doing it someday. Almost.

Sata requested another fishing trip, and this time they invited Glorm, who got the biggest fish. Boro's and Sata's were so close that they declared it a tie.

Sata danced whenever she could, but spent almost no time with Mati during that station-day, except during missions.

Mati knew why.

What she had done in the observation tunnel of the simulated desert environment, and the events that followed, gnawed at her. She could now see that it may have damaged her friendship with Sata. She had asked her friend to help with something that had gotten one child killed and many others injured. It had not, as far as she could tell, done anyone any good. She remembered Rini predicting as much. She thanked the stars every day and every night that her actions had not caused any bad feelings with him. He seemed to accept her completely, even when she did stupid things.

Although no one seemed to openly blame her, she had a hunch, deep down inside, that it would someday come back to haunt her.

* * *

The next evening dance party began like any other. Decorations appeared, musicians and dancers warmed up, and food and drink came in from every kitchen.

But before the first song began, Melorania and Kerloran appeared, gathered form, and settled onto the floor in the middle of the main hall of Satamia Star Station. She wore a swirling blue gown that never completely ceased its motion, and he was covered with green scales and leaves.

More than a thousand Nebador citizens fell silent and looked at them with great respect. Most of those citizens sensed that something special was about to take place. The students from other star systems, seven transport-ships-full by this time, although still a bit timid, hovered in the air or slithered up walls so they could see.

When all was quiet, Kerloran spoke. "Mati and Sata, please come forward."

A moment of panic brought tears to Mati's eyes as she desperately looked around for her crutch. Rini sensed that if she found it, she would not use it to approach Kerloran, but instead to hobble away and hide in the deepest, darkest corner she could find.

Sata stood nearby, waiting for her friend to collect herself. She could feel her own body trembling, but had known this moment would come. She just wished it didn't have to be in front of everyone.

Eventually Mati remembered that her crutch was on the Manessa Kwi, under her bed. She looked down and saw her two good legs. Embarrassed chuckles began to mix with her tears.

Kerloran and Melorania waited patiently.

Mati and Sata looked at each other.

Sata knew, from the pathetic look on Mati's face, that Mati was deeply sorry for dragging her friend into this mess. Sata smiled slightly, and offered her hand to the friend whose fate had been intertwined with her own ever since they met.

Hand in hand, on shaking legs, they crossed the open floor toward the mysterious head of the Transport Service and the master of the star station. Both seemed to tower over the two girls.

"Most civilizations," Melorania began for all to hear, "would put you in prison for what you did, possibly execute you."

Two pairs of eyes dropped toward the floor. Four other response-ship crew members felt their hearts jump into their throats. Few others, anywhere in the star station hall, were breathing.

"But this is Nebador," Kerloran continued. "We do things a bit differently here."

Sata squeezed Mati's hand, and a tiny bit of hope entered both girls' hearts.

"We realized that we were being handed an opportunity that would be hard to arrange — perhaps even hard to imagine — if it had not happened as it did." He looked up and spoke to the entire room. "Yes, I assure you all, there is greater knowledge and wisdom elsewhere in the universe, and some things remain hidden, at least for a while, even from us."

A faint chuckling sound rippled through the star station.

"Mati and Sata," Melorania began, "you both acted out of love. Mati craves to share the freedom she now enjoys with all other creatures, and Sata has a deep need to prove herself to her fellow crew members, especially to Mati. You had the courage to put your necks on the line for a handful of homeless reptiles. Now I must ask you a very important question. Do you, or do you not, also have the courage to do what it takes to fully understand them, so you can help in the search for their new home, and possibly succeed where others have failed? In other words, do you have the courage to finish what you started?"

Mati and Sata tried to breathe, but it was not easy under the circumstances. Eventually they got some air into their lungs, but had to struggle for another long moment to swallow and clear their throats.

Mati knew in her heart she was more responsible for what happened than Sata. "It's . . ." She struggled to make her voice work. "It's . . . all my fault . . . and I want to take . . . the punishment for Sata. Someone died . . . because of me . . . and I don't deserve . . . to be a pilot . . . anymore."

Kerloran let the silence lengthen, then smiled. "You are very new here, my dear little monkey mammal. I will not attempt to teach you a lifetime of wisdom right here and now, as all these precious citizens want to dance and play."

More chuckles coursed through the huge room.

"But I will tell you three things very firmly."

Mati swallowed and tried to look at the majestic green master of Satamia Star Station, but the sight almost hurt her eyes.

"First of all, your friend Sata is responsible for herself, and you cannot take that away from her."

Sata cringed and nodded at the same time.

"Second, mortals do not get to decide what they deserve or don't deserve. You do not have that perspective, and you would not want that responsibility, believe me."

Mati swallowed and blinked, but could not think of anything worth saying.

"Third, death is not the tragedy you have come to assume. Nothing real and enduring was lost. In fact, much was gained, and much more may still be gained."

Melorania spoke next. "But you *do* have the responsibility to answer the question. Are you willing to do all it takes to understand the homeless creatures that we hold in the palms of our hands?"

"I . . ." Mati forced herself to begin. "I . . . have a hunch . . . that if I don't . . . I'm in big trouble."

"That's correct," Kerloran said firmly, leaving no doubt.

"Um . . . what would I . . . have to do?"

"I believe you would say something like, *walk in their shoes for a time*. They don't wear shoes, but the meaning applies."

"You mean . . . live with them? I don't think they like monkey mammals."

"You are right, they do not," Melorania replied, "especially after their recent experience."

Sata thought she heard Boro laugh somewhere behind her.

"But you would not live with them in the shape of humans," Melorania continued. "You would take *their* shape. That is the only way they would accept you enough to show you their true needs and desires."

Mati looked at Sata, still holding her hand.

"We have to," Sata whispered.

"I know," Mati whispered back.

Suddenly Rini was at Mati's side, looking up at Melorania and Kerloran, but he said nothing aloud.

"I see your concern," Kerloran said, looking at the freckled lad. "Yes, they will be females, and yes, they will be expected, by the other reptiles, to mate. If we accept your offer to accompany Mati, you must understand that you may have to fight off other males."

"I understand," Rini said for all to hear.

Suddenly Boro was beside Sata.

"Yes, Boro, you can go too," Melorania said with a smile.

Ilika and Kibi, near the back of the room, looked at each other with wide eyes.

✳   ✳   ✳

Chapter 29: Briefing

Melorania and Kerloran soon shooed the four humans away so the party could begin. The four wandered into a secluded corner, found an unused couch, and huddled together to try to figure out what they had just gotten themselves into.

Kibi started to move in that direction, but Ilika grabbed her hand. "I think they need some time without us. This will be *their* mission, and you and I don't have a part to play, as far as I can see. If I'm wrong, someone will let us know."

Kibi was torn, but eventually nodded. A lively song began, and her feet started moving almost by themselves, so she grinned and pulled Ilika toward the dance floor.

✳

"I am so sorry . . ." Mati began.

Rini gave her the sternest look he could muster. "Didn't you hear what they said? They are *glad* it happened. It gave them some . . . you know . . . volunteers . . . for something nobody else wanted to do."

"Yeah, but you and Boro will have to fight off a bunch of horny reptiles, with scales and claws, trying to get into Sata's and my pants! Except . . ." she continued thoughtfully, "we won't have pants . . ."

Boro laughed. "But *we* will have scales and claws, too!"

Sata nodded and smiled, and got the impression that Boro was looking forward to the experience.

✳

By morning, they had the schedule.

For the next Satamia day, the four volunteers would be in meetings, briefings, classes, and training sessions almost constantly. They looked for times they could eat and sleep, and found only breaks for snacks or short naps.

Ilika and Kibi were only invited to the first meeting.

A large white feline leapt onto a table at the front of the conference room. "I am Silmula Sorafax. Although this is not something we do often, I have as much experience in these matters as any mortal in Satamia. I have been placed in charge of this mission, although you must understand that I will remain on the outside, and not join you for the Great Transformation."

Mati had heard that term somewhere before, just recently, but couldn't remember where.

"As you may guess from your schedules, the four of you are off-duty concerning your ship, and all other training and activities, until this mission is completed. Please note that, captain."

Ilika nodded.

Boro raised his hand. "We have the . . . pre-mission schedule . . . but we were wondering how long the . . . um . . . transformation will last."

The big cat was silent for a moment and seemed to almost smile. "As I understand it, a year would do you good."

The four fellow crew members in the front row, currently off-duty, swallowed hard.

"But since there is some urgency in figuring out where we can resettle those beautiful reptiles, and since good response-ship crews don't grow on trees, I'm thinking that about twenty days might do the trick."

Sata could almost see Boro doing the math in his head, then realizing, with wide eyes, how long twenty Satamia days would be.

"But the length will also depend on you four. This is not a vacation. You will be in there for a purpose, and to atone for what, as Melorania said, could easily be considered a crime."

Mati nodded, and mentally heard Rini's assurance that they would be together, no matter what.

✳

After several hours of basic information, Ilika, Kibi, and a few others departed. The meal break was so short, it was served from a cart by a large furry ape whose nimble hands quickly assembled trays for each species.

The hundred or more students in the back of the room gathered into groups where they were comfortable, introduced themselves to each other, and chatted about the fascinating adventure they were witnessing.

Silmula Sorafax and about a dozen other advisors and teachers took a large table and talked as they ate. Even though the group included four reptiles, they could offer little insight into the situation that the large cat did not already know. Avians, ursines, a four-legged equine, and two humans completed the team.

Boro glanced at the two monkey mammals. "I wonder why we've never met them before."

Sata, holding his hand, shrugged. "Maybe they came in one of those ships that brought students. Come on, I have . . . something I want to say."

They grabbed a tray, saw that Mati and Rini were already huddled together, and picked a small table in a corner.

As soon as they sat down, Sata scooted her chair close to Boro, put her arms around his neck, and began the deepest, longest kiss he had ever received.

"Wow . . ." he began when she finally, reluctantly, let a little space come between them. "I guess I did . . . something right," he went on with a shy smile.

She grinned at him with smoldering eyes. "You certainly did! And I've been aching to get some time alone with you to tell you. I'd like to do *more* than tell you . . ."

Boro looked embarrassed. "Um . . . we've got less than a quarter hour, AND we have to inhale this food."

"It's very simple," she continued. "When you stepped up and agreed to go in there with me, I *knew* I was going to be yours, and only yours, whether we're reptiles, monkey mammals, or anything else . . ."

❋

It seemed to Mati that a thousand different people had a million thoughts about the homeless reptiles, and she and her friends were going to have to sit through every minute of it.

Luckily, Silmula Sorafax was very skilled at breaking up the presentations, leaving time for questions, demonstrations, toilet breaks, snacks, and even little games and dances.

Even so, after about six hours, Mati was asleep on a couch, with Boro not far behind on another couch. The large white cat seemed to have anticipated this, and lessons and discussions continued as long as any two of the four humans were awake.

❋

Rini awoke from a short nap to find Mati munching on fruit slices and nuts. She formed thoughts while chewing. *Hi. I saved you some.*

The slender boy sat up and yawned. *Did the equine ever quit talking about safety protocols? His deep voice put me right to sleep.*

Mati smiled. *Yeah. He became embarrassed when Boro and Sata both joined you in dreamland. But then Sata woke up, so we listened to a bird who's learned a bit of the reptiles' language.*

It's weird that none of the Nebador reptiles can speak it, Rini shared while eating.

They say it's mostly genetic. The homeless reptiles are born speaking it, and it's not like anything they've ever heard.

I was awake then. Did you hear that spider saying it's almost like some insect languages?

No, I missed that, Mati admitted. *I wonder how reptiles got an insect language . . .*

Maybe we'll find out.

After a long pause, Mati formed a new thought. *No matter what stupid things I do, you'll always be with me, won't you?*

Rini popped a few nuts into his mouth. *That's right. But . . . I'll be with you when you do smart things, too!*

Silmula Sorafax leapt onto a table and cleared her throat. "We're going to take some questions and comments from the students from other star systems . . ."

*

Ilika and Kibi walked through the boarding tunnel hand in hand, then strolled around the Manessa Kwi, half-heartedly making sure everything was stocked and ready.

"I always like time alone with you," Ilika began as they descended in the lift, "but this wasn't exactly what I had in mind."

Kibi laughed nervously. "Do you think . . . they'll be okay?"

Ilika thought about her question as they entered the utility room. He touched a symbol and an access panel opened. "They have no idea what they've gotten themselves into, and all the briefing and training can hardly begin to prepare them for the experience of living in another creature's skin."

Kibi took a deep breath as she watched Ilika begin a diagnostic. "I gathered as much, since no one else is volunteering to go in their place, or even with them."

"Yeah," Ilika confirmed, closing the panel. "I've only done it with another mammal, of similar intelligence, and I'm not looking forward to the next time."

"What kind?"

"Equine. Beautiful creatures, but they live with more than their share of fear. Fear, as I'm sure you know by now, is the enemy of intelligence and wisdom. Horses have worked hard, on many different planets, to overcome that handicap."

Kibi nodded and opened her water filter cabinet. "So . . . the greater the difference in the creatures, the harder it is to live in their skin?"

"I'm not sure 'harder' is the right word. I'd say more like 'shocking.'"

"Oh," Kibi responded without voice. She finished looking over the supplies, and closed the cabinet. "So there's . . . real danger?"

Ilika's laugh was full of tension. "Oh, yeah! In addition to the claws and all that, there's the very real possibility of forgetting who you were, or just not wanting to come back. You have to *choose* to end the mission. Equine fear makes that very hard. There are things going on in this situation that will also make it a supreme decision for our friends."

Kibi swallowed, then took a deep breath to clear her head. "We won't be getting any missions while it's just you and me, will we?"

Before Ilika could answer, both their bracelets chimed.

※   ※   ※

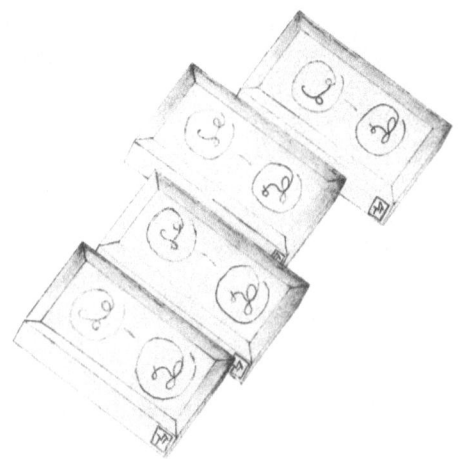

Chapter 30: The Great Transformation

As evening on Satamia Star Station approached once again, the main hall appeared far from ready for a party. Instead, four golden boxes sat alone in the middle of the hall, all about the size and shape of a wide coffin, and all glowing with an inner light.

Many creatures were at work, but not hanging decorations. The entire briefing team was present, under the firm leadership of the large white feline, Silmula Sorafax. They poured over checklists on knowledge pads, organized the visiting students into teams, and conferred with fuzzy, glowing orbs who came and went.

Eventually Kerloran whirled into the room and spun himself into a majestic green bird, larger even than a fanator. A moment later, Melorania appeared and became a wise old woman with sparkling youthful eyes. Silmula Sorafax approached them and the three spoke silently.

Mati, Sata, Boro, and Rini had not been back to the Manessa Kwi since the process began. They had occasionally, during the four days of lessons and briefings, been able to use a bathing room, but the crowded schedule had never allowed any leisure.

Kibi and Ilika had visited once or twice a day and shared their own process of learning to run the ship with a crew of only two. It was not easy, they emphasized, was never going to be easy, and they really looked forward to their friends returning to duty.

Now the captain and his steward stood off to the side of the main hall, trying to stay out of the way. A few minutes after Melorania and Kerloran materialized, Mati and Rini entered hand in hand. Behind them, Sata and Boro appeared.

Kibi looked into their faces and hearts. Mati might have been going to her own funeral, although Rini seemed content. A moment later, Rini looked deeply worried, and Mati suddenly became calm and ready for anything. Sata had tears on her face, but was smiling. Boro looked around warily, as if expecting wild, hungry wolves to be lurking, then stumbled over the corner of a bench and laughed at himself.

Kerloran, Melorania, and Silmula Sorafax turned and looked at the four monkey mammals. Everyone else in the huge room fell silent.

Kibi noticed all four of their moods shift once again.

"Mati of Sonmatia Three," Melorania began in a voice that everyone in the station, in every hall and room, could hear. "When you accepted Ilika Imni's offer to become the pilot of a deep-space response ship of the Nebador Transport Service, you jumped ahead of the people of your world, in some ways, by thousands of years. In other ways, they can never experience the marvels you have seen, and will continue to see, in the many long years ahead of you."

"But," Mati squeaked, tears suddenly springing from her eyes, "I have to . . ."

". . . experience transformation, Mati, and gain the wisdom that can only come with transformation, while most of the people of your little planet cower in fear of such changes."

Mati swallowed several times, wiped her tears on her sleeve, and nodded. Sata stood crying silently. Boro looked steeled for some dire fate, and Rini was not quite smiling.

"Have you decided, truly decided?" Kerloran asked.

Mati sniffled. "You'll take care of my . . . my body? I worked really hard to get two good knees."

Chuckles of sympathy rippled through the room. Kerloran nodded and Melorania smiled.

"Okay . . . then I guess . . . I'd better . . . do it."

"Sata?" Silmula Sorafax inquired.

"Um . . . yes," she said through tears. "I did a stupid thing, right along with my friend. It took me a long time to learn to stand on my own two feet, even though my knees were good, and I'm not going to stop now."

Mati cracked a tiny smile.

"Boro?" the large cat continued.

He nodded. "I wouldn't be worth my salt, as a man, if I didn't go with Sata."

"Rini?"

"I go where Mati goes, and some reptile is only going to mate with her over my dead body!"

More chuckles rippled through the crowd.

"As we have discussed, Rini," Silmula Sorafax began, "more than one reptile may try to arrange that."

"I know. They won't find it easy."

"Same here," Boro assured everyone.

✳

When nothing more remained to be said, the large white cat walked to the first golden box. "Mati, as you led the misguided effort to free the homeless reptiles, so you are now the leader, if anyone is, of this little team. Think of it as flight command."

Mati shuddered for a moment, then approached the glowing box. Silmula Sorafax touched a symbol and the box opened. The blue female reptile curled up within, deeply-asleep if even alive, appeared to be perfect, as if newly-made.

"She's . . . beautiful," Mati muttered.

"She is completely yours, and has no life of her own," the cat explained.

Mati knew what she had to do. It was one of the last lessons given by the briefing team, and they had made sure everyone was awake. She climbed into the box with the sleeping lizard, curled around it until she could feel its scales touching her body in many places, and tried to relax.

Silmula Sorafax touched another symbol and the box closed.

Sata climbed in with her green female, slightly larger than Mati's blue.

Rini curled around his gray male lizard and closed his eyes.

Boro's orange male had large muscles and sharp claws, and Boro was glad.

Unseen by those in the boxes, four glowing purple entities descended from somewhere near the ceiling of the main hall. One came to rest over each golden box, and spread wings of light completely around each container and its precious cargo.

The room remained silent as the minutes passed, and Kibi at first thought she was going to explode with anxiety. Then she glanced around, and saw that everyone else in the room, from Ilika to the floating creatures from a distant star system, were all meditating. After laughing at herself silently for a moment, she closed her eyes and began to slow her breathing.

✳

To Kibi, it seemed like hours later, but may have been mere minutes. The purple entities retracted their wings of light and drifted away into the upper balconies. Kerloran leapt into the air on giant wings, swept over the assembled Nebador citizens, and vanished into a corridor. Melorania began to swirl, became a blur, and disappeared. Only beings of flesh and blood remained in the huge room.

Silmula Sorafax stretched her long feline body, and stepped to Boro's box.

When it opened to her touch, an orange reptile slowly lifted his head, then looked down at the sleeping monkey mammal beside him in the box. After blinking and considering the situation for a long minute, he looked up, climbed out, and said something in throaty sounds and hisses that only one bird could understand, and then only a little.

A lanky gray lizard emerged from Rini's box, and scanned the room with a contented look.

Sata, in her new form, looked back and forth from the sleeping human in the box, to the large cat.

The blue female came out last, testing her legs to make sure all four knees worked.

"As you know," Silmula Sorafax began, addressing the four reptiles, "we can understand very little of your speech. If you succeed in your mission and return to us, you can tell us all you learned. If you do not return to us, that knowledge will be lost, and we may never find those noble creatures a suitable home."

*

The four golden boxes, with their sleeping monkey mammals, were closed and floated into the medical center.

Ilika and Kibi spent a quarter hour with the four new reptiles, assuring them they would be missed, and promising that the Manessa Kwi would await their return. Drrrim-na, Glorm, Dakalio, and other friends came by. They could do little but wish their friends well. All those who visited looked at the four with great respect, and also a tinge of worry.

Finally, with preparations for the evening party going on all around them, Silmula Sorafax declared that it was time. The four reptiles took one last look around them at the decorations and musical instruments, shared clumsy embraces with Ilika and Kibi, and followed the white feline toward the simulated desert environment.

*   *   *

Chapter 31: Newcomers

The door that looked like a rock closed behind them.

It was far from the one Mati had left ajar days earlier, selected for its distance from the cavern of the homeless reptiles, designed to make anyone coming through it seem like they had just crossed the vast open desert.

Boro remembered well that they could not return to their lives in Satamia Star Station, and in the Nebador Transport Service, by going back through that door. But just to be sure, he used his new claws, quite long and sharp as claws went, to try to open the door. After a long effort, he gave up. "It's locked," he said with deep throaty sounds and hisses. "Like they said, the only way back is . . ."

"We know," Mati assured with a hiss. "It's strange *hearing* reptile sounds, and yet *understanding* them, just like you were talking our language."

"It's genetic," Rini recalled with a throaty gurgle. "This would be a lot harder otherwise."

"But that bird," Sata began with a wavering growl, "the one who knew the language a little, said there would be some idioms we wouldn't know."

"That's where the story about coming from far away will help us," Boro reminded them.

They all fell silent for a while, looking around at the rocks and sand.

The scales around Mati's eyes tightened. "I know they put me in command, but I don't think that'll look good here. Boro, I want you to be in command most of the time, unless I override something. Even then, I want you to *look* like you're in command."

Boro stood up on his hind legs and filled his chest with the dry air. Sata stood close beside him, letting her scales touch his.

Rini smiled without letting it show.

"We stay in pairs," Boro began, "as every male in this place — about a hundred of them — are looking for females willing to mate."

Mati nodded. "We're here for twenty Satamia days, not an hour more, and hopefully less if we discover what we're here to learn. Rini, will you keep track of that?"

"Sure. It's a hundred and forty simulated days in this place. I'll make marks on a rock somewhere," he promised, flexing the sharp nail of one finger.

Mati looked at Sata, who was rubbing up against Boro. "And don't forget what we *can't* do, with reptiles here, *or* each other, to have any chance of going home."

Sata collected herself and let some space come between her and the large orange male who was making her feel very affectionate.

*

When the four new lizards arrived at the main cavern, they were immediately surrounded by about two hundred reptiles, mostly female, who immediately began showering the newcomers with questions.

Boro stood tall and silent, obviously in charge, while Mati, Rini, and Sata did most of the talking.

"We were in a small cavern across the desert when the ground started shaking," Mati began the story that had been suggested by the equine on the briefing team. "Many were killed when the cavern collapsed . . ."

"Ours did too!" many reptilian voices shared.

". . . and more of us died on the long desert crossing," Rini took up the story. "Our only hope was to find the great tribe our legends told us we once came from, long before we hatched."

"You have found it!" a very large male suddenly boomed, standing upright and towering over the females.

The four newcomers looked at him with respect, as they knew they must.

"But alas, we have little," he continued, dropping back to all fours. "The stars are wrong here, the water does not flow right, and most females are so upset, they never go into heat. We discovered a Rip in the fabric of the universe, but our scouts returned trembling with fear and muttering about sights and sounds that made no sense. The Rip will no longer open. We are a dying people. You are welcome to die here with us, perhaps distract us with stories from your cavern."

As Boro listened to the heart-felt words of the cavern's leader, he became aware that two young males were edging close to Sata, sniffing and reaching toward her. He took a deep breath, felt the muscles in his spiked tail respond to his will, and slapped the ground right in front of the two males, sending them scurrying backwards. "She's mine. Don't get any ideas."

An older male sniffed the air. "She's in heat. You'd better mate with her, or someone else will."

Boro growled, but the older male just shrugged and walked away.

The females quickly surrounded the new arrivals. "Come into the cavern!" an older female, wearing several pieces of jewelry, invited. "We just collected grubs. Not as tasty as the ones in our old cavern, but they'll fill an empty belly!"

Mati walked beside Sata and spoke in a soft voice. "*Why* are you in heat?"

"I don't know! I just got this reptile body an hour ago, remember?"

Mati sighed and continued following the other reptiles toward the cavern entrance.

✳   ✳   ✳

Chapter 32: Getting Comfortable in New Shoes

Kibi greeted the three avians and two small mammals who came through the boarding tunnel, but frowned when one bird stepped into the galley and began opening cupboards, and another hopped into the steward's chair.

Ilika, working on a flight plan at navigation, caught her eye and motioned toward the watch station. "They know we're short-handed. Try to ignore your human territorial instincts. That bird in your chair has more flight experience than you and me put together. The watch station is where I need your skills today, and probably at navigation too."

Kibi swallowed and began activating external sensors. "Why am I more worried about Sata than I am about Mati?"

"Anything we should tell Silmula Sorafax?"

"Nothing I can put my finger on, just my over-active intuition."

"That intuition of yours is one of the most important strengths of Manessa's crew."

Kibi smiled. "Am I still second-in-command?"

"Oh, yes. And the avian up there will respect that. Also, you can, and should, monitor what he does from here. Think of it like this — with just you and me on the crew, you are too valuable to use your time as steward when Nebador citizens can easily take care of themselves."

Kibi smiled, and felt her territorial instincts melt away. She placed a copy of the steward's status list in the corner of the watch station display, and noticed that the bird in her chair had almost completed his checklist. "Hey, you're good!"

"Glad to be of service, bok."

A moment later, Kibi squinted at her display. "Ilika, why are there four thousand seven hundred and fifty people on the passenger list? Manessa isn't as big as a star station, you know."

The captain chuckled, but shrugged.

One of the small mammals looked up from a knowledge pad. "They're non-material. It's a specialized type that can't go outside a gravity field. They're checking in with Manessa as they arrive, but are invisible to us."

Kibi glanced at the acting steward.

"All but eight are here, bok," he began. "There, the last group just checked in."

"Close hatch, retract boarding tunnel," Ilika commanded from the pilot's chair. "Kibi, I need you at navigation for the first leg of the flight plan . . ."

✳

The main cavern of the homeless reptiles seemed almost perfect, with a sandy floor, many smaller alcoves and caves for storage or privacy, and rock balconies that overlooked the large public space. On one of these, the cavern leader ate grubs while surveying his tribe with sad eyes.

Water, apparently from higher in the mountains, gushed from a crack in the ceiling of a side-cave, then collected in a pool big enough for swimming. It flowed into a smaller pool, then disappeared, along with any waste, into another crack. The residents of the cavern had no idea where it went after that.

The surviving reptiles had found this new home almost immediately after a violent storm and earthquake collapsed the cavern they had inhabited for countless generations. It had seemed so close to their old territory that they wondered why they hadn't found it before, and could make no sense of the riddle. Their vague memories of that terrible time contained blanks they couldn't fill, gaps in their recollection that must have been, they presumed, caused by the fear and chaos of that frightening day.

Mati, Rini, Sata, and Boro were served wiggling insect larva, slimy fungus, and spiny cactus fruit. Their new bodies rejoiced at the sight and aroma of the fresh food, but their human minds were much less thrilled.

Rini noticed his friends hesitating. "This is all there is to eat," he mumbled softly, "and all there's gonna be."

Boro grumbled a little, then noticed Sata swallowing a grub. Her eyes lit up with pleasure, and she quickly grabbed another. He cautiously tried one. To his new reptile tongue, it was quite delicious. Noticing other reptiles watching, he puffed himself up. "Better than the grubs in our cavern! If you had even better in *your* cavern, I'm sorry our ancestors left!"

The watchers seemed delighted that their new guests were happy. They strutted with pride at the memory of their beloved old cavern.

＊ ＊ ＊

Chapter 33: Temptations

Nightfall soon came to the simulated desert environment, and the newcomers were shown to a small sleeping cave with a sandy floor, vacant because so few babies were hatching.

They curled up in the sand. Boro tried to leave some space between himself and Sata, but no matter how he placed himself, she quickly wiggled closer until their bodies were in contact. "Are you sure you want to tempt fate?" he asked softly.

"Yes," she replied without hesitation.

He sighed, put his arm around her, and wrestled with his own feelings for more than an hour, before finally drifting off to sleep.

*

Three times during the night, Boro's instincts woke him to find young males lurking near the entrance to the sleeping cave. He growled and they scurried away. Each time, Sata lifted her head, looked at him with sparkling reptilian eyes, then curled up beside him again, closer than before.

During that short night, strange dreams haunted all four newcomers. The half-remembered images seemed completely out of place for a desert reptile species. Shades of green colored everything, mists and dripping water formed a constant background, and all manner of living creatures lurked in every shadow.

*

Morning brought females with invitations to join food-collecting parties or mushroom-tending teams. Mati quickly indicated, by example, that they should fit right in and do their part. The other females assured Boro and Rini that their girls would be safe, and they could join the males playing Bones or brewing *shmur*.

Without an override from Mati, Boro decided to stand his ground. "Our cavern was not so fortunate, and the males could only . . . brew *shmur* and . . .

play Bones when other work was done."

Sata's reptilian eyes sparkled with pride, and she brushed against Boro lovingly.

Mati remained silent, so Boro continued assertively. "I will be on the gathering team, to carry heavy loads and protect ... anyone who needs protecting . . . from anything."

"And I can learn to tend mushrooms," Rini said calmly. For Mati's mind only, he added, *If I remember the lessons correctly, you'll probably go into heat sometime while we're here.*

Mati's eyes snapped open wide and she swallowed.

The other females giggled among themselves about the males who insisted on helping to gather food.

*

Silmula Sorafax sat alone in the observation tunnel, watching Mati and Rini sprinkle water from a hollow gourd onto the reptiles' fungus garden. Three other females worked with them, talking with throaty sounds as they worked. Mati and Rini only spoke when responding to one of the females. When interacting with each other, they remained silent, but their glances often revealed something about their secret conversations.

The large white feline enjoyed trying to guess. Just then, someone licked her neck, and she knew by his scent who it was. She purred and turned to greet Toran Takil. "I am the luckiest cat in the universe to have a handsome male like you!"

He purred. "I'm just as lucky! How's your project?"

"They're just getting settled," she said, turning back to the observation window. "Days in there pass very quickly, six to our one. I don't think Mati and her crewmates have any idea how to find the information they need."

"Do you?"

"Of course not! Kerloran never makes things *that* easy! And with Melorania involved, it's *bound* to be a nearly unsolvable puzzle!"

Toran Takil sat on his haunches close beside the female cat and looked into the mushroom cave. "I almost wish Kibi was in there. It would be good for her. You're not mad at me for leading her on for a few minutes?"

"As I understand it, you led her on just long enough to get her to Psychic Development. And I *completely* understand her reaction to your presence. I experience it daily, you know."

The male cat growled lovingly. "But you get much more than she did . . ."

She licked his mouth. "That's right, and I plan to continue getting . . ."

Just then a large bird came waddling along the tunnel and the cats ceased their intimate conversation.

"Boro just had to fight off *another* male, bok, who was trying to get close to Sata. This time a little blood was spilled."

Silmula Sorafax chuckled in her feline way. "That's good for him, but not really a test. It's Rini who will be tested when Mati goes into heat."

The bird thought back to the day the process began. "But he was the first to step up and volunteer to go in ..."

"Only because he's mentally quicker, and realized what would happen if he didn't," the white cat added.

The bird nodded. "It's going to be a strong crew, isn't it?"

"I think so, after they fully understand Nebador and work off some rough edges." She turned and looked at her lover.

"I was worried about Mati right after the escape, but now my gut tells me Sata has the biggest test coming up. But I agree about Rini, too."

At that moment, Toran Takil's mission bracelet chimed. "They want me at Mission Assignment."

"I'll come along. I want to talk to the ursine in charge of the planet search."

The two cats bowed to the large bird, who stayed to observe the fungus gardening.

*

"WHY are you keeping all the males away from this perfectly ripe and beautiful female, but not mating with her *yourself?*" the cavern leader asked as he held Boro's gaze with his penetrating eyes. "If you'd just *mate* with her, her scent would quit driving the others crazy!"

Boro stood his ground. "Because, where I come from, we don't *force* females to mate! And she says she's not ready."

Sata rubbed up against Boro. "Well ... actually ..." She stopped herself and took a deep breath. "Yeah. He's right. I'm not ready."

The leader rolled his reptilian eyes and walked away, muttering, "It's your blood ..."

Soon they were alone. "I'm sorry," Sata began with a shaking voice. "It's just ... my whole body is screaming at me, day and night, and it's becoming harder and harder to ignore."

Boro wrapped his arms and claws around her. "I just want us to be able to go home ..."

"Me too. I'll do my best to ignore it."

"And I'll keep fighting off other males, but ..." He held her at arm's length and looked into her eyes. "... if you work against me, I'll quit trying."

Sata swallowed hard and slowly nodded.

* * *

Chapter 34: Grubs and Bones

After dreaming of dripping ferns and roaring streams leaping under and over slimy tree roots, the four newcomers awoke on their fourth day in the simulated desert environment.

With a tasty breakfast of fresh grubs and cactus fruit in his belly, Boro again hoisted up the big grub basket, allowing six females to concentrate on collecting, instead of carrying.

The team of more than thirty reptiles followed a carefully-planned route through the small, rocky caves that riddled one entire mountainside not far from the cavern. The winding route visited only the insect nests that hadn't been harvested in many days. The reptiles crept along quietly, knowing from experience going back countless generations that the insects would fly away with the fewest grubs if the gatherers arrived silently and worked quickly.

Claws were inserted into the nests of dried mud, slicing with precision where the scaly hunters knew the largest grubs could be found. The insects quickly went into action, about half attacking the lizards, the other half flying away with their wiggling young as quickly as possible.

Boro and Sata had flinched the first time several thousand angry flying creatures began hammering them, but quickly noticed that all the other reptiles completely ignored it. The reason was soon clear — the insects simply had no way to penetrate the lizard's scaly hides.

Today, Boro was again increasing the harvest by cupping his claws for those females working on nests near the ceiling, saving them from jumping down with each load of grubs. Sata noticed, and quickly started helping with the highest nests.

On the way back to the cavern, the females told stories of grubs their grandmothers collected that were twice this size. They even muttered half-remembered tales about grubs so big that one would make an entire meal.

The younger females shook their heads in disbelief.

✳

Kibi's eyes were wide as the little ship approached Rontilia Star Station, much smaller than Satamia, yet glowing like a bright diamond in space.

With an effort of will, she tore her eyes away from the visual display and made the selection Ilika requested at the navigation console. With another part of her mind, she continued to monitor the watch station, often with voice commands to Manessa, occasionally just by reaching over.

The small docking tunnel only had berths for two response ships and one transport, all currently empty.

"Sssssss," came the voice of the docking controller. "Berth one pleassse, captain. It'sss very quiet inssside. Half the ssstation isss at Sssatamia for the Great Transsssformation. I wishsh I could go, but sssomeone musssst run the ssstation."

Kibi smiled as she slipped back to the watch console. "Docking visuals on channel four. Any news about our naughty crew members?"

"Sssata now undersssstands how powerful her body'sss urgesss can be, and Boro hasss been injured ssseveral timesss. Many obsssserversss ththink Sssata isss on the verge of mating withth . . . whoever isss handy."

Kibi swallowed, and remembered her body's reaction to Toran Takil. The silver and gold docking fingers wrapped themselves around the ship, and a boarding tunnel made contact with the hull.

"Bok. Welcome to Rontilia," the acting steward announced. "I know the Great Transformation will be challenging for your friends, bok, but understanding the lives of simple creatures is very important. Bok."

✳

Many more nights passed as Mati and her friends dreamed about warm rain and huge insects of all sorts. During those nights, Sata became more and more affectionate. Even though she didn't do anything to directly invite him, or any other male, to mate with her, her indirect signals were becoming all but impossible to ignore, both for Boro, and a hundred other male lizards.

He cared very much about her, but he also wanted to go home and be the engineer of a deep-space response ship again, and perhaps something more challenging someday, like a star station docking controller.

As evening came to the simulated desert environment once more, Boro made a decision. *He* had had enough. *He* was going home. If Sata couldn't resist the temptation to mate with a reptile, it wasn't going to be him.

He approached a group of males about his age who were laughing and joking as they gathered the necessary ingredients from a storage cave. "I haven't played Bones and brewed *shmur* in a long time. You guys have room for one more?"

They welcomed him with slaps on the back that nearly drew blood.

Boro had to think fast that evening, as the rules to the game of Bones had not been known to the briefing team. *Shmur* contained several mysterious ingredients, one of which came from a different, much smaller, mushroom garden. Boro pretended that the rules and the ingredients had changed a little over the generations at his old cavern, so he humbled himself to learn theirs.

Soon a large hollow gourd bubbled with a frothy brew that went right to Boro's head when he took a drink. The other males laughed, drank deeply, and spent several minutes arm-wrestling.

Eventually Boro learned to play Bones.

It was not the loser of a round that had to fight the others, as Boro had assumed, but the winner. It was considered an honor, and the *shmur* made all the players feel invulnerable, but at the same time, rather slow and clumsy. Serious injury, therefore, was almost impossible, given their tough reptilian hides.

Boro had to reach inside himself for instincts he had never before let out. His large size allowed him to hold his own, but it was the fifth round before he started feeling some actual joy at the prospect of winning a throw of the Bones.

During a pause to drink more *shmur*, one of the other males casually said, "It's almost midnight. That girl you were protecting — she's probably mated by now."

Boro tensed up for a moment, ready to run and do his duty as Sata's protector. Then his *shmur*-clouded mind remembered the situation. "I protected her as long as I could. It's her problem now."

The others laughed heartily.

"When you asked to join us for Bones," one male said, "I almost offered to stay behind and . . . you know . . . try my luck!"

Boro laughed deeply and reached for the *shmur*.

Chapter 35: Failure

"I'm not in heat any more!" Sata announced with pride when Boro staggered into the cavern the following morning.

Boro's head felt like it had been run over by a transport ship, or maybe the star station itself. He had to struggle to understand what she was saying, and the implications of it. "Um . . . I bet that's a relief. Who was the lucky guy?"

Sata frowned. "Boro! I didn't *mate* with anyone! When I realized you were gone, I knew I had to stand on my own two feet. And besides, Mati's in heat now, so Rini's very busy protecting *her*."

When Sata's words finally penetrated his groggy brain, Boro threw his head back and laughed deeply.

"So with Rini busy," Sata continued, "I *really* had to think fast. I approached a group of older females. They let me sleep with them, and told me about some herbs. They made me a potion that tasted like it was straight from the Underworld, but it worked! Only problem is, it won't work on Mati until she's been in heat for at least a week."

At that moment, their attention was drawn to a commotion just outside one of the cavern entrances. When they arrived, others were already crowded around, three or four deep, trying to see.

"The little blue female is actually *helping* the skinny gray keep others away," they heard a tall male say. "I'd love to get my claws around *that* feisty girl."

Boro stretched up on his hind legs to see. Rini was bleeding in several places. He and Mati, side by side with their backs to a rock wall, were putting up a good fight. The large brown male, however, was not taking *no* for an answer.

Boro took one more breath, then muscled his way through the crowd, finally leaping into the fray beside Rini.

The brown male stopped in his tracks.

"What's wrong?" Boro roared. "Don't like a fair fight?"

The large brown reptile stood with his chest heaving, trying to catch his breath, and deal with his lusty feelings for the little blue female.

Boro glimpsed Sata appear at his side.

"What is *wrong* with you people?" the brown finally gasped out. "It's one thing that our females are too upset to go into heat. But you idiots won't even mate when you *are* in heat, and you have your pick of all the males! You don't like the ones who came with you, you've had offers from the largest, the strongest, and the fastest, and you refuse *everyone*. The population has dropped by seven just since you arrived. Don't you see what's going to happen if *someone* doesn't mate?"

"Don't *you* see that we're not *from* here?" Sata suddenly blurted out, breathing almost as hard as the brown male. "And we're not from some little cavern across the desert, we're from Satamia Star Station — what you call the Rip in the universe — and we are your *only* hope of finding a new home!"

After Sata fell silent, grains of sand could be heard sifting down through the rocks of the simulated desert environment.

Mati wasn't sure whether to laugh or cry, so she just rolled her eyes.

Rini smiled and started licking his cuts.

Boro stood his ground, but didn't have to do any fighting. The brown male stomped away, and the crowd silently dispersed, most of them wearing frowns.

✳

Rontilia Star Station's only large space, Silver Hall, gleamed with shiny crystal and bright metal. No great tree wound through the station, but small trees and bushes added color in many little gardens and big planters. One balcony overlooked the large silver floor.

So few people, of any species, were to be found in the station, that Ilika and Kibi had to fix their own lunch at one of the three eating places. Just as they picked up their trays, an ursine bustled in carrying a large carton.

"Sorry, had to run down to the storeroom, and couldn't resist stopping at a knowledge processor to see how the Great Transformation was going. Did you find everything you needed?"

The pair of monkey mammals smiled and nodded, then wandered away to pick a table.

"Are we the only ones not following Mati's and Sata's every move?" Kibi asked with amusement.

Ilika laughed. "Melorania knew we'd just worry if we didn't keep busy."

"At least now we can catch up on news . . ."

"Actually, no. While you were getting stuff out of the refrigerator, my bracelet chimed. We have an urgent cargo run."

Kibi chuckled and started eating faster.

When they slipped their trays into the dishwashing room, no one was working within, but they noticed a lone reptile, wearing an apron, glued to a nearby knowledge processor.

Ilika smiled when they discovered the supply room completely unattended.

"What do we do?" Kibi asked. "You said the cargo run was urgent."

"This isn't hard," Ilika replied, grabbing an empty pallet and a knowledge pad.

Kibi looked with wide eyes down the long rows of shelves. "There must be a thousand different things in here!"

"Probably more like twenty or thirty thousand," Ilika said. After touching some symbols on the knowledge pad, the pallet began to float slightly above the floor. "Your first piloting lesson," he said, handing the pad to Kibi.

She chuckled as she got used to the controls while the pallet bumped into nearby shelves, but soon had it moving down the first aisle.

As they began loading cartons and canisters onto the pallet, they heard someone else come in and prepare another pallet. Soon a large fanator was coming down the aisle behind them, lifting cartons with his beak through the loop at the top of each item.

Kibi hadn't really thought about it before, but could now see that every package had half a dozen ways to lift it. "There's so much to learn in Nebador."

"Little things and big things, bok," the huge bird said after placing a carton on his pallet. "It's your kind in the Great Transformation. How are you taking the bad news?"

Kibi swallowed and felt her entire body become tense.

Ilika glanced at her and chose his words carefully. "We've been very busy, and haven't had a chance to follow the news."

"The observers are saying it looks like a complete failure," the fanator revealed with a sad voice. "Bok."

Ilika could see the tears on Kibi face, and feel the huge knot in his own stomach.

"Bok. I'm sorry," the bird began. "I didn't realize you were emotionally involved . . ."

"They're our friends," Kibi whispered through her swollen throat.

The fanator came close and wrapped his large wings around the pair of grieving monkey mammals.

Kibi began crying freely.

"Don't give up hope," Ilika whispered. "Strange things can happen during Great Transformations . . ."

＊

Silmula Sorafax trembled slightly as she waited in a small chamber near the Mission Assignment Room. It was unusual to wait so long for a conference with Kerloran, especially when he himself had requested the conference.

But the white cat knew a lot was happening in the star station. Dozens of visiting students were grumbling about all the things going wrong with the Great Transformation. Most members of the briefing team were asking for new assignments in the deepest, darkest corners of the star station, or even, if possible, off-station.

As the leader of the mission, Silmula Sorafax knew she could not hide from her responsibilities, and what now appeared to be her failure. She was a fully-trained graduate of the Psychic Development program, and about twenty other specialized programs, so she had no temptation to even try to avoid facing . . . whatever judgment was about to descend upon her.

Kerloran appeared suddenly, as if in haste, a green swirling cloud that filled most of the little room.

The cat nearly jumped out of her skin, then instinctively licked her paws and hung her head while purring.

The master of Satamia Star Station smiled to himself.

I . . . I was so ashamed, she began, *when Boro left Sata alone, still in heat, to fend for herself. I have made a list of training points that need to be emphasized in the future if any monkey mammal . . .*

Boro went off to play games and get drunk, the towering non-material presence said flatly.

The big cat flopped onto her belly with shame, and was about to cover her head with her paws, but stopped herself. *Yes, I was so tempted to open an access door, jump in there, and give him a good slap. I'm not sure I would have kept my claws retracted!*

You believe he should have stayed at Sata's side no matter what . . .

Silmula Sorafax rolled onto her back and presented her soft belly. *He promised to, and the need for them to support each other was stressed many times during the briefing. I don't think Rini ever left Mati's side . . .*

And then Sata broke one of the most important rules of the Great Transformation.

I have been going over the records of the briefing, the cat responded, sitting up on her haunches and hanging her head again, *and I cannot see how she missed the importance of non-disclosure, but I take complete responsibility for the failure of the mission, and plan to . . .*

Relax, little one, Kerloran said in a soothing tone, shrinking down to a small green ball.

Silmula Sorafax looked up into the swirling presence, and sensed a depth of intelligence and wisdom she could not even begin to understand.

The green ball continued to speak to the cat's mind. *The visiting students will need to see the entire process unfold, but you, as leader of the mission, do not have that luxury. Know that Boro's decision to cease protecting Sata was the best thing for both of them, and for the mission. Know also that Sata's disclosure was the only possible path to the success of the mission. Ponder these things. Hold your head up and do not grovel. You work for me, and I am well-pleased with your work. In you I place my trust.*

The green presence faded and was gone, leaving Silmula Sorafax blinking, trembling, and knowing she had a lot to learn.

* * *

Chapter 36: Shunned

The four crew members of the Manessa Kwi, currently in reptile form, walked from the scene of the last fight, and Sata's strange disclosure, toward their sleeping cave near the main cavern.

Mati smiled at a young lizard who had been friendly when they tended mushrooms together, but received only a brief icy stare.

Boro waved to one of his *shmur*-drinking buddies, but the other male hissed and walked away.

Sata greeted an older female who had helped make the potion the evening before, but the female turned away and began talking with someone else about grubs.

Once in their sleeping cave, they huddled close and spoke softly.

"I . . . I blew it, didn't I?" Sata asked with a trembling voice. "First I was in heat, and came very close to mating with . . . anyone. Then I told the one thing I wasn't supposed to tell, ever."

"I . . . don't know," Rini replied.

Mati smiled with sympathy.

Boro was tempted to confirm Sata's suspicion that she had made huge mistakes, but decided to remain silent.

After a long pause, Mati said, "Actually, I don't care. If they can't handle the truth, that's their problem. I just wanna go home, so we either have to figure out why they don't like any of the desert planets they've been offered, or just survive another . . ." She looked at Rini.

"Fifty-six days."

Mati rolled her eyes again. "With me and Sata going in and out of heat, and Boro and Rini bleeding half the time, trying to protect us, I'm not sure we're gonna make it."

"But we never have *time* to figure out what kind of home they want!" Sata blurted out with frustration. "Now, because of my stupid mistake, they won't even *talk* to us."

The other three were silent for a long moment, but eventually had to nod agreement.

※

The grub collecting teams departed without the newcomers, mushroom gardens were tended as usual, and cactus fruit was gathered and cleaned as it had been every day since long before any of the reptiles could remember.

Rini worked up the courage to humbly approach the food storage caves, but found several large males guarding them, and was chased all the way back to the group's sleeping cave.

The four outcasts talked quietly or dozed for the rest of the day. Sata carried her shame like a great weight, until late in the afternoon when Mati hissed at her. "The only way they would have accepted us, in the long run, is if you and me both mated, laid eggs, and hatched out lots of little lizards."

"She's right," a young reptilian voice came from above them.

They all looked up. A half-grown orange female perched on a rock shelf near the ceiling. As soon as she had their attention, she tossed down a dried gourd with a hinged lid.

Boro caught it, looked inside, and discovered lots of wiggling grubs.

"It's not a feast, but it's all I could get without making them suspicious."

"Thank you!" Mati said softly.

"Most of the people are scared and just want you to go away. Some, mostly males, want to kill you, or at least . . . you know . . . two of you. A few people . . . very few . . . mostly my friends . . . want to talk to you about this . . . star thing . . . and how you could help us."

"The ones who want to kill us . . ." Boro began, "how soon do you think they'll . . ."

"Probably tonight. There's a little tunnel up here that leads to the outside, but only three of you will fit."

Boro nodded with understanding.

"I have to go tend mushrooms. There are insect caves higher on the mountain where the grown-ups never go. The grubs are small, but they'll keep you alive." She turned and vanished into the rocks.

Boro passed out the precious gift of grubs as they all pondered the situation.

※

Crouching between rocks at the entrance to their sleeping cave, Rini kept an eye on the cavern as nearly three hundred reptiles gathered for their evening meal. The mood was tense, he reported, with whispering and grumbling among the males, and repeated glances in their direction.

While Rini kept watch, Mati and Sata tried the little tunnel near the ceiling. Sata scraped herself a little, but could get through.

After they returned, Boro stuck his head in, then sighed. "I'll have to fight my way through the cavern. Right after they eat, they get a big drink of water, and are slow . . ."

"We know," the other three assured him.

Boro chuckled. "This feels good now that we know what we're doing, and have a plan."

Mati nodded. "We'll wait at the big boulder near the insect caves. Remember, you won't be protecting anyone, so just get away as fast as you can."

Boro blinked. "If I can catch them off-guard, I might get through without a scratch."

With all the details of the escape plan set, they fell silent. Rini reported that the meal was drawing to a close, and some were heading down to the water cave. A few young males crept near the sleeping cave, still attracted by Mati's scent, but older males warned them away.

Suddenly Rini frowned. "Not all the large males were at the evening meal . . ."

✳   ✳   ✳

Chapter 37: Escape

"Go, now, but be careful and silent!" Boro asserted in a whisper. "I think there's a trap somewhere, so I'm taking a round-about way."

Mati nodded and poked Sata, then motioned for Rini to follow her up to the escape tunnel.

Sata barely managed to hold her tongue as she squeezed herself through the rocks once more.

Mati followed Rini up to the tunnel near the ceiling. She looked back and saw Boro walk casually out of the sleeping cave. Instead of aiming for the nearest cavern entrance, he headed for the water cave. Mati smiled, turned, and wiggled through the rocks.

*

Boro's heart pounded in his chest as he did his best to look like just another lizard going down for a drink after eating his fill of grubs. Evening was at hand, and the passageway would soon be nearly dark. No one seemed to recognize him.

He drank little as he wanted to remain quick on his feet. As he pretended to drink, his mind raced, trying to decide which cavern entrance was least likely to be a trap.

He remained undecided on the way back to the cavern, but then stepped into enough light to be recognized.

"Hey, everyone! There's the freak!" a large male boomed.

The clearest path of escape was a small side entrance, so Boro judged it his best bet, perhaps his only bet. Most of the males, and some of the females, began calling loudly for blood. Boro started running as fast as his reptilian legs would go.

*

"Your friend will NOT get out unharmed," the half-grown female lizard informed them as the three outcasts crouched behind a boulder where twelve young lizards had awaited them, all wanting to know more about stars.

Mati set her jaw, looked into Rini's eyes in the fading light, then into Sata's. "We have to leave soon anyway, so we'll do it side-by-side with Boro."

Rini nodded.

Sata hesitated, whined a little, then collected herself with a deep breath and nodded also.

"We're coming too!" the young female declared.

Her friends all nodded vigorously.

Mati frowned.

"Don't give us that grown-up look! If we have to take risks to learn about the stars, then we'll do it."

Mati looked at the young reptile faces around them. Some were still children. The leader and a few others were old enough to mate, but barely.

Rini looked at Mati. "Whoever's going, we have to go now," he said aloud. "Boro would be here by now if he'd gotten out safely."

Just outside the minor cavern entrance, in the half-light of evening, Boro didn't see the first spiked tail swing toward him, but he felt it pierce his body deeply as pain shot from his inner-most organs, outward to every scale of his thick hide.

Remember, Boro, you'll be home soon, Kerloran whispered to Boro's mind.

Somehow, Boro found the courage to take a few more steps, only to feel another tail spike pierce his side.

Against his will, Boro fell onto the sand, and suddenly, all around him, a commotion of screaming and hissing erupted, forming a complete circle close around him. He glimpsed a green female he knew, just out of heat but still very beautiful. A blue female and a small gray male both moved too quickly for any of the big males to hit. But for some reason, many young reptile voices were also snapping and hissing, and occasionally yelling something about stars. Then everything went dark.

✳

For a minute that seemed to last an hour, tails swung, teeth snapped, and claws ripped at anything they could find. Soon, no one was sure exactly who they were fighting. The enemy was anyone within reach.

In the fury of the fight, the large brown male, who had proudly sunk his spikes into the outcast's belly, didn't notice when his tail caught a female child and sent her flying against a rock with a bone-breaking crunch.

"ENOUGH!" the leader of the cavern boomed in his loudest, deepest voice, standing tall on a nearby boulder.

With some reluctance, especially from the large males, the two sides parted, one into a ring completely surrounding the other. For a long moment, everything was still and silent.

Then the small gray male from the inner group walked boldly toward the outer ring. He looked so weak and harmless, walking alone, that the large males laughed and parted for him. They fell silent with shame when he collected the broken body of the little female and carried her back to the inner circle.

Her friends gathered around, threw back their heads, and screamed their grief to the first few stars of the gathering night, and anyone else who cared to listen.

The grown-ups in the outer ring, who had bravely protected their culture from the freaks who claimed to come from the dreaded Rip in the universe, slowly filtered away to eat cactus fruit or brew *shmur*.

✳   ✳   ✳

Chapter 38: The Mission

Having nothing else to work with, Sata and Mati clamped their claws over Boro's deep wounds, but had little success stopping the bleeding. Sata's eyes swirled with fear and grief, and she tried to say something, but couldn't make words come out.

Boro raised his head a little. "I . . . didn't do a very good job . . . getting to the meeting place . . ."

"Don't worry about it," Mati assured her friend. "None of us are very good reptiles, and this whole thing is all my fault . . ." she said, breaking into shaking sobs.

Rini left the dead female child with her friends, wrapped his mind around Mati's, and took over trying to stop Boro's bleeding.

"I . . . don't want to . . . stay here," Boro muttered between gasps. "Help me . . . get to the . . . insect caves."

As Boro struggled to stand, Rini and Sata took his weight as best they could, each keeping one claw on the worst wounds, those inflicted by tail spikes.

Mati, Rini spoke to her silently, *you'll have to carry the child. They're afraid to touch her.*

Mati blinked to clear her mind, gathered the lifeless child into her arms, and with eleven young reptiles trailing behind, followed Boro and his helpers across the sand in the twilight.

✳

Tapping into his deepest reserves of determination, when Boro arrived at the nearly-dark mountainside riddled with small caves, he didn't crawl into one of them as his friends had expected, but instead started climbing.

Rini and Sata had kept the blood loss to a small trickle until then, but when Boro started climbing, they were hard pressed to stay at his side, much less keep the bleeding under control. As he climbed, the rocks under his feet quickly turned red.

With a roar of relief, he came to the first of the small caves, much higher up, that were not used for grub harvesting. The first entrance was too small for him, so he reached down inside himself for one more burst of strength, somehow found it, and staggered to the next cave, nearly collapsing into the opening. After several long minutes of effort, with his friends powerless to help, Boro managed to drag himself inside so others could enter and again try to tend his wounds.

Feeling the need to keep a watch, Mati remained outside as the eleven young reptiles entered silently.

He's breathing easier, Rini reported to Mati from inside the small cave, *but is very weak, barely conscious most of the time, and won't be going another step in this reptile body.*

Mati was about to tell Rini that all was well outside, when she spotted the shadowy silhouette of an adult reptile creeping up the rocks toward their hiding place.

❋

Rini, inside the cave doing everything he could to stop Boro's bleeding and make him comfortable, immediately knew what Mati saw. He whispered the situation to Sata and the eleven young lizards. The eleven quickly scampered out and lined up on both sides of Mati to look down and see who was coming.

The shadowy figure continued to advance, hopping from rock to rock on the mountainside. When it got to a certain point, about a stone's throw away, all eleven youth hissed in unison. Mati added her reptilian voice to the chorus.

When the warning faded away, a lone female voice floated up to them. "I just want to talk. There are others who also want you to help us, but they are afraid to come. May I approach? Please?"

The young ones looked at Mati.

"Yes!" she hissed in a no-nonsense voice full of warning.

The adult female, with her heart in her throat, slowly climbed the rocks until she perched just one boulder below the line of watchers. The swirling anger in their eyes told her they were quite willing to tear her apart.

"I am a member of the Guard," she began timidly, "and have been through the Rip in the universe, although I understood little of what I saw. I was cornered and had to fight, but a strong mammal grabbed me and held me, without hurting me, until the fight drained out of me. I knew, as he held me, that I could never understand that place, and I had best go home. The next thing I knew, I was home."

Mati smiled to herself, knowing who she was talking about. In the cave, Rini smiled also.

"Please, we are a simple people, and our pride keeps us from understanding many things, but we shudder at the thought of seeing the last egg hatch, the last female fail to go into heat because of the fear in her heart, the last male grow old without finding a mate. Please, if you can, help us to find our home . . ."

Mati became choked with emotion as she listened to the female lizard. She had to swallow several times before she could speak. "As my friend revealed earlier today, we came here to do just that. We have eaten grubs and cactus fruit with you, tended mushrooms, and raided insect nests. We have asked questions, and listened to every story you could tell us about your people, your old home, and what makes you happy. But . . . I have to admit . . . we have completely failed. Many new homes have been offered to your people, and in each you shrivel and die, even faster than here in this . . . small temporary home. We have no idea why. I am sorry."

"But . . ." the lone female whined with desperation, "have you not dreamed of our home, as we do every night? You slept in the same cavern with us. Did you not glimpse, in your sleep, what we see all the time? We do not know what to call it . . ."

The female stopped talking. Suddenly the blue female's mouth hung open, the slender gray male behind her bounced with excitement, and the green female poked her head through the cave entrance.

"Yes!" Mati said as soon as she found her voice.

"That explains it!" Rini added from behind.

Mati turned to Sata, who still wore a puzzled look. "They aren't desert reptiles!"

Sata smiled with realization. "Of course! I've been dreaming about jungles ever since we arrived!"

"Jun . . . gles?" the female of the Guard tried to say, not recognizing the word.

Mati turned back to the visitor. "My friend was just doing her best to say a word from our language. Jungles are very wet, warm, and green."

"Yes! *That's* our home!"

✳   ✳   ✳

Chapter 39: Success

Although no one witnessed it, Kerloran smiled.

All over Satamia Star Station, groups of students, come to witness the Great Transformation, bounced, flapped, or swung from tree branches with excitement. Birds hugged reptiles, ursines embraced equines, cats rolled and laughed with monkeys as the tension and gloom was suddenly lifted.

The briefing team emerged from the conference room where they had been hiding.

Silmula Sorafax sat on the third balcony overlooking the main hall, her eyes sparkling with new knowledge and wisdom about how the mysterious universe worked.

✳

At an asteroid mining camp, Ilika and Kibi were helping to load canisters onto pallets. The strong ursine could carry four at a time. Ilika managed two. Kibi cradled one in her arms and called it good.

A large spider came bustling out of the control room, mandibles twitching and eight feet tapping on the floor with excitement. He stood right in Kibi's path.

Knowing something was up, Kibi set down her canister.

With gleams in his dozens of eyes, the spider shoved a knowledge pad into Kibi's hands.

After reading the first few words, Kibi's face lit up with a huge smile. She started bouncing and nearly hit the ceiling in the quarter-gravity cargo room.

As soon as she landed, Ilika was quickly at her side, reading over her shoulder. He looked up at the spider. "Are we the last ones in Satamia to find out?"

The spider's mandibles twitched again. "Probably."

✳

On one of the four golden boxes in the medical center of Satamia Star

Station, a symbol changed from yellow to green, and the top slowly opened. Healer Dakalio walked over and reminded Boro to move very slowly, as his body had not had any exercise for several Satamia days.

Boro felt for the bleeding holes in his belly and side, and was delighted to not find them.

When the young engineer felt ready, the older healer helped him to slowly sit up, then carefully stand. Boro held onto things as he made his way into a shower, then slipped on clean clothes. By then, he was ready to stand on his own.

He grabbed a nutrition drink on his way through the main hall, but was soon at his destination — a certain observation window in the dimly-lit tunnel that wound through the simulated desert environment.

Mammals, birds, large insects, and many others he couldn't name — all gathered around to watch the drama within — quickly recognized him and made a space.

✳   ✳   ✳

Chapter 40: The Hard Part

Rini soon returned to the cave to check on Boro. When he found no signs of life in his friend, Mati instantly knew. Sata, the eleven young reptiles, and the female of the Guard, all followed Mati into the cave and gathered around to pay their respects.

Rini could see Sata trembling with grief, so he put his arm around her. "Remember, he's home, probably sucking on a nutrition drink while watching us from an observation window."

Sata cracked a tiny smile, but her eyes still swirled with emotions.

Mati lifted the lifeless female child, from where she lay in one corner, and placed her close beside Boro.

"I'm sorry," the female of the Guard began. "It was stupid for the thick-headed males ... and some females ... to attack you. You were just trying to help us."

Mati swallowed and found her voice. "Same thing would have happened where we were born. Our teacher did nothing but help people, so they tried to kill him and burn our ship."

"What's a ... ship?"

Mati smiled. "Long story."

The leader of the group of youth cleared her throat. "If you're done with adult talk, can I ask a question?"

Rini looked at the girl.

After stammering with embarrassment for a long moment, she finally collected herself. "Um ... now that you know about our dreams, can you help us find that place again?"

Rini looked at Mati during a moment of silence, then he spoke. "Your planet ... your old cavern ... was probably once like your dreams — wet and warm, with plants and huge insects everywhere. Then it slowly changed into a desert. You survived by learning to live in caves, eat smaller grubs, pick cactus fruit instead of jungle fruit, and water mushrooms that used to grow by themselves . . ."

"Wow . . ." the female of the Guard began. "We have no memory of that, except in our dreams."

"That entire . . . world . . . no longer exists. It was burnt to a crisp when your star . . . your sun . . . became very large. That happened soon after you were brought to this . . . new cavern. You are inside a star station where thousands of people live and work, all around you, and many of them have been working hard to find you a new home, a real home to call your own."

"Will they find one?" the half-grown female asked bluntly. She and all her friends looked at Rini intently.

Rini smiled and looked at Mati. She smiled back. "I think we know of one you'll like," he said.

✳

Ilika and Kibi were soon back in Satamia Star Station. Their patience was sorely tested as reptiles and ursines slowly unloaded the cargo from the asteroid mine. The moment the last pallet cleared the boarding tunnel, the captain and steward dashed to the simulated desert environment.

Ilika and Boro embraced, then parted and looked at each other. Ilika could see a new light of confidence in Boro's eyes, a light born of passing through the Great Transformation.

Kibi greeted Silmula Sorafax with a bow and a friendly touch.

The big cat experienced a moment of jealousy, but had plenty of practice dealing with other females, of many species, who had felt the magnetic qualities of her beloved Toran Takil. She returned Kibi's gentle touch.

"What's happening?" Ilika asked, nodding toward the observation window.

Boro took a deep breath. "They're all standing around my carcass, talking about something. I don't understand a word of it anymore, but the bird over there is getting the gist of it. They're from a jungle, not a desert. I vaguely remember the dreams."

Ilika looked where Boro had gestured, and could see a large bird, his face nearly pressed against the window, muttering into a knowledge pad. Others followed on their own pads.

The captain of the Manessa Kwi turned to the big cat in charge of the mission. "Now that we know what to look for, we'd be happy to help find the reptiles' new planet . . ."

Silmula Sorafax licked a paw. "I'm sure Kerloran and Melorania will expect you to."

✳

"We must leave you now," Mati announced after everything had been said that anyone could think of to say.

"Will you . . . see if that . . . jungle . . . is still available?" the female of the Guard asked.

"Someone might already be doing it. Our people are watching over us constantly, day and night."

"How will you leave? The Rip in the universe will no longer open."

Mati looked at Rini and he answered. "We came in through another Rip, but can't leave that way. We need . . . a high cliff where we can . . . fly."

The female of the Guard opened her eyes wide, but eventually nodded. "There is one near here. Morning light will allow us to find it."

Boro and the little female were left alone in the silence of death. Out under the simulated stars, the living curled up together in a sandy hollow not far away. Mati, Rini, Sata, and the female of the Guard took turns keeping watch. The rest dreamed of dripping ferns, mushrooms springing from the wet forest floor, and big, juicy grubs.

✳

"I had it easy," Boro said as he worked his way through a hearty meal with his captain and steward on the second balcony of Violet Hall. "I was fatally wounded. I can't imagine how hard it's gonna be for the others."

Kibi nodded and smiled weakly. "That's one of the final tests in Psychic Development. I wonder what kind of creature I'll get to be . . ."

"Whatever you'd learn the most from," Ilika guessed.

"In other words, whatever would be hardest," Kibi decoded with a smirk.

Ilika smiled.

✳

When everyone was awake, the three visitors and one adult followed the eleven youth to some nearby caves where the grubs were small but tasty. After a light breakfast, they followed the female of the Guard to a cliff that overlooked a sheer drop of more than a hundred meters.

The adult female and the eleven youth stepped back from the edge to give the three visitors some space.

Mati looked at Sata, then at Rini. "I'm in command of this mission, right?"

"Right," Rini said firmly.

"Right," Sata whispered after a pause.

"Okay," Mati began. "Rini, I have an assignment for you. You already know what it is, but I need to say it out loud so Sata will know. You will be in the middle. You will hold our claws tightly and take us over the edge with you. Can you do that?"

"Yes," Rini said aloud, "but you both must be willing to step to the edge and take my claws. I won't go until you're both with me. We all go or we all stay."

"Fair enough," Mati responded. "You okay with that, Sata?"

"Um . . . yes," she said with a slight whine.

Rini stepped to the edge, facing outward, and stretched out both arms. He knew what he had to do, and it did not involve leaving any extra time for thought, worry, or fear. The instant he felt Mati's claw touch his on one side, and Sata's on the other side, he grabbed both by the wrists and launched all three of them into the air.

*

Eleven youth and one adult reptile stepped to the edge of the cliff and looked down.

"They . . . didn't fly," the half-grown female said with sadness.

"No," the female of the Guard agreed. "I don't think they intended to. I think they just said that so we wouldn't worry."

They all stood in respectful silence for a long minute. Eventually one of the young males said what many were thinking. "I wonder how long it will take the star-people to find us a . . . jungle."

"Probably many days," the female of the Guard replied.

"We're going to stay on the mountain and wait," the leader of the eleven said, "eat small grubs and lick morning dew. You are welcome to wait with us."

"Thank you," she said. "That would be nice."

* * *

Chapter 41: Debriefing

In the medical center of Satamia Star Station, three golden boxes opened at the same time.

The avian healer on duty squawked as Ilika, Kibi, and Boro came running in the door.

As soon as Sata blinked enough to focus her eyes, she saw Boro grinning down at her while catching his breath. She smiled and breathed a sigh of relief.

Mati was greeted by Kibi, and Rini by Ilika.

The bird ran around, trying to explain to three monkey mammals at once what they needed to know about recovering from the Great Transformation.

None of them were paying much attention.

✳

After showers, clean clothes, and nutrition drinks for the new arrivals, six mission bracelets chimed at once.

The large audience hall was packed with visiting students, the entire briefing team, and many friends and observers. Melorania, in the form of a beautiful lady with swirling blue gown, and Silmula Sorafax, whose sleek white fur seemed to sparkle, stood side-by-side at the front.

When the crew of the Manessa Kwi finally squeezed themselves into the room, a few pokes from Ilika were necessary to get the four honored guests moving down the aisle.

Boro, Sata, Mati, and Rini approached the head of the Transport Service and the large cat. The room fell silent.

"Boro and Rini," Melorania began, "you both willingly experienced the Great Transformation to support and protect your beloved girls. You did well, and neither I, nor Kerloran, have any complaint about the decisions you made. Some observers had negative judgments at some points in your journey, but they are pondering and learning from the process, now that it has completely unfolded. You two may sit and listen."

Boro and Rini smiled at each other with mixed pride and embarrassment. Seeing no empty seats or benches, they settled onto the soft floor.

Melorania looked at the navigator of the Manessa Kwi. "Sata, you were tempted by primal instincts, experienced deep emotional challenges, and remained true to yourself, your friends, and Nebador."

Sata smiled.

"And you violated THE most important rule of the Great Transformation, a rule that must have been repeated a hundred times during your days of preparation."

Sata's chin fell onto her chest and tears filled her eyes.

"Good Work."

It took Sata a long minute to recover, wipe her tears, and look up to see the smile on Melorania's face. Chuckles rippled through the audience.

"Rules are necessary for intelligent people, but as we approach wisdom, they must often be broken. This is especially hard for avians . . ."

Many feathered heads in the room ducked with embarrassment.

". . . and monkey mammals."

All six crew members of the Manessa Kwi, and the three or four other humans in the room, cringed.

"You, Sata," Melorania continued, "performed a great service by giving an excellent example, which just about everyone in Satamia was watching, of a situation in which a rule needed breaking. Most importantly, you did it *knowing* the rule. People who break rules without awareness are just simple mortals stumbling through life. We love them, but they cannot work in the Nebador Services."

Everyone in the room was thoughtful during a long silence.

"To break a rule with wisdom, you must first know the rule, and be willing to follow it most of the time. But, I'll admit that for a little while during your Great Transformation, we, who can see far into the past and future, could see no path to the success of your mission. You, Sata, changed that. Suddenly, when you broke that rule, new possibilities sprang into existence. A group of reptiles who had been powerless . . ."

"The young ones!" Sata interrupted.

"Yes, those born since coming to the star station. You created the moment, and they seized it. The rest of the story . . . you know."

Sata took several deep breaths to settle the many emotions she was feeling.

"But don't let it go to your head," Melorania warned. "Breaking the rules, with knowledge and wisdom, will serve you well as a starship navigator, as long as you do it carefully, knowing that every one of those rules was written with blood."

Sata looked puzzled.

"Every rule was written because they usually, in most situations, give the best chance of people coming back *alive* from their missions."

Sata nodded with understanding.

"You may sit, Sata."

✳

"Mati of Sonmatia Three, crippled slave, Tera's first companion, starship pilot, Rini's beloved."

Mati was suddenly filled with amazement at all the things she had already been and done in her short life. She tried to look up, but Melorania's face was almost too bright to endure.

"You were the leader of the mission, and partly for that reason, you worked hard to avoid some of the feelings and experiences that Sata endured and learned from."

Mati cringed, and tears threatened to come.

"Kerloran is of the opinion that it would be very good for you to live an entire lifetime with the reptiles, including mating and raising little scaly children."

Rini quickly rose and stood close beside Mati, taking her hand in his.

Melorania smiled. "I agree with Kerloran completely. But I told him that you also have many things to learn as a deep-space response ship pilot, and good pilots, especially good monkey-mammal pilots, are very rare, and always will be."

Mati tried to collect herself, and Rini relaxed a little, but didn't leave Mati's side.

"Kerloran agreed, and offered as an alternative that you, Mati, begin Psychic Development training, which will include another Great Transformation as part of your final tests, although a shorter one."

Rini started to open his mouth.

"And I assured him," Melorania said before the freckled lad could speak, "that I would not allow Rini to begin *his* training until you, Mati, had completed yours."

Rini closed his mouth.

"Kerloran was satisfied with that. He apologizes for not being here, but is doing something very important right now."

✳

Mati and Rini embraced, and a moment later Boro and Sata stood and did the same, a little more slowly.

"Citizens of Nebador," Melorania called out in a loud, clear voice, "I give you the full crew of the Manessa Kwi, all monkey mammals again, all able to walk, and all back on active duty!"

Claws and wings nudged Ilika and Kibi until they went up to join in the joyous moment, as everyone in the room stood, flapped, cheered, screeched, or howled.

✳

With another Satamia day nearing its end, most of the creatures soon began to filter out of the large audience hall, their minds turning to decorations, food, drink, and music. Ilika and Kibi knelt down and chatted with the large white cat about helping with the planet search.

"Melorania . . ." Mati began when finally, many minutes later, no one was talking to the head of the Transport Service. "I want you to know that the eleven young reptiles who helped us, and one adult female, are probably outcasts now . . ." She stopped when she saw the knowing smile on Melorania's face.

"Come, all of you, I want to show you something."

Melorania floated out of the audience hall, along a corridor, and onto a balcony. The six humans, one large cat, and a few others, all ran along behind. Eventually they came to a balcony railing that looked down into Yellow Hall.

The hall was nearly empty, as many citizens were already at work in the main hall to prepare for the evening party, but a group of reptiles stayed close together as a much larger lizard, bright green with leaves twined around his head and arms, led them along.

"Kerloran . . ." Rini whispered.

"It's . . . it's . . ." Sata began excitedly, almost bouncing up and down.

"It's our friends!" Mati declared. "Can we go down and talk to them?"

Melorania looked askance at Mati, but remained silent.

Mati looked at Rini and Sata, both of whom were holding in laughter. Then she realized the problem, rolled her eyes, and laughed at herself. "They wouldn't recognize us!"

"Worse than that," Rini began, "we couldn't understand a word of each other's languages."

Mati sighed and turned back to the balcony railing to watch as Kerloran gestured toward a huge branch of the great station tree and spoke with reptilian throaty sounds. Most of the lizards turned circles with amazement at everything they saw.

"There's one too many," Rini said. "An adult male."

"They're going to be re-settled separately from the rest of the cavern," Melorania explained, "and the adult female selected a mate. He's not one of those who tried to kill you."

"That's good!" Boro said with relief.

They watched in silence as Kerloran and the thirteen reptiles entered a corridor and disappeared from sight.

"I wonder how they'll remember the star station . . ." Rini pondered aloud.

"They'll probably start a new religion about it," Melorania speculated. "That's what most creatures do after glimpsing Nebador. It'll be a mixture of what they saw and learned, and their own stories and myths."

"Their gods will be you and Kerloran, I bet," Boro said.

"No, they haven't met me, and Kerloran is just pretending to be another reptile so he can talk to them and be their guide." Then Melorania grinned.

"If I had to guess, I'd say their new religion will probably have *four* gods."

Mati's eyes suddenly opened wide with wonder and embarrassment.

Somewhat to Kibi's surprise, her friends who had just experienced the Great Transformation were quiet and thoughtful at the evening party. Some of the visiting students from far-away star systems also lingered on the edges, not used to the melodies and rhythms of Satamia. Others plunged into the merry-making, ready to try moving their tentacles to anything with a good beat.

Boro and Sata, hand in hand, wandered among the snack tables, not sure what they wanted. Eventually some wiggling insect grubs caught their eyes. They looked at each other, popped grubs into their mouths, and then stopped chewing as sour looks came to both their faces at once.

"They were a lot better when we were reptiles," Boro admitted as he bravely swallowed what he had already chewed.

Sata nodded. "Shall we . . . go find some fruit?"

"Yeah!"

Although Mati's knees could now handle a little careful dancing, she and Rini seemed happiest when snuggling close together on a small couch. Thoughts and secrets passed between them that no ears could catch.

If we had stayed reptiles, I would have missed the music, Rini shared.

I think the reptiles — at least the little group that's here now — will soon have music, Mati responded. *They're up on the fourth balcony with Kerloran, listening and watching. How could anyone hear the music of Nebador and not want to make their own music?*

Rini nodded, then noticed his two shipmates at the snack tables. *I think Boro and Sata are ready to . . . you know . . . hold each other.*

Mati followed Rini's eyes. Their friends had plates of food, but had stopped to share a long kiss. *I think Boro had to make promises about that, for Sata to avoid mating with anyone who wanted her, on about the first day of the Great Transformation.*

Rini chuckled.

Kibi and Ilika were enjoying a circle dance with a half-dozen large avians when four of the birds' mission collars chimed. The four danced their way toward a corridor. The two monkey mammals and two remaining birds tightened the circle and picked up the lively beat of the song.

When the piece ended with a flurry of notes from a spider's keyboard, the captain and steward bowed to the two avians and wandered over to the food and drink tables.

Kibi selected a cold, fruity beverage and took a long pull to wet her throat. "When we first arrived, I thought I'd never get used to all the different kinds of people. Now the usual Satamia types seem pretty mild compared to the strange creatures from far away."

Ilika looked at his lover and grinned. "You haven't seen *anything* yet!"

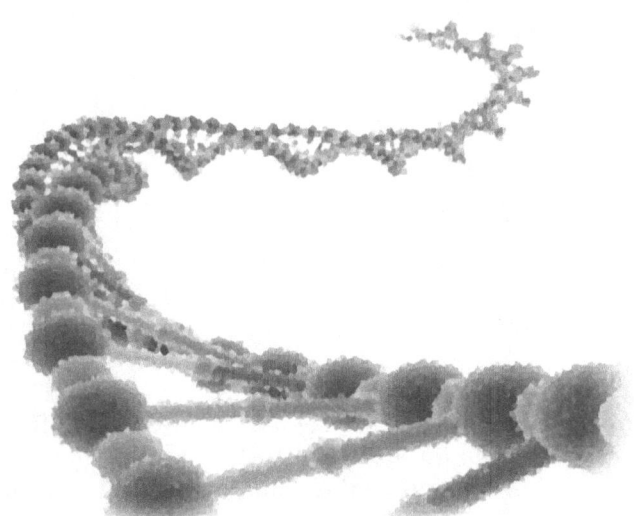

Chapter 42: The Search

Finding a jungle home for their reptilian friends wasn't quite as easy as Mati had imagined. She thought they could just be loaded into a transport ship and delivered to a jungle on her home planet.

Instead, she and her shipmates were invited to observe a much more complex process. Scientists began huddling around knowledge processors and combing through the hundreds of planets in Satamia with a tropical rain forest — a jungle. Twisted molecules glowed on big screens as the biochemical signatures of the planets were compared with that of the homeless reptiles. Simulations allowed the molecules to interact. Many Nebador citizens of flesh and blood discussed the results with each other and with the mysterious beings of color and light who came and went. Eventually, after nearly two Satamia days of work, many planets were eliminated, including, to Mati's disappointment, her own Sonmatia Three.

Silmula Sorafax explained that on those planets, the reptiles simply couldn't eat anything. Every insect grub, every mushroom, and every piece of fruit would be, at best, empty fiber without nutrition, and at worst, poison.

The specialists turned their attention to the hundred or so planets that had, in theory, a biochemical design that would allow the homeless reptiles to become part of the ecosystem.

Mati, Sata, Rini, and Boro were encouraged to recall any further details about their reptilian dreams. Birds listened, ursines took notes, and fuzzy balls of light observed.

Boro became very frustrated. Nothing was happening that he could sink his teeth into. "Watch, listen, and learn," Silmula Sorafax coaxed. Boro tried, but it wasn't easy. He even started to wish for a simple cargo run, but the Manessa Kwi remained at dock, while every other crew on the station, it seemed, was busy.

Finally, to Boro's relief, after another Satamia day of work by the scientists, the lists came out. The Manessa Kwi and Drrrim-na's life-monitor ship, the Tirilana Kril, were going to work.

✳

Four biochemists — reptile, arachnid, fanator, and ursine — each with an assistant, gave Kibi eight passengers to look after. They set to work with knowledge pads at Manessa's big table, long before the crew had the ship ready.

Kibi felt a little nervous at first, but the guests soon proved they could take care of themselves and stay out of the way. Seeing that Ilika was on the bridge, working with Sata on a flight plan that would take them to twenty different worlds, Kibi relaxed and strode through the hatch to get the supplies she needed.

She slapped hands with Boro in the waiting room as he guided a pallet of fuel canisters toward the boarding tunnel.

Mati and Rini emerged from the medical center, the pilot wearing an especially big smile. *Did you see how short my no-no list is getting? I'm so happy!*

I bet Boro and Sata will take us swimming after we get the lizards re-settled.

Yeah! Let's head for the ship. I need to review docking tunnel rules. It's been a while.

And I have to replace a sensor crystal before we go. It should be on the pallet with Boro's fuel.

✳

Finally, about two hours later, the steward declared the ship stocked and ready, the navigator sent the flight plan to the pilot, and the docking controller cleared them for departure. The Tirilana Kril, with six scientists, their assistants, and thirty worlds to visit, would soon follow.

Ilika smiled with pride when all his crew members quickly relaxed and cleared their minds for the first star transit.

✳

The crew of the Manessa Kwi settled into a routine that lasted an entire Satamia day. Ilika rotated station assignments, with Kibi sometimes covering watch, Boro taking navigation on easy flight legs, and Sata piloting during non-critical maneuvers. Ilika would cover one or two stations, and send a couple of crew members below for sleep, baths, or play, as they needed.

At each planet, after locating a tropical rain forest, the huge bird and her assistant took wing with plenty of sample bags, the lizard and bear explored on foot, if safe, and the spider crept into dark places, returning with bags of mushrooms and grubs.

When walking around was not safe, Kibi extended a small porch and the scientists picked fruit from trees and vines while Manessa hovered.

Every sample bag was carefully labeled and placed into temperature-controlled boxes in the rear of the passenger area.

As soon as each specialist's task was completed on a planet, they would curl up in a passenger seat for a nap before arriving at the next planet.

The five crew members from a medieval world paid close attention to how real Nebador citizens did their work on a real mission. They all knew that little cargo runs were easy, but they guessed that someday their missions would be much more challenging.

✳

When the ship arrived back at the star station, the scientists and their helpers guided the pallet of sample boxes toward the laboratory, and Silmula Sorafax greeted the crew with a serious look in her eyes. "I have to talk to you about the next step, so you will all . . . be prepared for what might happen."

They followed the cat to a small conference room.

"Eight years ago, the sapient reptiles' population was two thousand one hundred and forty-three, and very slowly, year by year, dropping by two or three — hardly enough for them to notice — as the climate grew hotter and drier.

"When their star began to experience rapid shifts in mass and gravity, all of the planets of the system were affected. As tremors and earthquakes caused their caverns to collapse, most of the reptiles died. When our ships arrived, less than a day later, only one group of three hundred and twenty-five could be found, wandering in the desert, dazed, confused, and hungry. We put them to sleep, brought them into our ships, and collected every plant and animal we could find that might be important to their survival.

"When Mati took pity on them and left an access door open . . ."

The pilot closed her eyes for a moment, took a deep breath, and wondered what she had been thinking.

". . . the lizards' population was down to two hundred and seventy-five, mostly because the birth rate is nearly zero. Four of you understand why, even better than I do. Today the population stands at two hundred and forty-seven. At this rate, they will be unable to function as a society in a year or two, and completely extinct in less than a decade."

Sata made a slight whimpering sound, and Boro put his arm around her.

"With the help of what you learned in the Great Transformation, our scientists began using every possible tool to find our friends a new home. Many planets, as you know, were removed from the list because we could predict the biochemical reactions. Now, with the instrument readings and samples you and the Tirilana Kril brought back, we will be able to eliminate many more planets. That work will begin immediately, and proceed as quickly as possible.

"But I must prepare you for the final phase of the search, for it will probably cause you some grief. Not all biochemical problems can be detected in the laboratory. Before a planet is selected, we will have to offer its possible foods to your reptile friends. They will be able to eliminate some by taste and smell, of course, but not all. Some of the reptiles will probably get sick, and we will care for them as best we can. A few may die."

Boro's hand shot into the air. "I think you should offer stuff to the big group first, you know, the thick-headed adults."

Silmula Sorafax cracked a slight smile.

✳

The scientists on the two ships had been able to eliminate almost half the possible planets from their instrument readings and observations in the field. Once the samples were analyzed in the laboratory at Satamia Star Station, another fifteen worlds dropped away. Eleven remained.

The females of the simulated desert environment chatted happily as they gathered cactus fruit. An egg had hatched that morning, bringing new hope for the future to their hearts. One cactus they came to bore a strange fruit they had not seen before. An elder female sniffed it, found it sweet, and took a bite. She moaned in pain as her stomach twisted and she vomited the fruit, and everything else she had eaten that morning, back onto the sand.

Eight planets remained.

A large male looked at the gourd full of grubs he was handed, big and juicy, but a slightly different color than usual. He found them quite delicious so he ate them all, got a drink, and curled up for a nap. His strange dreams faded into a darkness from which he never awoke.

The list shrank to seven planets.

A new mushroom appeared in the supply cave, right next to those for *shmur*, and of a similar color. A young male, newly arrived at manhood and looking for a mate, grabbed a claw-full of mushrooms and the other ingredients he needed. An hour later, he and his friends began drinking the heady brew and rolling the bones. But unlike the usual evening laughter and harmless wrestling, they were all soon fighting to the death and had to be separated and restrained by older males.

Another planet was crossed off.

✳

The following day, simulated desert environment time, Boro and Sata joined a scientist at an observation window. Two half-grown lizards sniffed at some fruit they didn't recognize.

Sata frowned. "Even though they're not in the group of kids who visited the star station, I hope they don't get sick."

Suddenly both reptilian youth turned around, backed up, and peed all over the new fruit, then walked away.

Boro and Sata rolled with laughter, and the bird taking notes honked and flapped his wings.

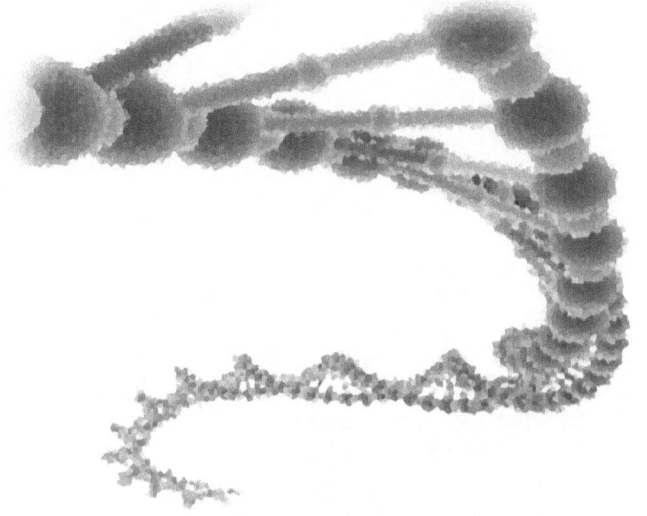

Chapter 43: Re-settlement

The fruits, grubs, and mushrooms of only three planets were offered to the eleven youth and two adults of the special group. Unlike the main group, these thirteen knew what was happening.

Kerloran, in his bright-green lizard form, divided them into four groups, three reptiles at each of the three trays of food, the other two receiving the grubs and cactus fruit from their original home.

They knew the same foods had already been consumed, with no ill effects, by the main group. They looked at each other, sensed the importance of the moment, and started eating.

✳

The scientists and specialists took another Satamia day to make sure no biochemical surprises lurked in the complex molecules of lizards, insect grubs, jungle fruits, or rain forest mushrooms. Even on the three planets that looked best, there were many things the reptiles could not eat. The scientists just had to be sure there were many things they *could* eat.

The Great Transformation briefing team, the crew of the Manessa Kwi, and the crew of the Palantia Lisa, a large passenger transport ship, were all summoned to a conference room. Visiting students squeezed in wherever they could.

With neither Kerloran nor Melorania present, Silmula Sorafax trembled inside, knowing the huge responsibility she bore. After a slow, deep breath, she leapt onto a table at the front of the room. Everyone fell silent.

"Our beloved Kerloran is very pleased with the course of events that have brought us to this point . . . as am I."

The room erupted with cheering and clapping, then respectful silence returned.

"Our reptilian charges, whom we know much better now after the mischief of a certain monkey-mammal pilot . . ."

Mati grinned with embarrassment as others chuckled or honked.

". . . will be re-settled on all three of the planets that can sustain them. On one, a sapient equine race lives in the temperate zone, and they will someday interact. On another, a global avian race is already highly sapient. The reptiles will grow in their shadow, and hopefully someday learn wisdom from them."

Many heads nodded and sounds of approval rippled through the room.

"The planet with no sapient life will be given to the small group who befriended our dear monkey mammals, and have seen a star station. They will, most likely, become the dominant form of life on the planet, and we will watch over them closely as they grow."

The room broke into cheering again as wings flapped and feet stomped.

"Captain Kam'rrral-ta?"

A large bird stood.

"Two hundred and thirty-one sleeping reptiles, and their meager belongings, will be delivered to the Palantia Lisa later today. Please prepare your ship. You will have two destinations, and a Local Universe Guardian will accompany you to protect your passengers from the effects of star transit."

The captain nodded and reached for the knowledge pad at her side.

"Captain Imni?"

Ilika stood.

"You have the honor — or problem, I'm not sure which — of transporting two adults and eleven youth, with their eyes wide open and their claws *itching* to touch everything."

The room filled with laughter and Ilika smiled. "I think we can handle it."

"Just remember," the large cat warned, "even the children have tail spikes."

Boro grinned knowingly.

✳

Kibi was relieved when Kerloran stepped into the Manessa Kwi with the thirteen passengers following behind. She knew that if anyone could keep them in line, he could.

But she quickly frowned when one of the youngest reptiles hopped into the steward's chair and began pounding on her console. She glanced at Kerloran, but he only returned her glance with smiling eyes.

She sighed, tapped the sleep code into her bracelet, and gathered the limp lizard child into her arms. "Please translate for me, Kerloran. If anyone wants to be *awake* during the journey to your new home, you will sit in your seats *calmly*, unless you are using the toilet."

The master of Satamia Star Station nodded his approval, then repeated the gist of Kibi's warning in sounds the passengers could understand.

They settled a little, but still wiggled with excitement. Then Kibi brought out her secret weapon.

As soon as the video of jungle sights and sounds began on the large screen over the steward's station, all twelve reptiles who were still awake, from the youngest to the two adults, sat completely still and stared. Somehow, their dreams were playing before their very eyes.

Kerloran smiled, and Kibi went through the passenger area securing inertia straps, even though the flight was expected to be completely smooth.

✴

With all his crew members at their primary stations, Ilika hardly had to say a word.

"Flight plan is on channel five. Satamia Control, Manessa Kwi at dock C-Eleven requests station departure."

"Manessa Kwi, you are cleared on the orange path to inner marker B."

"I need anti-mass one and maneuvering thrusters, please."

"All engines green. Plenty of fuel."

"Hatch closed, boarding tunnel away, ship and passengers secured for flight."

"Sensors active. No unusual energy signatures. Visuals on channel four."

As the crew fell silent and Mati piloted the ship through the docking tunnel, she had a moment of fright. Something was missing — something that had always been near, leaning on the console beside her, ready whenever she needed it.

It's in your cabin. I could go get it for you if you want ... Rini silently offered.

Mati, still guiding the ship along the orange line, took some deep breaths to settle her nerves. *That would be pretty silly.*

The freckled young man at the watch station smiled.

A quarter hour later, Kerloran protected all thirteen reptiles from the effects of star transit. None of them noticed the twenty-second nap they took while gazing at dripping leaves, buzzing insects, and sprouting mushrooms.

The crew of the Manessa Kwi had to take care of themselves.

✴

Once back in space and time, Kerloran asked Kibi to switch to a view of the planet they were approaching.

Most of the young reptiles gasped and hissed.

"This is what a world looks like," Kerloran began in the reptilian tongue. "You will not see it again, from a distance, for many long ages. It has everything you need, but it is also very much alone. We place it in your hands, as there are no other creatures here who can grow in knowledge and power, as you can. You will make many mistakes. They are yours to make, and yours to fix. We will watch over you, but not help you solve the problems you create.

"Someday, if your children of many hatchings become noble and wise, they will visit star stations again, walk and talk with us, and help with the work of the universe. Until then, you must follow your hearts."

Kerloran, however, would not allow the passengers to see the ship's planetary approach. Kibi switched the big screen back to the jungle video, but happened to glance at her console just as the surface zoomed toward them. Suddenly the view froze as Mati stopped the ship at four thousand meters. Kibi swallowed and remembered how frightening that had once seemed, not so very long ago.

"Finished with ion drive," the pilot said calmly. "Maneuvering thrusters, please."

A few minutes later, the Manessa Kwi settled into a small clearing in the jungle. Mists lurked about in the trees, birds called to each other in curious voices, and a small waterfall splashed into a crystal-clear pool. Two dark cave entrances stood nearby.

As soon a Kibi opened the hatch and extended the ramp, Kerloran strode out and the thirteen passengers followed. They looked around with wide eyes and open mouths, anxious to explore, reluctant to leave the safety of the ship.

The crew watched from the top of the ramp.

"Although you do not really need them anymore," the tall, bright-green lizard declared with throaty sounds, "we knew you would find comfort in caves. But unlike the dry, dusty, desert caves of your recent memories, these caves already contain other creatures, some of whom may not want to share."

Eyes swirled with determination, mouths snapped, and spiked tails swung back and forth to show Kerloran they were up to the challenge.

"I will remain here for seven days, so that you may share, if you wish, your stories as you begin to explore your new home."

After speaking those words, the master of Satamia Star Station curled up at the foot of the ramp as if to take a nap.

✳

For the remainder of that day, the youngest reptiles hardly dared leave the clearing, until the two adults and the older youth returned with stories of tasty fruit and juicy grubs. But by nightfall, all thirteen were back to tell Kerloran their stories, ask questions, gaze up at the passing moons, and eventually sleep.

On the second day, the caves were carefully explored, and indeed many spiders and snakes already dwelled within. The spiders were shy and willing to share. The snakes retreated to smaller caves after learning their fangs could not penetrate lizard hides, and after feeling tail spikes that easily pierced snakeskin. The thirteen returned to the clearing, as evening fell, to tell Kerloran of their adventures and ask him questions about spiders and snakes.

During the third day, Kerloran saw his charges often, and heard of fruits that made them sick and mushrooms that made their heads spin. As evening gathered once again, only the children returned to the clearing to sleep near him.

The following day, with no real reptiles in sight, Ilika allowed the crew to stretch their legs and gather tropical fruit. About noon, Kerloran shooed them all back into the ship, and soon the reptiles appeared, telling of a cave with fingers of rock on the floor and ceiling, pools of delicious water, and dry nooks for sleeping. After another visit from his charges as the sun prepared to set, Kerloran slept alone that night.

The fifth day brought a few scattered visitors, sharing that the older youth had dared to climb high into trees where they found insect nests with huge, tasty grubs, and all the fruit they could ever want. But the evening was quiet, with only monkey mammals to keep Kerloran company.

Only two reptiles visited the clearing on the sixth day. The two adults announced shyly but proudly that soon eggs would be laid and babies hatched. After sharing their news, the pair returned to the edge of the jungle, but glanced back at the bright-green lizard of great power and wisdom who had brought them to their new home, and the mammals behind who did his bidding. Then they scampered away in search of grubs.

All during the seventh day, the tropical mists lurked through the trees, insects buzzed, and birds called. No one came to tell him stories or ask him questions, so Kerloran rested.

Chapter 44: Unfinished Business

When the crew of the Manessa Kwi arrived back at Satamia Star Station, most of the visiting students had departed, and the simulated desert environment was in the process of being cleaned.   Silmula Sorafax, the briefing team, and the six humans gathered in a conference room and listened for hours as the specialists and the crew of the Palantia Lisa shared stories from the re-settlement of the other two groups.

When the others finally wandered away, the large white cat looked at the four monkey mammals who had lived, for several Satamia days, as sapient reptiles. "Even though it feels like this project is complete, it has just entered a new phase that will stretch on for thousands of years. Non-material beings will watch over the reptiles constantly, and several times a year, a ship will visit the three planets to see how they are doing. For the rest of our lives, I, and you four, will be part of that process. As long as you are all together on the Manessa Kwi, it will probably be the ship assigned to make those visits."

"I must admit," Boro began with a slight smile, "I'll be curious to see — from a safe distance, of course — what kind of world they make for themselves."

The large cat curled her lips and nodded. "And Mati now begins Psychic Development training."

The pilot cringed slightly.

"Kibi can show you the way, but it is best, Kibi, to not attempt to describe the experience, as it is different for each person. Boro's introductory class, for example, was disguised as juggling lessons, and Sata began the process by joining a dance troop."

Boro's mouth opened with surprise for a moment, then changed to a knowing smile. Sata just stared with wide, curious eyes.

"Perhaps both of you will someday choose to go through the whole program. I do not know. For now, farewell. I will see you in the station often, and occasionally on missions." The large cat brought her mouth to each of their necks and gave them a lick. She saved Kibi for last, and made it especially wet. Then she walked out of the room.

✳

Life on Satamia Star Station began to settle down for the crew of the Manessa Kwi, as much as life can ever settle down for members of the Transport Service who are always on call for whatever universe work might arise.

Kibi returned to her training, and a day later, Mati stepped into the simple doorway beyond the little bubbling fountain. Sata returned to her dance troop with a new light in her eyes and more passion in her movements than ever before. Boro introduced Rini and Mati to the joys of swimming and fishing in the underwater world beneath the halls and balconies of the star station.

Ilika and Kibi worked with Melorania to plan the lessons and cross-training that each crew member needed, and the types of missions that would best build their knowledge and skills. They agreed that the little ship was ready to move beyond simple cargo runs, but the head of the Transport Service didn't yet say what she had in mind.

✳

Two slender monkey mammals strolled, hand in hand, along the first balcony overlooking Green Hall. A chuckle would occasionally come from one or the other, even though no spoken words passed between them.

Suddenly Rini recognized the place he had been looking for. Leaves of the great station tree shielded a small bench from view, so he steered Mati toward it.

Mati knew something was up, but Rini carefully hid his intentions in a corner of his mind. She sat down and couldn't help but smile.

Rini didn't sit. Instead he went to his knees in front of her and pulled a small box from his pocket. He opened it to reveal a tiny pastry, good for two bites at the most.

Mati laughed deeply as she relived the bitter-sweet memory of watching Rini accidentally marry a desert girl.

He waited until she recovered from her laughter and dried her tears. *I once made a big mistake*, he began, *and I did my best to fix it. Back on Sonmatia Seven, you asked me to marry you, but then things got really busy.*

Mati grinned. *Really, really busy!*

If you're still interested, I think we can find the time now, he continued, offering her the pastry.

She took a bite, then placed the other half in Rini's mouth. *Let me think . . .* she pondered for him to hear, *I have to meditate with some bears this afternoon, then I'm helping to put up decorations for the party . . . yeah, I think we can squeeze it in.*

Rini chuckled, then joined Mati on the bench. *Only problem is, I don't know how they do it here.*

Mati pulled a knowledge pad from her pocket and touched a key. "Who do we talk to about getting married?"

A map appeared on the screen. *Blue Hall, balcony two*, she silently shared.

The pair hopped up and strode toward a ramp with purpose and determination in every step they took.

※

The glowing purple ball of light listened to Mati and Rini describe their desire to be married. It overheard the unspoken thoughts that passed between them, and peered into their memories of childhood, slavery, test, journey, and selection. Finally, it scanned the universe records of their service on the Manessa Kwi, including the recent Great Transformation they endured together.

"I see the problem," the being of color and light said when the two monkey mammals had said all they could think of to say. "Because of the culture into which you were born, you conceive of marriage as something that someone else does *to* you — a priest, whatever that is. I'm sorry, but you are about as married as any two creatures can be. What you really want to know, it seems to me, is how you can *celebrate* your marriage, and share your happiness with the citizens of Nebador. Am I not correct?"

Rini and Mati looked at each other. Several thoughts passed between them before Mati spoke. "And ... we want to know ... that our marriage won't be a problem for anyone ... and if it ever is ... they'll tell us and ... you know ... help us fix it ..."

"You can assume all that," the glowing purple light assured. "Your captain watches over you, as do your other teachers and trainers. Melorania and Kerloran, and others even greater, know what is in your hearts at all times."

After a long silence, Mati and Rini both nodded. "So ... how can we ... celebrate?" Rini asked.

"There's a very creative equine who's in charge of the party this evening. Let's go talk to him, shall we?"

※

After a long day of excitement that included the successful completion of the reptile re-settlement mission, the Satamia sun once again began to set relative to the star station's main hall. Ilika and Kibi wandered up from the ship after checking the galley stocks. They didn't see any of their other crew members anywhere.

Kibi looked worried, but Ilika grabbed her and pulled her toward one of the kitchens that obviously needed help carrying food out to the tables. "They've earned our trust, and both relationships are deepening after their recent experiences. We can always find them with their bracelets if we really need them."

Kibi let out a long breath. "You're right. Mati said she'd be hanging decorations. I'm just so used to her hobbling along on a crutch ..."

"I bet she'll be dancing tonight!"

Kibi smiled. "I will be, too!"

They helped birds and reptiles push carts and carry trays for half an hour, then found a bench where they could snuggle close together as brilliant music announced the star station's evening party. But for some reason, the dance floor remained closed, roped off by a blue cord. People gathered on couches, benches, and perches, or just floated on the surface of the large pool, hundreds of sparkling eyes wondering what surprise might be in store.

The first song ended, and an ursine drummer took up a slow, steady beat as a spotlight found a slender female monkey mammal riding on the back of a large golden equine. Horse and human approached the dance floor, and long legs easily stepped over the ribbon.

The human slid off the sleek golden fur, but instead of standing, crumpled to the ground. The audience gasped. A spider stepped forward and handed her an old, tattered crutch.

Kibi and Ilika looked at each other, both grinning.

The horse walked away, and with dramatic effort, the girl got to her feet and stood alone.

Suddenly another musician plunged furry fingers into his keyboard, just as a fanator swooped into the main hall and circled, a slender human boy riding. Huge wings beat the air and sent leaves fluttering and decorations swinging as the giant bird brought itself and its passenger to a halt just above the dance floor, then settled with strong webbed feet right in front of the girl and her crutch.

Kibi put her arm around Ilika as they continued to watch.

The boy stepped down clumsily, clearly not used to riding, and the audience chuckled. The fanator departed, and the boy bowed to the girl, who pretended to be embarrassed and shy.

Just then a large monkey mammal, wearing crude wool clothing, stepped onto the dance floor. He grabbed the girl and started pulling her away. A musician somewhere added tense, dramatic music.

The slender boy stood alone with sad, downcast eyes.

The girl suddenly lifted her crutch and started swinging at the large man. He cowered and backed away, and the girl ran into the boy's waiting arms.

The audience cheered and honked with happiness, but fell silent when another human girl, dressed in a flowing green gown, danced toward them with seductive movements. She hid her face with a long green scarf as she coyly took the boy's hand, causing him to forget, it seemed, all about the girl he had just embraced. In a trance, he joined in her sensuous dance and followed her.

The audience moaned and screeched with anger.

The music changed to a fast and anxious rhythm as the boy shook himself out of the trance, planted his feet, and crossed his arms.

The audience cheered and the seductive girl danced away, even as the boy returned to the girl's arms. They took hands and bowed in several directions to the many creatures around them.

When the room finally fell silent, the girl spoke. "I am Mati, a simple monkey mammal from a backward little world called Sonmatia Three. I am honored to be the pilot of the Manessa Kwi, and happy beyond words to tell all of you that I *love* this freckled boy, and will be his girl as long as I have life."

The hundreds of Nebador citizens in the room roared and squawked with approval.

"I am Rini, same backward little planet."

Chuckles rippled through the huge room.

"I was a slave, and now I am Manessa's watch. I love this girl, and will be her boy as long as she will have me."

The audience roared with approval, and on cue, the musicians began a slow, intimate song. The two slender youth began to dance, alone on the dance floor, together in the limelight. Their timid, clumsy movements brought smiles to many watchers, who waited silently outside the blue cord.

When the first dance ended, the pair of monkey mammals bowed, helpers quickly removed the cord, and dozens of creatures headed for the dance floor.

As thrilled as Mati was to be sharing her marriage with all the people of Satamia Star Station, her knee soon yelled at her to slow down and spend time on a cozy couch. Many creatures came by to congratulate the couple, and often they carried baskets or trays from the snack tables.

Silmula Sorafax and Toran Takil appeared about an hour later. They sat side by side on the floor in front of the couch, which placed their heads at the same level as Mati's and Rini's.

"You two are married, aren't you?" Mati inquired.

"Yes," the female cat said with glowing eyes. "And there are forms of marriage that go beyond mortal life, beyond what most people call marriage."

"You two have such a bond," Toran Takil began, "because of your mental link. We have another type that will, if we are strong and true, survive death."

Rini and Mati sat silently, pondering what the large cats had just shared, and looking into their beautiful feline eyes. Mati looked mostly at Toran Takil, and could feel her heart beating faster and her skin becoming hot.

Boro appeared. "Sata's in a circle dance with some reptiles. May I dance with my pilot?"

Mati quickly hopped up, glad for a reason to break the male cat's spell.

Rini smiled, having easily seen and felt Mati's reaction to Toran Takil. As soon as Boro and Mati were gone, he turned back to the cats. "I have a funny question."

The cats' ears twitched as they looked at him.

"Why do I get the feeling that . . . Kerloran and Melorania knew, all along, that the homeless reptiles needed a jungle?"

Toran Takil looked at his mate with a sparkle in his eyes.

"Of course they did," the female cat answered. "It is not the purpose of the universe to get things done as quickly and efficiently as possible. That's a mortal preoccupation, especially strong in monkey mammals, but we all feel it to one degree or another. The purpose of the universe is experience and personal growth. If Melorania, Kerloran, and others like them, just did everything without helpers like us, none of the citizens of Nebador would get any training. Small minds with a little knowledge and power try to keep it to themselves. Real wisdom is for sharing."

Rini nodded thoughtfully.

Boro and Mati soon returned from the dance floor, and a moment later Sata appeared, nearly out of breath but smiling.

Toran Takil touched Silmula on the shoulder, and they bowed and slipped away.

A minute later, Ilika and Kibi wandered over, arms around each other.

Kibi looked at Mati and Rini. "You two have gotten us talking about marriage. We agree we're not as ready as you, but we're thinking about it."

Boro exchanged looks of understanding with his captain, and Sata grinned at Kibi.

Mati danced whenever the music moved her, but also listened to her new muscles and joints, and often found a couch where she could snuggle with her beloved Rini. More creatures wished them well in their marriage, and sometimes left invitations to eat or play together.

Kibi noticed the tenderness growing between Sata and Boro, and it made her even more determined to learn, along with everything else she was learning, how to be Ilika's faithful companion and lover.

Sata was on the dance floor almost constantly, with Boro, or anyone else who would dance with her. But her mind often recalled what Silmula Sorafax had said, that her dance training was just an introduction to something greater.

Boro could feel dreams and desires inside himself coming to the surface. As he watched Sata dance with some nimble-footed birds, he knew he was no longer too gentle for man's work or too clumsy for woman's work. By combining the two, he was just right.

Rini sensed he had become part of something bigger than anything he had ever imagined. Mati, the Manessa Kwi, and the homeless reptiles were all parts of it, but it stretched far out into the universe, farther than his mind could follow. He smiled, knowing he would just have to wait and see.

Ilika looked around at his solid engineer, his bright-eyed watch, his brave pilot, his young but rapidly growing navigator, and, longest of all, at his sweet steward. For perhaps the first time, he felt confident that they had all firmly planted their feet on the path to becoming citizens of Nebador.

After a few more songs, just as the crew of the Manessa Kwi was beginning to yawn and think about cozy beds in their cabins, all six mission bracelets chimed.

They looked at each other and laughed.

Afterthoughts

As *Book Six: Star Station* is being published, *Book Seven: The Local Universe* has been written, *Book Eight: Witness* is about half-written, and *Book Nine* (not yet titled) has been "assigned." The Muse (or whatever you would like to call Her) is obviously not done with Nebador. And yet, this is a good time to pause. The essential Nebador story has been told, and most of the unanswered questions from the earlier books have been answered.

As I'm sure you know by now, this story isn't really science fiction. That genre has done the great service of hosting (and, in a sense, protecting) those stories that attempt to explore our place in the universe. Ideally, that would be the task of religion, but it isn't ready to take up that role yet. Perhaps it will be someday.

In the meantime, while waiting for *Book Seven* and beyond, the author invites all readers to dig deeper. The *Deep Learning Notes*, available both on the www.nebador.com internet site and in printed book form, are a good place to start.

But the most important "depth" can only be pursued in each of our lives, minute by minute, day by day. If the Nebador stories have anything to leave to the world, it's a glimpse of the difference between REALITY, and the many layers of assumptions and myths that most people live by. If, while reading these stories, you have experienced even a tiny peek beyond normal "monkey mammal" thinking, then you have set your feet on the path to "Nebador" (by whatever name).

Good journey to you!

J. Z. Colby
2012

Neti's Temptation

By Karen Buchanan

This story takes place the morning after the group is trapped by high tide on the rocky coast in *Book Two: Journey.*

Neti couldn't sleep. She didn't toss and turn because she didn't want to wake Miko, so she just looked up at the sky and counted stars. It was kind of fun because she had just learned to count not long before.

But soon she got bored with it. Something that happened the day before really bothered her. For the first time in months, maybe years, she wasn't sure if Miko was the right boy for her.

After lying there for a long time, sometimes counting stars and sometimes just fuming, she saw a little morning light creep into the sky. She carefully slipped out from under her blankets.

"Neti?" Miko called in a groggy voice.

"Have to pee," she whispered.

"Ok, good ni . . ."

Neti tiptoed through the camp, being careful not to make anyone. Ilika and Kibi were snuggled close, and Buna and Toli were near each other but not touching. Boro and Sata weren't sleeping close together yet, but Neti knew they would be someday. When she got near the beach, she climbed a small sand dune partly covered with wiry grass. She sat down on top and looked out over the wide beach and the calm water of the bay.

With her chin in her hands, she sat with her feelings, but no clear thoughts about anything came to her. Suddenly a sea gull landed on a nearby driftwood log and looked up at her.

"What is it about boys?" she asked the sea gull.

The sea gull cocked it head but didn't say anything.

"I suppose you might be a boy. If you are, maybe you know the answer. Why do we love boys, but they're never as good as we think they should be?"

The sea gull squawked at Neti.

She felt in her cloak pocket and found a little piece of stale bread. "You're lucky. There was a time this would have been my breakfast, and I wouldn't have shared it with you! Here you go!" She tossed the bread toward the driftwood log.

The sea gull kept an eye on Neti as it hopped off the log and grabbed the bread. Before it got back to its log, a man came walking along the beach, so the bird spread its wing and took off.

"Hey! You didn't answer my question!"

But the sea gull didn't come back, so Neti gave up and looked at the man. She knew she should go back to the camp and wake someone, just in case the man gave her any trouble, but she was still in a bad mood because of Miko, so she stayed on top of the dune.

The man wasn't very old, maybe about Ilika's age, and was dressed like any fisherman. He carried a bucket brimming with clams. When he got close, he stopped and looked up at Neti.

"Hello, fair maiden."

Neti could feel her heart pounding. "Hello."

"Are you all alone?"

"Sort of."

He came closer, and Neti could see that he was handsome. Her heart pounded louder.

"Would you like to help me clean these clams, then make a stew? My house is not far."

Neti couldn't speak for a minute, so she coughed and tried to breathe. The young man noticed her confusion and smiled.

"Um . . . maybe . . . if you'll answer a question for me first."

"If it will help me win your heart, I'll tell you anything!"

That's what Neti was afraid of. Maybe the sea gull hadn't been so bad. But she took a breath and decided to give it a try. "Why do girls always think boys are so wonderful and perfect, but they never are?"

The young fisherman squirmed and shrugged. "Um . . . because . . . no . . . maybe because . . . I don't know . . ."

Now Neti was *sure* the sea gull had been more honest.

Suddenly the young man found his thoughts and said, "I guess girls are just made that way, and boys . . . are made like they are!"

Neti thought about his answer, then asked, "So what would you do if you were in a waterfall bowl and the tide was rising?"

"Easy. Sing fishing songs until the tide went out, or carve a piece of driftwood if I had my knife."

"And if you came to a place where there's hot steam hissing out of the ground?"

He backed up, frowned, and made signs to protect himself from evil. "That's from the Underworld, and I wouldn't go near the place without a priest at my side!"

Neti smiled. She had just learned something, but knew she couldn't tell the young, handsome fisherman. She almost wished the sea gull would come back.

The fisherman, with his bucket of clams, was still frowning. "Did you go near such a place? Places like that can put curses on people, you know."

Neti laughed out loud.

"Mocking spirits and demons is dangerous!" He looked around with fear in his eyes. "Are you going to clean these clams with me, or not? If you won't, there's a girl up the beach about a mile who will."

Neti was torn, just for a moment. Then she smiled and said, "I'm glad you have someone to share your clams with. I think . . . I'll stay here."

"Good day to you," he said with a slight bow and headed along the beach, swinging his bucket of clams and whistling.

Neti stayed on the sand dune for another half hour, thinking about what she had learned. The sea gull came back, and another, and they walked back and forth on the driftwood log, sometimes looking at each other, sometimes clicking their beaks together. Neti somehow knew that one of them was a boy, the other a girl, but she couldn't tell which was which. She decided not to interrupt them with her thoughts, so she just watched.

After a few minutes, both sea gulls looked at Neti and squawked, but she didn't have any more bread, so they flew away together.

When she finally tiptoed back to camp, Miko was still dead asleep, but Ilika was just coming out of the trees, so she went up to him, smiling.

"Guess what I just learned!" she said.

✳   ✳   ✳

About the Authors

Born in the Mojave Desert, J. Z. Colby now lives and writes deep in a forest of the Pacific Northwest.

He has studied many subjects, formally and informally, including psychology, philosophy, education, and performing arts, but remains a generalist. His primary profession as a mental health counselor, specializing with families and young adults, gives him many stories of personal growth, and the motivation to develop his team of young critiquers and readers.

All his life, he has been drawn toward a broad understanding of human nature, especially those physical, emotional, mental, and spiritual situations in which our capacity to function seems to reach its limits. He finds fascinating those few individuals who can transcend the limits of our common human nature and the dictates of our cultures.

In his spare time, he flies helicopters and airplanes.

He may be contacted at the email address listed on the internet site www.nebador.com.

*

Karen Buchanan, 15, is a native of Quebec, Canada. She speaks both English and French fluently, is learning Spanish, and wants to learn German and Chinese someday. But she has discovered, in the last year, that there are much more important things in life, and is considering literature or art history at university.